CHAIN OF EVIDENCE

The Burren Mysteries by Cora Harrison

* available from Severn House

CHAIN OF EVIDENCE

A Burren Mystery

Cora Harrison

Severn House Large Print
London & New York

This first large print edition published 2018
in Great Britain and the USA by
SEVERN HOUSE PUBLISHERS LTD of
Eardley House, 4 Uxbridge Street, London W8 7SY.
First world regular print edition published 2012 by
Severn House Publishers Ltd.

British Library Cataloguing in Publication Data
A CIP catalogue record for this title is available from the British Library.

ISBN-13: 9780727893550

Severn House Publishers support the Forest Stewardship Council™
[FSC™], the leading international forest certification organisation. All
our titles that are printed on FSC certified paper carry the FSC logo.

Typeset by Palimpsest Book Production Ltd.,
Falkirk, Stirlingshire, Scotland.
Printed and bound in Great Britain by
T J International, Padstow, Cornwall.

This book is dedicated to my dear friend, Cath Thompson, supportive colleague of my working days and now equally supportive in the occupation of my retirement: writing novels.

It takes a certain nobility, well over and beyond the bounds of friendship, to read and report back on forty-five books written by a friend and I am very grateful for her continued support and valuable advice.

Acknowledgements

Thanks are due to all, such as Fergus Kelly and Daniel Binchy, who laboured in the field of medieval Gaelic writings of the early Irish law.

All gratitude to my agent, Peter Buckman, for his zest, his prompt and decisive verdicts on my preliminary typescripts, his support through the long process of publication and for his continuing enthusiasm for Mara, Brehon of the Burren.

Thanks, also, to the team at Severn House, in particular my editor, Anna Telfer, who has to cope with a writer whose mind runs ahead of her typing skills.

One

Cáin Lánamna
(The Law of Marriage)

There are nine forms of union:
1. *The union of joint property where both partners contribute to the wealth of the couple.*
2. *The union of a woman on a man's property.*
3. *The union of a man on a woman's property.*
4. *The union of a man visiting with the approval of her kin.*
5. *The union of a man and a willing woman without the approval of her kin.*
6. *The union of a man and an abducted woman.*
7. *The union of a man and a secretly visited woman.*
8. *The union that follows rape.*
9. *The union of two insane people.*

It had been an early spring in the west of Ireland.

In the kingdom of the Burren, mild south-westerly winds from the nearby Atlantic Ocean had put a temporary end to winter frosts by the middle of January. By the second day of February the sunken lanes in its valleys had been filled with pale yellow primroses and dark purple violets. Soon afterwards the willow had begun to quicken and burst forth into fluffy

1

buds, the pink haze of the tiny herb robert spread over the ditches and the grass of the fields was sprinkled with cowslips. An early spring, said the optimists who began making plans for moving their cows to summer pasture.

But by the thirty-first day of March, just as soon as the bare thorny twigs of hedgerows had become covered with white blossoms, the traditional saying 'the little winter of the black-thorn' had come true and the air turned icy. Winds from the north-east scoured the land. Showers of hail and of heavy, icy rain drowned the dry fields and puddles sprang up even on the limestone lands of the Burren. The cattle, over-wintering on the clumps of sweet grass that grew between the heat-retaining limestone rocks of the High Burren, grouped together in the shelter of stone walls and turned their backs on the arctic winds. Farmers slept little on these freezing nights, but continually checked on in-calf cows, trying to bring those near their time into the shelter of the stone barns or cabins close to their houses. Even as April neared to an end, the winds and the rain still continued and the grass made poor growth. The riches of the kingdom lay in its cattle and this late spring was a worry to the farmers. By now the cows should have been taken down from the high limestone plateaux and the mountain sides to feed on the lush grasses of the valleys, but it seemed as though winter still had a grip on the land.

A fit evening to mourn the dead, thought Mara, as she rode her horse up the Carron Mountain

2

towards the MacNamara tower house. The *tánaiste* (heir) of the clan, an unmarried man in his late sixties, had died and Garrett MacNamara, *taoiseach* (chieftain) of the MacNamaras was holding the funeral ceremonies at the castle.

As Brehon of the Burren, in charge of law and order, Mara felt obliged to attend every wake – those particularly Celtic occasions when the dead are mourned by a night of singing, dancing and storytelling; and by the consumption of large amounts of food and drink. It was, she knew, a time when the bonds between relatives and neighbours were renewed and she recognised the importance of honouring the life of the newly deceased. However, personally, on this particular evening, she grudged the time. This was a very busy season of the year for her. Tomorrow would be the eve of the festival of *Bealtaine*, and was traditionally judgement day in the kingdom. She had planned to spend this evening writing up her notes and preparing for the various law cases which would be brought before her on that occasion. Two of her scholars were due to sit their final examination in a month's time and she needed to make sure that they were well-prepared for this.

Nevertheless, it was impossible to evade these ceremonies, so after supper she set out reluctantly. Her assistant teacher, Fachtnan, rode beside her and her scholars followed. The two eighteen-year-olds, Moylan and Aidan, who would be taking their final examinations this summer; seventeen-year-old Fiona from Scotland; fifteen year-old Hugh, whose father was a wealthy silver merchant on the Burren; and fourteen-year-old Shane, son of the Brehon to O'Neill from Ulster, were all in good spirits. These wakes were always entertaining for the young and they looked forward eagerly to the feast that would be provided there.

The attendance at the wake promised to be huge; the steep hill, leading up to the castle at Carron, was lined with people drawing aside to allow the Brehon to pass and calling out greetings in a cheerful manner. There seemed to be little sorrow at this death of a man who was no longer even middle-aged and who had been in poor health for the majority of the time during his office of *tánaiste*. The general talk seemed to be more about the unseasonable weather; and the lowing of cows cooped up in the huge barn on the hill above the castle called forth a general discussion on the perils of calving in low temperatures. New life, rather than death, was the topic of conversation for the people of the Burren on this evening. And that was how it should be, thought Mara. Look ahead, not back, had always been her motto for life. She found that she could hardly recollect the features of the dead man and sighed to think how in a few minutes' time she would have to gaze respectfully down at the dead face inside the open coffin and say a few dignified and meaningful words about his life and time in the Burren. And later on in the evening she would hear, with a suppressed smile, her words passed from person to person as if they were gospel truth.

What on earth had possessed Garrett, four years

ago, to impose upon his clan such an elderly and obviously unfit heir? The thought was in Mara's mind as she greeted the *taoiseach* and his wife and then shepherded her scholars over to say a quick prayer for the repose of the soul of the deceased. Garrett himself was a man in his middle thirties who had inherited the position from his father a few years ago. At the time people had said that the newly married man had wanted to keep the position warm for his own son and to avoid electing his younger brother, Jarlath, but few had cared to oppose the strong-expressed views of their new leader.

But now? Who would be the new *tánaiste?*

Just as Mara crossed herself piously and murmured a prayer her eye was caught by a tanned young man accepting a drink from a servant. Surely that was Jarlath, himself, back from his sea voyages. Jarlath MacNamara was a successful merchant with his own ship and little of him had been seen on the Burren for the last ten years or so. He had arrived opportunely, thought Mara. The slim youth that she remembered had turned into a tall, broad-shouldered man with an air about him of command and authority. The clan would be impressed by him. Unobtrusively she dodged a few neighbours looking for a gossip with her and made her way across the room.

'Can it be you, Jarlath? Well, you have changed,' she said with her best smile and he bowed gracefully over her out-stretched hand.

'But not you, Brehon,' he said with a flash of white teeth in his tanned face. 'I swear that you

5

haven't aged a day since I saw you last. You still have your law school, do you? I heard that you have married since I saw you last.' His eyes went to Fiona, and their shade of pale blue darkened in appreciation of the pretty Scots girl with her primrose-fair curls and shapely figure. 'And I hear that you have a girl scholar, now,' he said. 'You must introduce me.'

'Your brother must have been pleased to see you back home again after all those years,' said Mara, ignoring this. If he wanted to flirt with Fiona, later in the evening would be the time for this. For now she would get to know him again. This time the clan would be reluctant to allow Garrett to ride rough-shod over them and to impose his choice of *tánaiste*. Garrett's father had been an immensely popular man and the clan had been happy to elect his son as *taoiseach*, but it had not proved to be a success – nor had Garrett's choice of an elderly man in very poor health for his heir been a good one. The MacNamara clan would be cautious this time, and no doubt many of them would be finding an excuse to ask her opinion about young Jarlath. She would take this opportunity to get to know the young man and assess his quality. There was no doubt that Garrett was not a well-loved *taoiseach*. A popular young *tánaiste* who could deputise for him, a man who knew how to talk, and how to listen to his people could help to alleviate some of the trivial disputes and complaints which seemed to arise continuously from the MacNamara clan and which took time and attention from her at every judgement day, during the intervening years and months since Garrett's election.

'So will you be staying at home for a while now, Jarlath?' she asked in a tone of innocent curiosity.

He shrugged and grinned. 'Yes, I'm home for a while, perhaps for good. Burned my boat, as they say. At least I sold it to the O'Donnell. Not a great boat, but he seemed happy with it. He was visiting the king of Scotland and we met at Mull of Kintyre. He was good enough to offer me a free passage down to the Burren as he had promised to drop off an Englishman, Stephen Gardiner, who wishes to study the ways and customs of Ireland, down here. And two others, also . . .' His voice tailed away and his eyes went to his brother. There was a twinkle in them which intrigued her, though part of her mind was pre-occupied in wondering what part O'Donnell and this Stephen Gardiner were playing in visiting James IV of Scotland when the Scottish king was rumoured to have signed a treaty with Louis of France against Henry VIII of England, master to both of these men.

'You'll be staying with Garrett, will you?' she asked. It would not be ideal so she was not surprised when he shook his head.

'Not for long, not here, not in this castle,' he said. 'Things are none too pleasant here at the moment. I didn't get much of a welcome when I arrived. But perhaps I will build myself a new house on one of the farms that belong to me, that were left to me when my father – may God have mercy on him – died. Anyway, I am home for the moment, not sure what I'm going to do next – in any case, I need to replace my ship; get a few repairs done to the fleet – it will take a while and I don't want to impose too long on Garrett.' His smile broadened. 'Things are a bit tense here. You see two of the three visitors I brought with me have caused a bit of an upset. Let me introduce you to them.'

Without saying any more, he took her arm and steered her across the room and towards the window that overlooked the valley. There were two people sitting on the window seat, almost hidden by the splendid curtains of woven brocade. One was a tall, strongly made woman, probably in her middle thirties, and the other was a thin boy of about fifteen. They were talking – or at least the woman was talking, whispering the words in the boy's ear, while he sat, head averted, sulkily gazing at the ground. From time to time she patted his hand as though he were a toddler, not an adolescent. He didn't look strong, Mara thought. He was very bony and his shoulders were bent over a hollow chest.

But then he looked up and at the sight of his face, Mara stopped abruptly. Not a good-looking boy, though adolescent boys of that age seldom were. But this boy with his fleshy, protruding nose and his heavily swelling lower lip jutting out from the receding chin bore a strong resemblance to someone else in the room. Mara's eyes turned towards the *taoiseach*, Garrett MacNamara, still greeting the visitors and accepting their condolences on the death of the *tánaiste*. The boy was the image of him.

'This is my brother's son, Peadar, and his mother Rhona,' said Jarlath with the air of someone enjoying the shock that he was causing. 'They are from Scotland; come and meet them,' he added and then introduced Mara to the woman, Rhona, whose eyes sparkled with interest as she heard Mara's office.

'We have a Brehon in the mountain area that I come from,' she said. 'I clean his house, help to milk his cattle and he gives me food and information. He it was who told me of my rights and what my son could expect.' She laughed suddenly, 'But I have never heard of a female Brehon. It's good to see a woman doing a job like that. Mostly it's the men telling us what to do and we knowing the right way to go before they even open their lips. That's what we say in Scotland, anyway,' she added.

'Well, then, if you come from Scotland, you must meet my scholar, Fiona,' said Mara, smiling. 'She, also, comes from that country and I think she gets homesick sometimes for it.'

'Come on, young Peadar, I'll introduce you to the beautiful girl scholar from your native land and we'll leave your mother to chat to the Brehon.' Jarlath took command in a lordly way, signalling to a maidservant to bring refreshments to Mara and taking his nephew by the arm and steering him across towards the group of scholars.

'You are surprised to see my Peadar!' Rhona eyed Mara appraisingly. Her Scottish accent was stronger than Fiona's but the Gaelic was near enough to the Irish form to make her quite comprehensible.

'Very,' said Mara frankly. 'I did not know that Garrett had a son.' She looked across at Garrett and his wife Slaney. Slaney had come from the English city of Galway, twenty miles away – not from the MacNamara clan or from any of the other three clans on the Burren. They had married quite soon after Garrett had succeeded to the office of *taoiseach*, but over four years had now passed and there was no sign of a child. Slaney, thought Mara, looked white and ill. She had never liked the woman much, finding her arrogant and intolerant, and uninterested in the customs and laws of her husband's clan, but now she felt sorry for her. This must be a terrible blow to her.

'Garrett has acknowledged Peadar as a son.' Rhona broke into her thoughts. 'And,' she added, watching Mara's face, 'he has invited me into the household as his second wife. There is talk of a divorce from his chief wife, but I don't know whether he's serious about that or not.' She shrugged her wide shoulders with an air of indifference.

I wonder what Slaney had to say about that? Mara suppressed the question and tried to smile in a natural fashion. 'You met in Scotland, did you?' she asked politely.

Rhona shook her head. 'On board ship we met; out in Spain. I was the ship's captain's wife. My husband's dead now.' Her voice was harsh and indifferent when she mentioned her husband's death, but Mara offered a conventional expression of sympathy. Her mind was whirring. Why had she not heard of this before now?

10

'When did you arrive, you and your son, Rhona?' she asked.

'Just recently,' the woman replied. 'We came on the same ship that Jarlath travelled on – from the north of Ireland. We had crossed over from Scotland a week ago with Jarlath when we heard that he was making the journey. Jarlath had already arranged to sell his ship to O'Donnell and in return to be allowed to journey down to the Burren on one of O'Donnell's boats.'

'So you came with Jarlath?' asked Mara, her mind grappling with the problem of Garrett taking a second wife. It was quite a common occurrence in Gaelic society, especially among the wealthy who could afford the expense, but Slaney had never been part of that society and she would find this even harder to accept than most wives would do.

'That's right,' said Rhona. 'O'Donnell was sending someone down here, and there was plenty of room for three more. Look, there's the man, over there. Jarlath invited him to come to stay with his brother. He's called Stephen Gardiner, that Englishman over there, the one that has gone over to talk to Slaney.' She pointed across the room to where Slaney, rigid and pale-faced, was endeavouring to smile upon the stranger.

Definitely English, thought Mara. This Stephen wore a small pointed beard, instead of Irish moustaches, and he was dressed in tight-fitting brightly-coloured hose, and an elaborate, bulky tunic, with a short cloak swinging from his shoulders. Middle to late twenties, thought Mara, about the same age as Jarlath, his travelling

11

companion, who must now be at least twenty-five; she dismissed him from her mind and turned back to the woman beside her.

'If you only arrived a little while ago,' she said, 'this explains why I have not heard of the matter. If Gareth has the intention to declare you formally as his wife of the second degree, then this should be done as soon as possible – preferably tomorrow – at the judgement day at Poulnabrone.' She hesitated a moment, her eyes going to Garrett – was the man really going to impose a second wife into the household? Slaney would find that a barbarous custom. Or did he intend to get a divorce from Slaney? And on what grounds? Infertility, perhaps; that was certainly grounds for divorce for either party in a marriage. It was obvious, now, that Garrett had fathered at least one child, so the fault must lie with Slaney. Still she would hear when he had made up his mind. She wouldn't disturb him now in the midst of this mourning for his cousin, the *tánaiste*, she decided. However, the legal status of this son and new wife would have to be ratified and the sooner the better.

'I think you should remind him of his obligations to put this on a legal footing, so do make sure, Rhona, that he, you and your son are at Poulnabrone for the judgement ceremonies tomorrow. He needs to declare in public to the people that Peadar is a true son of his and that you are his wife.'

When Rhona said nothing in reply to this, Mara wondered whether she should ask the question

12

in her mind; decided that it was none of her business, but still could not resist it.

'Is Slaney staying on at the castle?' she asked.

Rhona hunched an indifferent shoulder. 'You'll have to ask her that, Brehon.' Her smile broadened. 'Jarlath tells me that she comes from a family of wealthy merchants and I'm just the daughter of a poor cattle dealer in the mountains of Scotland. I know more about cows than I do about golden sovereigns. She doesn't even speak to me.'

Not surprising, thought Mara. She liked Rhona, she decided. She was no beauty with her broad, weather-beaten brown face, and her slightly rusty-blond hair but she had a straight-forward, honest look in her grey eyes. Her position in the household would not be an easy one. The position of a wife of the second degree seldom was. And then there was Garrett himself. Mara wondered whether an inde-pendent-looking woman like Rhona would be able to stand Garrett too long – not to mention his unpleasant wife, Slaney. Still mother-love was a potent force and no doubt Rhona was doing this for Peadar's sake and might only stay for long enough to make sure that he got his dues.

However, Mara had many people to greet so with a nod and smile at the Scottish woman she moved on to speak to other mourners. The MacNamara clan had turned out in big numbers for this wake – perhaps the rumour about the newcomers had spread and all had been curious to see the newly discovered son and the wife

13

of second degree. Many of them were unknown to her as they came from the bordering kingdom of Thomond, rather than from the Burren. The MacNamara clan had moved east, though their *taoiseach*'s place of residence remained here, high on the rocky cliff that overlooked the fertile valley at Carron. But whether they came from Burren or Thomond, all seemed eager to find out how the wife of Garrett was taking the arrival of these two from Scotland.

Mara began to feel rather sorry for Slaney, who was pretending to make indifferent conversation with this Stephen Gardiner from London. Slaney had ridden high and had ridden roughshod over her husband and his clan since their marriage four years ago and now she had to share the position of wife with this stranger from Scotland. She had, poor woman, proved barren and another's son would inherit what should have been given to her offspring. Would Slaney wait for Garrett to divorce her? Or would she, now before there were any scandals aired, go straight back to her people in Galway? She would get plenty of sympathy there; the right of a man to take a second wife would certainly be declared to be a pagan custom in that anglicised city which regulated its conduct by English laws and English customs.

'Not too happy,' said Maol MacNamara, Garrett's steward, breaking into Mara's thoughts. He gave a nod towards Slaney. His face wore a malicious smile.

'A death is always a sad occasion,' said Mara coolly, deliberately misunderstanding him. She

14

had no very high opinion of Maol. A steward should be loyal to his master. Maol was a poor manager, a gossip and a spreader of information. He was honest enough, she reckoned; at least she had not heard any rumours to the contrary, but that might not be any credit to him. Garrett, with his obsession about money, would be a difficult man to cheat and Maol would not have the brains to deceive him.

'What do you think about this terrible weather, Maol?' she said briskly. The weather was usually a safe source for conversation in this land of farming, but it didn't seem to work well this time. Maol's face darkened.

'Nothing I can do about the weather, Brehon,' he said with the air of one who was glad to air a grievance. 'It wasn't my fault that the spring sowing of the oats failed.' He cast a furious look across the room at his *taoiseach*. 'How could I know that the weather would take a turn for the worse? If I sowed too late then I would be found to be in the wrong, too.'

'As the good book says: "He that observeth the wind shall not sow; and he that regardeth the clouds shall not reap,"' said Mara with a bland smile. She had often found that a store of quotes from the Bible had been of great use in situations like this; a respectful pause usually ensued and the subject could be changed.

Maol, however, did not avail himself of this opportunity.

'I feel that I have been very badly treated, Brehon,' he pronounced ponderously.

Mara sighed inwardly, but after all her years

15

as Brehon of the Burren, she was well used to the way that people brought up the trickiest of law problems on these social occasions. She hastily banished from her memory the scorn expressed by her own farm manager at Maol's poor judgement and of how Cumhal had laughed when he saw the MacNamara fields sown with oat seed on a blustery day of freezing north-easterly winds.

'You feel that your *taoiseach* has not been fair to you,' she remarked mildly, observing that Maol's face had darkened to an almost purple shade.

'He has threatened to dismiss me,' said Maol bluntly. She noticed that his right hand had doubled itself into a fist, clenching so tightly that, when he undid it and held the hand dramatically out to her, she could see nail marks on his palms.

'I ask you, Brehon,' he said, his voice breaking with emotion, 'what am I going to do if he carries out his threat? I will be disgraced entirely. He'll do it, too. He's a hard master. He dismissed his cowman, Brennan, just because the dun cow miscarried of a heifer calf – so he said.'

Mara thought about it; Brennan would probably go back to stay with his brother over the border with Thomond, but for this man to lose the job of a steward was a more serious matter. Maol had been a small farmer at the foot of the Oughtmama hills to the north of the kingdom of the Burren and he had given that farm up when he had been appointed. Most had been surprised when Garrett had chosen him as steward; openly

16

hinting that Maol had gained his position, less by ability, than by his shameless flattery of the newly-appointed *taoiseach*.

'Come and see me at Cahermacnaghten,' she said with an inward sigh, but a firm resolution not to be pushed into giving an opinion before she was in position of all the facts. 'We'll talk it all over then and you can tell me what you feel and what has been said. After that I will see your *taoiseach* and hear his side of the story.'

Maol grunted, not too pleased at this response and Mara sought to divert his attention before he could persist.

'How well Jarlath is looking,' she remarked, glancing across at the tall, well-tanned figure of Garrett's very much younger brother. 'It must be almost ten years since I have seen him. The life of a merchant has certainly suited him.'

Maol's face lit up with enthusiasm. 'A man who is interested in the land and in the people of the clan,' he agreed.

'You've met him, then?' asked Mara.

'I have, indeed,' said Maol. 'He has made a point of visiting all of his clansmen. The image of his father, he is. That's what we all say. It's like having the old man back again.' His face darkened. 'I could count on the fingers of one hand the number of times that *himself* has been inside my cottage.'

It was as she had thought; Garrett had not endeared himself to his clansmen since he had taken up his position in 1509. Four years should have been enough for the man to establish himself, but instead these years had only served to erase the memory of his popular father and create a desire for something new in the minds of the MacNamara clan.

'Come and see me next Monday,' she said firmly and moved away before he could reply. Monday would give a cooling-off period of five days and would give her time to think and to make a few discreet enquiries. She crossed the room and joined Jarlath and his cousin, the newly arrived Peadar from Scotland.

'Tell me what you have been doing since I saw you last, Jarlath,' she invited the young man cordially. He certainly would be popular with the clan. Jarlath did not resemble his brother, but had the same clear, light-coloured blue eyes, well-modelled nose and curly black hair that his father had possessed and these assets were enhanced by the deeply tanned skin which had resulted from his many sea voyages.

'How have you prospered?' she added.

To her surprise and admiration he did not seize on this as an occasion to boast but smiled deprecatingly. 'I'd bore you if I told you about every scrape I fell into, every piece of idiocy that I committed, every time that I was cheated,' he said modestly, and Mara saw that the boy Peadar looked at him with surprise and a touch of disappointment. No doubt he had been expecting to hear some very different stories about daring deeds on the high seas and of near-misses and feats of valour. Her opinion of Jarlath went up. How different he was to his elder brother, she thought, glancing across the room at Garrett.

There was some sort of quarrel going on; she could see that. Garrett was surrounded by some prominent members of his clan from both kingdoms. The blacksmith, Fintan MacNamara, whose forge was on the western side of the Burren, was speaking now and even though, for Fintan, the tone of voice was lowered, a man such as Fintan, built like a bull, reared in a forge where there was incessant clamour of beaten iron, could never successfully talk quietly.

'It's for the clan to elect the *tánaiste*,' he was saying, 'and with all respect to you, my lord, I say that we do it here and now; the clan is present, the Brehon, herself, is present; no reason why it can't be all signed and sealed while the night is young.'

Garrett said something, his long face flushed with anger. Mara could not hear his words but the response was instant.

'I see no disrespect to the dead, my lord,' bellowed Fintan. 'Lord have mercy on him, the poor man was a good and loyal member of the clan and he's probably wishing that we would get on with the business and appoint his successor and allow him to enjoy his eternal rest.' Fintan cast a glance up towards the high carved ceiling of the great hall and crossed himself piously. The rest of clan followed suit, and having, thought Mara suppressing a smile, checked the wishes of the deceased, they turned angry faces back towards their *taoiseach*. She put down her goblet of sour Spanish wine and made her way swiftly across to the cluster around Garrett. Trouble, she found, could often be averted by

19

her mere presence. Garrett's lower lip was jutting out like the curved edge of a platter and his eyes were full of anger.

Many of the men gathered around him were unknown to her as most of the MacNamara land lay east of the kingdom of the Burren, in Corcomroe and Thomond, but all knew her; as the only woman Brehon in Ireland she was famous and in addition her marriage three years ago to Turlough Donn O'Brien, king of the three kingdoms of Thomond, Corcomroe and Burren, made her well known to all of his subjects. Voices ceased and men stood back as she joined the group.

'We were discussing the subject of the election of the new *tánaiste*, Brehon,' said Niall MacNamara, a neighbour of Fintan. Niall was attached to Fintan and grateful to him because he had a half brother, Balor; a huge strong man, but mentally retarded whom Fintan employed. Balor was extremely happy working at the forge; he was good with animals and proud of his enormous strength which allowed him to swing the heaviest hammer. It was no wonder, thought Mara, that Niall would support Fintan in this matter.

'The clan favours Jarlath,' said Niall. 'We of the Burren have decided that is our wish. And Tomás, here—' he indicated a dark-haired man with an air of authority, who was standing beside Garrett – 'he's from Thomond, Brehon; well, he favours electing Jarlath as the *tánaiste* as well.' He cast a dubious glance at Garrett's bad-tempered face, and stepped back hastily, murmuring, 'We're all in favour of doing it here and now, Brehon, if that suits you.'

Niall was a peaceful man and obviously did not want to anger his *taoiseach*, Garrett, too much. Fintan, on the other hand, was too aggressive. This Tomás looked like a man who would be cautious and sensible in what he said so Mara addressed herself to him.

'Are all the clans represented here tonight?' she asked.

'All of them, Brehon,' he said respectfully. Garrett made an inarticulate sound, but Mara ignored him. When relationships were good then a *taoiseach* usually picked out his heir, but by law the decision was one for the clan to make. The king had to be involved in the election of the *taoiseach,* but his presence and approval was not necessary for the election of a *tánaiste.*

'And you are all agreed?' she asked looking around at the cluster of MacNamara clan members. Several, who had been standing in other parts of the room, sidled across to join them. There was a murmur of assent as Mara looked from one face to the other.

'Well, in that case, perhaps you will let me have the name of your choice,' she said. 'If you are all of the one mind, the ceremony can be held tonight if you wish. The king is not present, but I can act on his behalf.'

'We would like Jarlath, the brother of the *taoiseach*, to be the new *tánaiste,*' Tomás raised his voice slightly and spoke firmly. He looked straight ahead.

Garrett lifted a peremptory finger and beckoned

the young lad, Peadar, his newly-discovered son. Peadar came over, but his mother, Rhona, remained where she was, watching the scene with an amused smile.

'This is my choice for *tánaiste*,' he said, slipping an arm around the boy's shoulders. 'My son, Peadar, bred of my bone and acknowledged by me.'

There was a dead silence. All of the MacNamara clan exchanged glances with each other, but none looked at Garrett, or at his newly discovered son. Jarlath strolled over and stood beside the two, his eyebrows slightly raised. The contrast between his tall, broad-shouldered figure and the slight, underdeveloped adolescent boy at his side was enough to start a murmur among the clan. The rest of the neighbours from the Burren watched with interest. Even those praying beside the coffin returned their rosary beads to their pouches and went to stand by the fireplace and to watch the drama that had unexpectedly unfolded.

'Perhaps, Brehon, we could vote on the choice before us,' suggested the man named Tomás and there was an eager murmur of agreement from the clan.

'Those in favour of electing Jarlath MacNamara as *tánaiste* please raise your right hand,' said Mara, looking around at the faces.

Every hand was raised except that of Garrett and of his son.

'For Peadar?' queried Mara.

Only Garrett's hand went up. Peadar looked unsure and then embarrassed. Rhona strolled away and stood looking out through the window.

Slaney glanced away from Stephen Gardiner, surveyed the crowd with a look of disdain and then turned back to him again.

'I refuse to allow this matter to go forward,' stated Garrett. He thrust his lower lip forward and glared belligerently at his clan members.

Mara touched Garrett on the arm and withdrew towards one of the window seats, leaving him to follow her.

'You don't feel that Jarlath will make a good *tánaiste*, is that correct, *taoiseach*?' she asked. She made sure that her low-spoken words could not be overheard by the clan and that her voice was calm and sounded neutral. She could not afford to take sides against one of the chieftains in the kingdom where she was responsible for maintaining law and order. Fights and even battles could flare up at a moment's notice among these martial clans. Or worse, outsiders might be embroiled in the quarrel and could bring war into the peaceful kingdom of the Burren.

'What's the problem, Garrett?' she asked briskly, seating herself on the broad window seat and signalling him to sit beside her. At least his appalling wife, Slaney, hadn't moved away from her seat by the fire to follow them. She was too engaged in her conversation with Stephen Gardiner. Garrett did not even glance in her direction. Up to now, thought Mara, Garrett had always appeared to be completely under the thumb of his Galway-born, English-speaking wife. How on earth had he found the courage to introduce a new wife and a fifteen-year-old son into the household?

'What have you against the appointment of Jarlath as your *tánaiste*?' she asked when he said nothing.

'No objection,' he mumbled. 'It's just that I hoped, in fact I was sure, that my son, Peadar, would be elected to the position. It seemed like providence when he arrived in the very hour when I first heard of the *tánaiste*'s death,' he explained.

Mara stared at him. Was the man mad? Sure? How could he possibly have been sure?

'What, a fifteen-year-old boy who has just arrived into the country – totally unknown to your clan! That would never be approved of, Garrett. I wonder that you should have thought that.' Mara decided that she would not waste any more time. The clan was uneasy and rebellious. Her instincts told her that there could be trouble. The MacNamara clan was never part of the Burren in the way as the O'Brien, the O'Lochlainn or even the O'Connor clan with its roots in west Corcomroe.

'Well, he is my son and I have accepted him,' he argued.

'And rightly so,' said Mara soothingly with an eye on his high colour. The man looked about to explode. 'He does seem to bear the family face and I presume you are happy with the date of birth and with Rhona's testimony.'

He nodded vigorously. 'She's a good woman, Rhona. I should have married her instead of . . .'

'However, that does not alter the fact that the boy is only fifteen years old and is quite unknown to the clan,' continued Mara firmly. 'The clan is, by courtesy, consulting you about this matter and I don't see that you can have any complaint when they are proposing to choose your brother. And it does make sense to get through the legal business tonight when so many members of such a widespread clan as yours are present. We can deal with the declaration of Peadar to be your son and Rhona to be your wife of the second degree tomorrow, but the election of Jarlath can perfectly well take place tonight.' She watched his frowning face for a moment and added quietly. 'I would do it with as good grace as you can muster, Garrett. In the end, the choice will not be yours. What say you? Shall we do it now?' She did not wait for an answer but got to her feet decisively and moved back to where the clan stood.

'We will deal with this affair now,' she said briskly.

The north-easterly wind was freezing when the MacNamara clan moved out of doors to inaugurate their new *tánaiste*. Mara was glad of her fur-lined woollen mantle and the heir-elect, Jarlath, made a great show of shivering dramatically. He was very well-liked, Mara could see, as the clan surged forward to gather under the newly-budded branches of the huge ash tree. Many clapped him on the back and joked with him about the warmth in Spain and of the beauty of the sunburnt ladies in that country. Mara gathered her mantle more closely around her as they went down the path into the small hidden place where these events took place. At least

25

they were sheltered from the wind here, she thought, as she climbed up onto the raised platform of heavy stone slabs beside the cairn, the inauguration place of the MacNamara clan on the Burren. Jarlath took his place on one side of her and Garrett on the other. Slaney, Mara was interested to note, had hesitated for a moment, but then joined them, casting a look of loathing at Garrett. Rhona and her son Peadar remained on the ground below, slightly outside the enclosure space, standing beside the smooth-barked trunk of the giant ash tree. Curious glances were cast at them but both stared straight ahead and ignored these.

'Let's get this over as quickly as possible,' muttered Jarlath and Mara frowned. This inauguration of a *tánaiste* was one of the prehistoric ceremonies of Gaelic Ireland and one that would be lost in the future if the young king of England, Henry VIII, had his way. Already the new *taoiseach* of the O'Donnell clan in northern Ireland had given up his ancient title of *Ri* (king) and accepted an earldom from the English king. Never again would the O'Donnell clan have an opportunity to elect the most suitable candidate to rule over them. From now on the inheritance would pass from father to son, generation after generation, even if the son were a mere infant in arms when the father died. Even when the heir was unsuitable, unpopular, or unstable, son would follow father as surely as night followed day.

I hope I never have to see such a situation here in the Burren during my lifetime, thought Mara and turned a face filled with solemnity towards the crowd. There was an instant silence, a silence that she allowed to last for a long minute before raising her well-trained voice.

'I, Mara, Brehon of the Burren, by the power devolved on me by Turlough Donn O'Brien, King of Thomond, Corcomroe and Burren; son of Teige; son of Turlough Beg; son of Brian; son of Mahon; son of Murrtough; son of Turlough; true descendent of the *derbhfine* of Brian, son of Cinnéide; now inaugurate Jarlath MacNamara as the new *tánaiste* of the MacNamara clan here in the Kingdom of Burren.'

Jarlath knelt and placed his hands within Mara's, as representative of the king. This was the ceremony of *imbas* where authority flowed from king to recipient. And the MacNamara clan broke out in thunderous applause when she released his hands, kissed him lightly on the cheek and turned to Garrett.

'My lord,' she said, 'I present to you Jarlath, *tánaiste* of the MacNamara clan.'

Two

Berrad Airecht
(Court Procedure)

*The judgements of a Brehon must be open to all
in the kingdom. They should be held in a place
where the clans may gather and it should be a
place that is sacred, such as an ancient burial
site, a dolmen or a cairn. All should be able to
see and to hear.*

*All of the people of the kingdom should hold
themselves ready to be called as a witness.*

'Garrett MacNamara isn't here, Brehon,' said
Fachtnan. He handed her a satchel, which she
placed on the flat surface of the dolmen's table
stone at Poulnabrone, while he set up a desk for
himself, arranging vellum, well sharpened quills
and an ink horn on a low, flat stone beside the
dolmen. Poulnabrone was the ancient judgement
place for the people of the kingdom of the Burren.
The dolmen was at the southern end of a large,
rough field, paved with great slabs of limestone
and littered with large, rounded boulders. A place
of great solemnity, but also of great beauty, Mara
always thought. In the grykes between the clints
of limestone the small flowers of the Burren grew
abundantly. Delicately pale flowers of the daisy-
like mountain avens contrasted with the tight,

28

pink, bud-like flowers of cat's paw and stiff columns of dark-purple early orchids rose up from between the slabs of rock everywhere. The field was a large one and stretched northwards for a couple of hundred yards, and the stones that littered its surface made convenient seats for the audience. Mara undid her satchel, took from it a couple of scrolls which she placed on the flat table-like surface of the dolmen and then stored the satchel itself beside one of the upright supporting slabs. She looked around. No, there was no sign of Garrett, anywhere. She would have expected to find him beside her, fussing in his usual fashion and trying to emphasise his own importance.

'Rhona and Peadar are coming down the road,' said Aidan. 'He's not with them, though.'

'Well, it's the last case to be heard,' said Mara, casting a quick glance around. Today was the eve of Bealtaine and the custom was to climb the mountain of Mullaghmore as soon as the judgement day cases had been resolved. I'm not waiting for him, she decided, and greeted the people of the kingdom, opening the proceedings with her usual briskness.

The first case, involving a matter of a shared stream, was fairly quickly dealt with, each landowner agreeing heartily to Mara's suggestion that they both devote a day's labour to clearing the silt and pebbles from the stream's pathway, thus ensuring that there was a plentiful supply of water and sufficient for both farms. The second was a divorce – not acrimonious, but a careful division of property had been made and the details had to be checked in public. The third was another straightforward affair of a boundary stone being moved and a long strip of land being stolen in order to plant extra oats. Mara imposed a fine, declared her intention of checking that the stone had been replaced and then looked around.

'He's definitely not here, Brehon,' said Fachtnan in a low voice. 'Nor is Slaney.'

Mara looked all around. No, there was no sign of Garrett anywhere. She saw Rhona was also looking around, her hand shielding her eyes, so Mara sent Aidan over to fetch her. Already some of the younger men had moved over to the stone wall where dozens of bundles of hazel rods had been laid out, ready for the traditional bonfire and others were shouldering leather bags containing wine from Spain. Soon her husband, King Turlough Donn, would arrive and then all would begin the climb which would culminate in an enormous bonfire lit on the summit of Mullaghmore at the hour of midnight. This business with Garrett and his introduction of a new son and wife to his household would only take minutes, but Garrett had to be there and had to make the formal application.

'He spoke to me this morning; told me that he would be here, but I haven't seen him since.' Rhona looked bewildered, her fair eyebrows drawn together in a frown and her grey eyes full of anxiety. 'I thought all was settled,' she said in a low voice.

'He's made a fool of you; he's not going to accept me as his son after all.' The boy, Peadar,

30

looked sulkily angry. He glared at Mara as if it were all her fault. His dignity had been badly hurt, she guessed, so resisted the temptation to frown and just nodded politely. Boys of that age were very sensitive, she knew and she felt sorry for him.

'This matter can easily be dealt with on the next judgement day – there is no hurry about it. It's after all a private matter and just a courtesy custom for the kingdom to be informed,' she said soothingly. 'But now we are all going to climb Mullaghmore Mountain for the Bealtaine bonfire. We hold it here every year on the eve of the feast. The bell from the abbey will sound at midnight and then the fire will be lit. Perhaps you and your mother would like to come, Peadar? Hugh, you could do with some help in carrying wood, couldn't you? Peadar will go with you and Shane. Where is Shane?'

'He's talking to that English man, Brehon,' said Aidan. 'Come on, Peadar, you come with us.'

Mara waved them away and turned to Rhona. 'He'll be better in the company of other boys,' she said. 'Otherwise he will just spend the evening wondering if his father has let him down. Will you come, also? You will enjoy it.' She spoke cordially but was somewhat distracted by searching for Shane. 'The Englishman' that Aidan referred to must mean Stephen Gardiner, but what was he talking or interrogating Shane about?

'There they are, over there.' Rhona pointed in the opposite direction to where Mara

31

had been looking. The Englishman had, like Fachtnan, used one of the flat stones as a desk. He was seated on another stone and, quill in hand, was making notes while Shane, perched on the table stone in front of him, seemed to be busily talking.

Mara moved quickly and was near them in a moment. Shane was in full flow, speaking fluent English, describing to Stephen Gardiner the studies that he and his fellow scholars undertook.

'And you study Latin, also, is that right?' the Englishman asked and then before Shane could answer he continued, '"*Arma virumque cano.*" Do you know what that means?'

Shane smiled with a slight look of disdain as he fluently continued the quotation from Vergil's first book of the *Aeneid*. '"*Troiae qui primus ab oris Italiam, fato profugus, Laviniaque venit, litora, multum ille et terris iactatus et alto vi superum saevae memorem Iunonis ob iram . . .*"'

'Don't show off, Shane,' said Mara, seating herself beside him on the flat stone and looking down at the book filled with exquisitely written notes. 'You are interested in what my scholars study?' She raised her eyebrows in a query to the young stranger. Who was he? And what was he doing here in this Gaelic kingdom? And why had Garrett invited him? She turned back a page and grimaced at some sketches of shock-headed men with exaggeratedly huge moustaches, entitled '*the wilde irishe*' in English. Turlough, her husband, had often said that he did not trust

32

Garrett and now she wondered whether he was right. What was this Englishman doing, staying with a Gaelic chieftain in the heart of a Gaelic kingdom?

'Who are these notes for?' she asked bluntly when he had not replied to her first question. The book must be at least half full.

'For my master, Cardinal Wolsey,' he said, finishing off his note and then shaking some fine dry sand from a small canister over the page. He looked up and smiled engagingly at her.

'And who is Cardinal Wolsey?' she asked tartly, annoyed that he had interrogated one of her scholars without asking permission.

Stephen Gardiner looked at her with astonishment. 'Have you never heard of him? Cardinal Wolsey is the most important man in England – after the king, of course.'

'And he is interested in Brehon law?' Mara glanced down at the closely written page of notes. 'Brehon law is now once again widespread throughout Ireland except for an area of only about ten miles around Dublin,' she read.

'Of course; it's regarded as a big drawback to the civilisation of Ireland,' said Stephen Gardiner. He smiled disarmingly and added, 'In the Latin sense, you understand.'

Mara laughed. She liked young men with sharp wits. 'So you think that Ireland would be improved if it were turned into a country full of city states,' she said her eyes looking with satisfaction across the landscape of green fields and rounded mountains. 'Come up the mountain with

33

us and you can fill another page of your notebook about the May Day customs of those strange Irish people.'

'He's been telling me about the court of Henry VIII and how no one can come near him without passing through fifty guards, all armed to the teeth,' said Shane, sounding impressed.

'Come and meet another king, who walks among his people with no fear,' said Mara. Her sharp eyes had spotted the tall, burly figure of her husband vaulting the wall from the road and striding forward, carrying a small boy perched on his shoulder. Jarlath MacNamara was with him, she noticed, but he hung back and allowed the king to make his way through the throng of people, greeting them and enquiring about their cows, their elderly relations, their new babies.

Turlough Donn had become king of Thomond, Corcomroe and Burren in the year 1499 so had now held the office for almost fourteen years. He was a heavily built man – in his middle-fifties, though he looked younger as his brown hair, which had given him the nickname of 'Donn', was only just beginning to turn grey. He had light green eyes, a pleasant open face and a pair of huge moustaches. He and Mara had married at Christmas in the year 1509 and their son, Cormac, had been born in the following June.

'I'm climbing the mountain,' yelled three-year-old Cormac as they came near. He eyed his mother triumphantly. 'You said I'd have to wait until next year and you were wrong,' he remarked.

34

'And I don't suppose that you remembered to tell your father that I had already said no,' remarked Mara.

'He's as full of tricks as a barrel load of eels,' said Turlough with simple pride. He looked inquisitively at the stranger and Mara presented Stephen who made him a courtly bow and then shook hands heartily.

'I've heard of you, my lord,' he said eyeing the king with curiosity and Turlough beamed happily at him.

'I suppose it was the Earl of Kildare – I know what he said about me,' he remarked with a laugh. 'Do you know what he said about your father, Cormac? He said that I was the most terrible man in Ireland and the greatest enemy to England.'

'I'm much, much, more terribler that you,' said Cormac emphatically. He plucked a hazel rod from the bundle carried by Hugh and began whacking it against a rock with war-like cries and then neatly sliced the head from an early purple orchid and looked around for applause. Stephen Gardiner laughed and the people of the Burren, all waiting for their king and their Brehon to lead the way towards the mountain, rewarded him with smiles and murmurs of admiration, but Mara said firmly, 'No warrior cuts the heads off flowers; just silly babies.'

Cormac, she thought, was getting very spoilt. He was made much of by everyone on the Burren and as he had a lordly disposition he enjoyed the attention that he got. He was still rather too young for school, but the sooner he started with some regular work there, the better for his character. Turlough had adult sons and nephews to inherit his titles – the plan for Cormac was that he, like his mother and her father, Cormac's grandfather, would be a lawyer, not a king. His foster mother was teaching both him and his foster brother to read and to write – she herself was learning the skill alongside the two little boys – and Cormac was picking it up with great rapidity. He had a retentive memory and would be well able to start memorising law texts and learning some Latin verbs by next September. He was scowling at her now, but then his face cleared as Bran, Mara's magnificent, pure-white wolfhound, joined them with wagging tail and a rough pink tongue with which he washed behind Cormac's ears.

'Me and Bran will go first and lead you all the right way,' he announced and swaggered off with one hand gripping the wolfhound's collar.

'Sorry,' said Turlough apologetically to his wife, 'I didn't know that you had told him he couldn't go.'

'He would take good care not to tell; never mind,' she added in a lower voice. 'It will give us a good excuse to come back down when we reach the third or fourth terrace. I get bored hanging around waiting until midnight.' She would leave Fachtnan in charge of the boys – all of whom were old enough and sensible enough, but Fiona was a problem. The girl would be rightly annoyed if she were dragged away before the fun had begun, but she was conscious of her responsibility to Fiona's father, a one-time schoolmate of hers, to keep his daughter safe from young men who were attracted to her like bees to may blossom flowers. There would be a lot of drinking tonight, thought Mara. Most of the men had leather flasks, filled with rough red Spanish wine, slung across their backs. She wondered what to do.

And then Mara's face cleared. She beckoned to Fiona, included Hugh and Shane in her gesture and went across to where the Scottish woman, Rhona, once more accompanied by her son, Peadar, was sitting looking rather lonely and embarrassed on the edge of one of the huge flat stones or clints which littered the High Burren.

'Stay with them for the evening; they're strangers and deserve courtesy at our hands,' she said to her three scholars. 'Fiona, would you find Fachtnan?'

To Rhona she said, 'My scholars will look after you and see that you both have a good time this evening.' And then in low voice she added, 'And I would be very obliged if you would keep an eye on Fiona and make sure that she doesn't drink too much or go out of your sight. Fachtnan will manage the boys but he has no control over Fiona.'

'In love with her, probably; she is a pretty girl.' Rhona gave an amused glance after Fiona and said thoughtfully, 'The local boys will be careful as they will have you to reckon with – I know how respected our Brehon is, back home in Scotland – but I'll make sure that Stephen Gardiner behaves himself. It looks as though he is coming also.'

* * *

Despite the cold wind, the mountain of Mullaghmore was as beautiful as ever. Orchids, violets, primroses and tiny gentians, as darkly blue as the Atlantic Ocean itself, lined the pathway as they began the climb. Mara and Turlough went slowly allowing the younger and fitter people of the kingdom to go ahead of them, stopping from time to time to admire the orchids, much to Cormac's annoyance. He'd tire soon, she knew from experience, and then Turlough could carry him for while and after that they would have a good excuse to go back down and relax over one of Brigid's splendid dinners. Her housekeeper was a wonderful cook and at the time that Mara had left for Poulnabrone she had been already brewing sauces from sundried mushrooms and making a wonderful paste from the well-preserved small tart fruits of the bird cherry tree that grew in the little woodland outside Mara's house.

'What's this about Garrett MacNamara taking a second wife and suddenly producing a son of fifteen?' Teige O'Brien, cousin to Turlough and *taoiseach* of the O'Brien clan on the Burren, joined them.

'And never turned up today to ratify the whole business, or so they've been telling me,' said Turlough. 'Strange fellow – wanted his fifteen-year-old son to be elected as *tánaiste* instead of young Jarlath over there. Fine fellow, Jarlath, you'll get on well with him, Teige. We met at the crossroad and came on here together. I liked him. Had some great tales to tell of his sea voyages.' He whispered something in Teige's ear and the two of them laughed uproariously as if they were back in the days when they had been foster brothers and schoolboys together and Turlough's uncle, Conor na Srona – he of the big nose – had been lord of the three kingdoms, Thomond, Corcomroe and Burren.

Jarlath, as well as Stephen Gardiner, noticed Mara, had joined the party of her scholars and the couple from Scotland. Fiona would be having fun, she guessed, but felt confident that Rhona would keep matters under control. The woman had a firm look about her. Her grey eyes were full of resolution and her height and broad-shouldered figure gave her a look of authority.

'I'm going to ride on Bran's back,' announced Cormac after another five minutes had elapsed.

'No, you're not,' said Mara firmly. 'A dog's back is not strong enough for a big boy like you; see if you can get up to the next terrace and then we'll all have a rest.' It was good for him, she thought, to know that actions had consequences. She had explained to him that he was too young to climb a mountain and he had insisted on coming with his indulgent father. He would be exhausted tonight but it would do him no harm. She would get Fergal and Conall, her husband's bodyguards, to carry him in a 'wounded man's lift' for part of the way back and that would delight him.

'We'll have to get him a little pony,' said Turlough, looking lovingly after his youngest son.

'And one for Art,' said Mara firmly. It was a rule with her that anything Cormac had, his little foster brother had to have, also. She didn't want her son growing up thinking he had to have special privileges. He'd soon settle down once he started school and had his daily tasks and the discipline, she told herself and looked around at the beauty that surrounded them – the silvered limestone mountains all around and the very blue lakes below.

Mullaghmore, like most of the other mountains on the Burren, was a rounded mountain, shaped into spiralling terraces of limestone rock, layered one on top of the other. The young and the fit climbed straight up, making for the top terrace in the most direct way even if at times it meant hanging on with fingers and toes. Mara and Turlough followed the general crowd and sauntered around the terraces, content to make slow progress with their rapidly tiring son.

'We'll just walk around this terrace and then quietly come back down on the other side,' said Mara as Turlough swept Cormac into his arms. 'Go on, Bran, go and find Fachtnan. Good boy. Stay with Fachtnan.'

He was a well-trained dog and though he looked at her for a moment to make quite sure that she did really mean it, he obeyed her almost instantly. She had a momentary qualm about sending him from her side, but he would enjoy himself with the boys; it would have been disappointing for Bran to return so soon and Fachtnan would take good care of him. Once again, she thanked her lucky stars that she had thought of keeping Fachtnan on as an assistant teacher when he had eventually scraped through his final examination. He was supposed to be studying for a qualification of *ollamh* (professor) but he had a terribly bad memory and study was a torment to him. He was now almost twenty-three years of age, and perhaps, she thought, he had gone as far as his capabilities would allow.

Cormac raised a protest when they turned to go back, but was distracted by the immense view of land and sky that spread out below them and of the lake in the distance which reminded him to demand to be taken out in a boat.

'In the summer,' said Mara as she seated herself on a rock and looked down at the empty fields below her. Cormac seemed drowsy and a short sleep would refresh him for the journey down. She was content to sit, sheltered from the cold wind by the mountainside and to look at what she firmly believed to be the most beautiful view in the world: the limestone shining silver and pink in the setting sun and the lake's deep blue reflecting the sky above. Spirits were high – the good weather of the day had brought a wave of hopefulness back to the farmers and she heard many plans being made for the month of May by those who passed them.

Almost the whole of the Burren were on the mountain by now, she thought. Very few houses had smoke coming from them, the roads were deserted, the fields empty . . . Her eyelids drooped as she leaned against Turlough's broad shoulder and a minute later she knew somewhere in the depths of her mind that she, like her little son, warm and heavy in her arms, had dropped off to sleep.

* * *

'Oh, *shluagh*, the cows are out,' said Cormac, using a favourite word of his foster mother's. He sat up very straight, instantly wide awake in the way that young children can be and Mara opened a sleepy eye.

'What!' she said. And then a moment later she heard the noise that his young ears had already caught. It was the sound of hoofs hammering onto a limestone surface. It was not just a few cows out from their field, though. This thundering that they were hearing came from hundreds and hundreds of cows. She stood up in alarm and moved over to the edge of the terrace and looked back down towards the south-east of the mountain. From above their heads came cries of anger.

And then the direction of the crowd turned abruptly. Men and boys who had been struggling to be first to the top of the mountain turned around and began to hurl themselves down the rocky slopes. They were stopped abruptly, though. Suddenly above the clamour of dismayed exclamations and oaths came the *'be-be-be'* mountaineering call. Everyone stopped and peered upwards at the low-set squat figure who had climbed to the high tip of a boulder. Muiris O'Hynes had taken charge, as he had done so often in times of danger or disaster.

'Don't waste your time going down that side. You'll be behind them,' he bellowed. 'I'm ashamed of you all. Aren't you cattlemen? Don't you know that the way to get cattle to run faster is to chase them? You saw the beasts – they'll be at Noughaval by now. Soon they will be running up the Carron Road, and then down past the castle. We know where they are going, don't you? They'll get them through the border of the kingdom, at Abbey Hill, and then they'll have them on O'Flaherty land and they can take their time. We'll go down on the north-east side and get in front of them before they reach the border, head them off.'

'And any man who can catch one of my young horses grazing in Glencolumkille valley is welcome to borrow it,' called Ardal O'Lochlainn, chieftain of his clan and a breeder of champion racehorses.

'What are we waiting for?' yelled Muiris, brandishing his knife. 'Let's go!'

So many knives were brandished, their polished surfaces catching the dying rays of red from the sun that for a moment it seemed as though the bonfire had been lit after all. No further words were spoken though; the people of the Burren were now grimly determined that no one was going to rob them of the fruits of their hard labour.

But into that sudden cessation of sound, the war cry from the raiders rose high above the thundering hoofs of the cows, 'O'Donnell *Abú*.'

The words were a shrill scream of defiance and Mara, looking sharply up at the group of her scholars who were being shepherded down the hill by Fachtnan, stared straight into the amused and unsurprised eyes of Stephen Gardiner.

Stephen Gardiner – Cardinal Wolsey – Henry VIII – Donegal – Territory of the O'Donnell – of

O'Donnell who had sold his birthright to bend the knee in front of an English king, Henry, the Eighth of that name; O'Donnell who had given up his birthright and his kingship in order to call himself 'Earl'.

Thoughts flashed rapidly through Mara's mind and suddenly she began to understand.

'Turlough,' she breathed as he got to his feet, deposited little Cormac on her lap and strode to the edge of the terrace. 'Turlough, I beseech you not to go. This is a trap. O'Donnell is trying to entrap you and perhaps send you to England. Don't go; I beseech you. Leave it to other, younger men.'

'O'Donnell! That lap dog of the English!' exclaimed Turlough in tones of such loathing that Mara realised she had made a mistake.

'Let's go back to my place, Turlough, and we'll pick up horses and men-at-arms there,' shouted Teige O'Brien. 'Go on, you fellows,' he dismissed his followers with a peremptory wave, 'get down the mountain as quickly as you can and meet us with some good horses.'

'By God,' said Turlough with satisfaction, 'we may not be in the front of them, but O'Donnell and his cattle raiders will wish that they had never been born by the time that we catch up with them from behind.'

Mara breathed a sigh of relief. If Turlough was with Teige O'Brien and a detachment of men-at-arms – and, in addition, was behind the raiding party and their pursuers, not much harm could come to him.

'My lord, may we go with you,' shouted Aidan

as the law scholars and their companions came tumbling down the steep, rocky path. Fiona, Mara hoped, was staying with Rhona and her son.

'Certainly not,' said Mara swiftly, before Turlough could say anything. 'I am responsible to your parents for you. In any case, Cormac and I need you to guard us and escort us back to the law school.'

'I'm going to beat up O'Donnell,' shouted Cormac.

'We'd better go back to Cahermacnaghten and get your sword first,' said Fachtnan swooping up the small boy and placing him on his shoulders. Mara looked at him with gratitude. He was loyal to her and would make sure that the scholars got back, unharmed, to the law school.

'You'll come, Jarlath, good man yourself?' shouted Turlough over his shoulder as he lowered his bulk down from a precarious hold on a protruding rock. Fergal and Conall, his bodyguards, swung themselves down behind him, their eyes racking the surrounding mountain anxiously.

'I'll be ahead of you, my lord,' called back Jarlath, bounding vigorously in the opposite direction, towards the north side of the mountain. 'I'll pick up a horse at Carron Castle and root out Garrett, too. We'll need ropes and things. He will lose all of his cattle, I'd say; by what I saw, they're headed in that direction, but hopefully we'll get them back.'

'And what about you, Stephen?' queried Mara ignoring the sulky faces of Aidan and Moylan.

This would be the moment, she thought, when he would slink away and find some means of joining up with O'Donnell and going back to England, probably on an O'Donnell ship. However, he surprised her.

'I'm not very war-like,' he said with a slight grimace. 'Could I form one of your escort – Cormac will protect me, won't you, Cormac?' He reached up and patted the little boy on the head.

'I'll chop the heads off all the O'Donnell clan when I get my sword,' promised Cormac with a patronising assurance. He shook Stephen's hand from his head, wriggled down out of Fachtnan's arms and marched ahead with dignity.

'What about Rhona and Peadar?' asked Fachtnan, looking back up the mountain.

'You shouldn't . . .' began Mara hastily and then stopped. She had been about to say, 'you shouldn't have come down without them', but then realised Fachtnan's dilemma: he had to stay with Moylan and Aidan; for two pins, these two would have been off chasing the cattle raiders. A slight discourtesy to Garrett's relations was of little importance compared with keeping safe the boys that she had placed under his care. She held her hand up to shield her eyes from the setting sun and then to her relief saw Fiona's bright yellow hair and behind her the tall figure of the Scots woman and behind that Peadar, all making their way slowly down from the terrace above. A few minutes later they were all in front of her.

'Will you come back with us to the law

school?' asked Mara hospitably, hoping that her housekeeper, Brigid, had enough food in her store cupboard for three unexpected guests. Turlough, she hoped, would be back within a couple of hours, with his bodyguards and probably Teige and some of his men might be with him. There would have to be a late-night supper prepared for them. Her celebration dinner for two people would have to be stretched to accommodate the pair from Scotland and the man from England.

'Do you think that I should?' said Rhona hesitantly. She took a step nearer to Mara with the air of one who wanted to say something in private and Mara moved with her away from the others.

'Should we go back to the Carron Castle, myself and Peadar; what do you think, Brehon? I hate having such bad feeling between us and Slaney. And between Garrett and Slaney, also. I haven't been able to talk to her, been able to explain, but now Garrett and Jarlath will be off chasing cows and Stephen will be with you, so perhaps it's a good time for the two of us to talk.'

'That's well thought of,' said Mara, feeling that she was liking this woman more and more as time went on. 'But if I know Slaney she will want to be out there directing operations,' she continued. 'I think you should leave it for the moment. Today will be full of anger and frustration if Garrett's cows are stolen. Do come back with us and give everything time to settle down.' Privately she thought that there was little that

Rhona could do about the situation. A woman like Slaney would not forgive easily.

Rhona agreed so readily that Mara suspected she was dreading an interview with Slaney. Allowing the younger ones to go ahead the two of them walked side by side and chatted. Rhona had been the daughter and only child of a cattle dealer who had built up a business in buying and selling the small, hardy cattle from the mountains of Scotland to lowland farms.

'He was disappointed that I married a sea-going man and then when my husband died and we, myself and Peadar, came back, he was furious that the boy spent all his time at the monastery, gardening for the monks and that he had no interest in cows. My father died last year and he left all his stock and the farm to his brother's son and Peadar and I were left with nothing.'

Well, that perhaps solved the puzzle of why Rhona had come over to Ireland to seek out Garrett after fifteen years. Under Brehon law the woman had a right to name the father of her son at any stage during her life, even when on her deathbed. But why had Rhona not contested her father's will, sought the help of this Brehon whom she had mentioned? None of my business, thought Mara. In any case, Rhona soon excused herself and went to walk beside her sulky-looking son, talking to him in hushed tones while Mara fell back to join her other guest.

'So how did you find the O'Donnell when you were in Donegal?' she asked casually as Stephen Gardiner gallantly offered her an arm down a steep section of the mountain. She scanned him narrowly as she asked the question. Was he here to cause trouble?

'The O'Donnell – oh, you mean the earl; you mean Earl O'Donnell,' he contradicted her with a pleasant smile. 'The king has ennobled him, you know. The first of many, it is hoped. I met him in Scotland with King James IV. I was on a mission to the Scottish court and when he heard about Cardinal Wolsey's project to write about Ireland, the noble earl extended an invitation to me.'

She looked at him with amusement. 'So the plan is to *ennoble* all of the leaders of the poor *wilde* Irish and to turn our country into a place of civilisation.'

'That's right,' he said eagerly, not noticing the irony in her voice. 'Of course, it will be difficult in the beginning – changing customs. But – well, you're an intelligent woman. You must see that laws such as you operate – these Brehon laws – these are laws for savages, not for civilised people. No wonder that there is no law and order when no proper penalties are imposed. Look at those cases today! Why, that man who stole some of his neighbour's land – he would have been hanged in England, and yet he only got a trivial fine. And then that woman wanting to divorce her husband . . . just because she objected to a little bit of rough treatment – what a terrible thing to allow a mere woman power like that! There is no way, in our country, in England, that a woman would be allowed to divorce her husband, no matter what

49

the reason was. I've made notes of the cases. They will interest my master, Cardinal Wolsey, because he is preparing a document for the king. It's called *The State of Ireland and Plan for its Reformation*. I am doing much of the work for him,' he finished modestly.

'It seems to me,' said Mara evenly, 'and I can only speak of my own part of the country, but I think that law and order is well-maintained here.'

He laughed aloud at that. 'And in the middle of your festival – rather a pagan festival, you must admit, but let that pass; in the middle of the festivities suddenly there is this cattle raid, and all, from the highest to the lowest in the land, rush off waving knives and swords.'

'Ah,' said Mara, 'but this cattle raid was instigated by one who had the privilege of being ennobled by King Henry himself. And I suspect that you had prior knowledge. Now, admit, you came down just to see a cattle raid in progress! You knew what was going to happen, didn't you? You knew that O'Donnell planned this.'

He said nothing, but a grin plucked at the corners of his well-cut mouth and his dark-brown eyes glinted with amusement.

'You couldn't resist the thought of what a great document you could write about the "wild Irish" could you,' she teased and he laughed good-humouredly as she went on, 'I can just imagine it – "Neighbour steals from neighbour" Good title, isn't it?'

'As long as no one is hurt; and they are all enjoying themselves,' he said lightly and she looked at him with interest. When he wrote about the cattle raid, he would suppress the information that it was the Earl O'Donnell who had instigated the raid, she guessed. It would not fit with the image of Ireland which would be portrayed in his master's book about the reformation of Ireland, where there would be a great distinction between the Irish who clung to their native ways and those who were loyal to the English crown and adopted English language, ways of dress and laws – like O'Donnell of Donegal and like the citizens of Galway city.

'Cows are very important to us,' she said gravely. 'It's a serious matter to steal cows – they are the wealth of the kingdom. It's one of our great laws.'

'Persons who steal cows must be killed,' called back Cormac in war-like tones and the scholars all laughed and Aidan clapped applause.

'There you are now,' said Mara sweetly. 'Three-year-old small boys agree with your English laws. Punish wrongdoers with death, says my little Cormac. You will have to tell Cardinal Wolsey that there is hope for Ireland, after all.'

She shivered a little in the icy wind and pulled the fur-lined hood of her cloak well over her head. The sun had been once more covered with clouds and rain threatened again. Despite her light tone she felt apprehensive about the future. She had spoken in jest, but would the new generation, would her grandson, Domhnall, now aged eight and due to start at the law school next September, would he keep faith with Brehon law, or would he bow the knee to the English king just as O'Donnell of Donegal did?

And what about her warlike little Cormac O'Brien? How would he grow up?

Three

MacSlechta
(son sections)

There are nine categories of sons who cannot inherit. These are known as 'sons of darkness'.

1. *The son who is conceived 'in the bushes' because there will always be doubt as to his paternity.*
2. *The son of a prostitute.*
3. *'The son of the road', an abandoned child who was found on the roadside and cared for.*
4. *The son of a woman who was having sexual relationships with many men at the time of his conception.*
5. *A late-discovered son who does not have the family voice, appearance and in behaviour and is not accepted as a son by the putative father.*
6. *The son of a 'girl in plaits', because the union was unlawful and without the permission of her family.*
7. *A son who has been outlawed from the kingdom and from his clan has no inheritance rights.*
8. *A son who neglects his ill or aged father and causes his death by lack of care.*

9. *A son who becomes a cleric after the Roman rule and will not have sons of his own.*

' "That all things may be fair and just in the inheritance of land, the division is the work of the youngest inheritor and then the shares are picked in order of age with the oldest choosing first and the youngest last." This ensures that the property has been divided into sections of equal worth.' Hugh recited the words in fluent English and Mara gave him a nod and a smile. He had grown in confidence since their stay in the city of Galway, she thought. She eyed Stephen Gardiner and saw his black eyebrows shoot up before he made a quick note on the page before him. The Scottish woman Rhona and her son Peadar had returned to Carron after spending the night at the law school's guest house, but Stephen Gardiner had requested to be allowed to remain for a while in the morning and watch a Brehon law school in progress so that he could write about it for his master in London, Cardinal Wolsey.

'Good,' she said aloud. 'Now, Shane, how does Hugh know this law?'

'Because he's learned off by heart "*Macslecta*",' said Shane with a grin. 'That means "son sections",' he added to Stephen.

'Who is counted as a son for the purpose of inheritance, Aidan?' asked Mara.

'For the purposes of inheritance all sons are equal,' replied Aidan, rising to his feet politely. 'A son born of a wife of the second degree is of equal status to the son born of the chief wife

54

and so is the son of a betrothed concubine.' His eyes slid over to meet Moylan's and then he hastily added, 'All sons who are publically recognised by their father are deemed to be entitled to their share in his wealth.'

'Goodness! Even when born out of wedlock; is that right?' muttered Stephen scribbling furiously. He had already filled pages, describing the Cahermacnaghten law school and how it was housed within an ancient circle of ten-foot thick walls enclosing a scholars' house, a girl scholar house, a kitchen house, the farm manager's house, a schoolhouse and a guesthouse; of how the scholars often began there at the age of five and studied for up to fifteen years, learning languages and poetry as well as the law; of their studies of the Latin and Greek languages, as well as English and some Spanish and French. Mara eyed him maliciously. She was not impressed by his air of piety. Why was it so outrageous to allow a son born out of wedlock, as he put it, to inherit when innocent small children could be hanged for stealing a loaf of bread or a pie? A nation that could justify to itself such laws, had, she reckoned, no grounds to turn up their noses at the laws of other countries.

'But there are nine categories of sons who cannot inherit,' Fiona informed him kindly. 'Shall I recite them for you? "The son conceived in the bushes," – that's Aidan's favourite one—'

'Fiona,' interrupted Mara and then she stopped. She knew the sound of the heavy step at the doorway. It was Cumhal, her farm manager, and he would not interrupt the morning school unless there was an emergency. He opened the door without knocking and thrust his head inside. Mara's heart stopped for an instant. Had anything happened to Turlough? She had not expected him back last night. Ardal O'Lochlainn had a secondary castle near to the border and she had guessed that he would have invited Turlough and Teige O'Brien to spend what remained of the night there in comfort. The morning was well-advanced, though, and she had anticipated his arrival at every minute, so she turned a worried face towards Cumhal.

'Brehon,' he said. 'There's news from Carron Castle. A body has been found. Someone has been found on the road below the castle.'

'Trampled to death,' said his wife, Brigid, from behind him. Her voice was shocked, but excited by the news. 'They do say that whoever it is – the word is that it might be Brennan the cattleman – they do say that he is ground to pulp like as though he had been under a mill stone.'

Mara shuddered. The image was too real. 'The poor man!' she exclaimed.

'There's a horse coming down the road,' said Aidan, alive with interest at the dramatic turn taken by the morning schooling. 'Coming fast, too; by the sound of it.'

Mara moved to the door of the schoolhouse. There was certainly the sound of rapid horse hoofs ringing out on the limestone-paved road and she went to stand by the great iron gates that led into the law school enclosure. A minute later a beautiful strawberry mare came into sight and her heart rose up thankfully. This was Ardal

O'Lochlainn, *taoiseach* of the O'Lochlainn clan. If he were safe, then Turlough and Teige were probably safe, also. Nevertheless, she held her breath until she saw his face and saw him nod reassuringly.

'I'm the first with the tale,' he said, 'but most of the cattle have been recovered and the King, thank God, is well. He and Teige will soon follow me.'

'He hasn't been injured?' she asked, but she knew the answer. Ardal did not waste words. He would have told her the truth instantly.

'No,' he replied. A smile lit up his blue eyes and spread over his handsome face. 'A bit disgusted that most of the action was over before he arrived, but otherwise unhurt. Muiris O'Hynes and his men managed very efficiently. They got to the peak of abbey hill well ahead of the herds. First of all they opened a gate to a meadow with a few cows belonging to the monks grazing and then they set up a road block right across the road with carts and such-like from the abbey. So when the herd came up the hill, going slowly now because of the steepness of it, the men from the Burren were behind the barrier waving sticks and shouting – O'Donnell's men were behind the herd, so the cows had no choice but to turn into the field. And glad they were, poor animals, to get in there and to drink from the trough and snatch a few mouthfuls of clean grass. And Muiris had the good sense to let the Donegal men go. All over safely, thank God.'

'Thank God,' said Mara, echoing his own words, but then waited. He had more to say, she knew the slight hesitancy with which he was now eyeing her.

'What is it?' she asked.

'I stopped at Carron Castle to tell them the cattle were on the way back,' said Ardal slowly. 'There's been an accident,' he added. 'A trampling . . .'

'I know – we heard,' said Mara, conscious that Stephen Gardiner was by her side, that her normally well-run school had dissolved into chaos and her scholars were all out on the road drinking in the news avidly, ready for any more horrifying details.

'Brennan, the cowman, that was the word,' said Brigid, giving a toss of her ginger hair. She liked to be the one who was always first with the news.

'Crushed to death by the stampeding cows,' said Aidan.

Mara looked severely at him. 'A terrible death for a man, a man who was doing his duty and probably trying to save his cows from being stolen,' she reminded him and then frowned. What was it that Maol, Garrett's steward, had said to her two nights ago when she was up at Carron Castle attending the wake of the *tánaiste*? Something about Garrett having dismissed his cowman . . . Yes, the name had been Brennan. Surely, if he had already been dismissed, this man, Brennan, would not interpose his body between the raiders and the marauding cow thieves.

'It's impossible to recognise a face,' said Ardal quietly. 'Even the clothing is . . .' He stopped with an eye on Fiona. Ardal was a very chivalrous man and he felt, thought Mara, that the small, sweet-looking Fiona with her primrose curls and large blue eyes looked too fragile to hear what he had been about to say.

'Unrecognisable with blood and dust and cattle droppings, I suppose,' finished Mara briskly. She had few worries about Fiona's toughness; Hugh, perhaps, but then her scholars were training to be law enforcers and she could not shield them from the harsh realities of life.

'That's it,' said Ardal, giving Fiona an uneasy glance. She stared back at him with her innocent blue eyes agog for more details.

'So no one knows whose body it is,' said Mara thoughtfully.

'And I don't suppose that we will know until all that *slógad* are back with the cattle,' said Brigid briskly.

'Is there anyone supposed to be missing from Carron Castle, my lord?' Moylan asked the question respectfully. Horses were an obsession with him and he was a great admirer of Ardal who bred several very successful strains of horse and was a great buyer and seller of racehorses as well as of trotting horses.

'Well, yes,' said Ardal reluctantly. 'There is, indeed, someone missing.' He looked at Mara and she moved back inside to within the enclosure but did not offer to him the privacy of the schoolhouse. Whoever was killed, there was no doubt that the news would be all over the Burren soon and she did not want to deny Brigid the chance to be one of the first to have the story.

'Who is missing, then?' she asked and then, from his appalled expression, guessed the answer.

'Garrett?' she asked and he nodded.

'It's still very unsure,' he said hastily. Ardal always liked to be certain of his facts. 'No one seems to know whether he was in the castle when the cattle stampeded past, not even the *taoiseach*'s wife knows that.'

'Which one of them?' Mara heard Aidan's mutter, but ignored him. Her mind was busy. Her eyes met Ardal's and saw her puzzlement reflected in his. Garrett MacNamara, she would have thought, was the last man in the kingdom to rush out in front of a herd of stampeding cows. It was one of the complaints about him that he had no interest in cattle, no knowledge of them and seemed to be only concerned with how much money he could wring from the clan in the way of rent. He would never have hazarded his life like that. Not even Muiris O'Heynes, the greatest cattle expert on the Burren, would have tried to do something of that nature.

'In God's name, what was he doing out on the road in the first place?' asked Brigid. 'We heard them over here. We heard them coming from Noughaval, heard them galloping down the road. Cumhal says to me, didn't you, Cumhal? – "that's a cattle raid if I'm a Christian" and out he goes and calls the cows into the barn and keeps them shut in there until the noise was well past.'

'I can always rely on Cumhal,' said Mara to Ardal, noticing that Stephen had gone back into the schoolhouse. No doubt he was filling another page on cattle raids among the 'wild Irish'.

'I guessed they were on their way to the border point at Abbey Hill, and that they wouldn't come so far out of their way,' muttered Cumhal, looking embarrassed at her praise. And then he added, 'But Brigid is right, Brehon. It would be surprising that the MacNamara would go walking down the road with that noise approaching. As for trying to stop them, well . . .'

'He was a terrible coward, anyway,' said Aidan candidly. 'Do you remember him when that bull got loose at the fair?' He whistled loudly to express his disgust at Garrett's lack of courage when faced with something as ordinary as a bull.

Mara looked at Ardal's still hesitant face. 'Go back inside all of you, I'll be in within a few minutes. Aidan, while you are waiting for me, perhaps you could explain to our visitor the importance of cows and how various fines can be paid in either silver or using a milch cow for each ounce of silver.'

They all disappeared instantly. Stephen would be bombarded with information, she guessed. Cumhal went back to his work of mending a fence on a roadside field and Brigid, after a second's hesitation, retired to the kitchen. Mara faced Ardal, looking keenly at his handsome face.

'There is something that worries you about this terrible accident, is that right?' she asked.

Ardal ran a hand through his copper-coloured hair and grimaced. 'It's probably nothing,' he said. 'The body is unrecognisable, but I suppose with washing we might be able to identify the clothes, but there is something else . . .' He hesitated.

61

Mara waited. It was never any good to try to rush Ardal.

'The body had a length of chain tied to its leg,' he said eventually.

Mara stared at him. 'Tied to his leg? His leg, is that right, Ardal? Well, that's an interesting piece of information.' She turned it over within her mind but could make nothing of it. The information that Garrett was missing was probably of more importance at the moment. If the tragic death by trampling was that of farm worker or cowman, well that was just a matter for the man's own family, but if it happened that the mutilated and unrecognisable body lying in the dust and filth of the road below the castle chanced to be that of the clan's chieftain, Garrett, then this matter concerned the Brehon and the king. A new *taoiseach* would have to be sworn in – young Jarlath would come to power more quickly than anyone could have foreseen – and a grand funeral would have to be arranged, the three other chieftains on the Burren, the O'Brien, the O'Connor and the O'Lochlainn all would have to be informed – as would, indeed, the whole of the MacNamara clan, many of whom lived outside the Burren in Thomond.

Thoughtfully Mara took leave of Ardal and went back into the schoolroom where Moylan, with a hint of condescension in his voice, was explaining the difference between cattle and milch cows to a rather bemused Stephen. She waited and he quickly finished and they all looked at her expectantly while Stephen made more notes in his book. Mara looked around at her scholars.

'Can any of you think of a reason why the dead man on the road below Carron might have a chain tied around his leg?' she asked. Her eyes were on Stephen when she said that. He looked at her wide-eyed, but then he seemed to have perfected that expression of astonishment at all of the strange goings-on in this western kingdom.

'What, the man that Cumhal was telling us about!' Aidan sounded pleased and excited by this extra spice to the story.

'Did the O'Lochlainn tell you that, Brehon?' asked Moylan curiously.

'Might have been a murder if it had been his neck,' said Hugh thoughtfully.

'But just his leg,' said Aidan with disgust. 'Perhaps he . . .' His voice tailed out. Not even Aidan with his fertile imagination could devise a reason for a man to have a piece of chain tied to his leg when chasing cattle raiders.

'Perhaps he was an escaped lunatic,' suggested Shane brightly. 'Some people do tie up lunatics by the leg so that they go a certain distance but can't stray and cause trouble. What do you think, Brehon?'

'It's in our laws,' explained Fiona to Stephen. 'We feel that the care of a mad person devolves onto the kin group. They must take it in turn to care for him, or her. They are then responsible for the lunatic's actions and must tie them up if they can't supervise them for a short period of time. A person may be excused for being late to a court hearing if he has to delay in order to tie up a lunatic. Let me explain to you the law about lunatics—'

'I believe,' said Stephen, clasping his head with mock horror, 'that I will leave you now.' He got to his feet after wiping his pen clean and replacing it, his ink horn and his notebook into his satchel. 'I think that I will ride up to Carron and see what's going on. I feel that I am suffering from an overload of information about Brehon law and its complexities. My studies of the law at Cambridge never seemed to offer so many difficulties.'

'That's a compliment, coming from a race that called Brehon law a set of rules for savages,' said Mara with a smile and she escorted him to the gate of the enclosure and saw him leave – with a sigh of relief. She would prefer him not to be here when Turlough came back. Turlough was very indiscreet and Mara did not want the remarks that her husband would undoubtedly make about this cattle raid to be carried back to O'Donnell's ears and to King Henry in England. The English, Mara thought, needed to be dealt with warily, treated with courtesy but kept at arm's length.

'What about this death, Brehon? Are we going to discuss this?' Aidan, despite the fact that he would face his final examinations in June, was eager for a change from routine.

'Only when we know more,' said Mara firmly. If it truly were the body of Garrett, she thought as she allocated tasks to her scholars, then why did not Slaney send a message to her – or had she already returned to Galway, perhaps she

64

had planned a flight before her shame of being set aside by her husband could be made public in the Burren.

'I don't think that either Maol MacNamara, the steward, or Brennan MacNamara, the cowman, were at the Bealtaine Festival yesterday evening,' said Aidan addressing his words to the air and then burying his nose in *Audacht Morainn,* a seventh-century text on kingship. 'I just thought that you might like to know that, Brehon,' he added hastily.

'I think that we will have half an hour of silent study,' said Mara turning the slimmest of the three sand glasses on its head. She had trained herself not to speculate until facts were before her and she would be doing her scholars an injustice if she encouraged them to conjecture before more was known. She took from the locked wooden press an enormous leather-bound book which contained notes on cases heard on judgement day. This book had been started over fifty years ago by her father who was then Brehon of the Burren and Mara, in her turn, faithfully recorded all her decisions. Now, with a faint sigh, she settled down to write up yesterday's cases. If it were true that the dead body was that of the chieftain of the MacNamara clan, then the most interesting case, that of Garrett's recognition of Peadar, his declaration that Rhona was to be his wife of second degree and his possible demand for a divorce from Slaney, would now never be heard.

Rhona, she thought and got to her feet. 'Fachtnan, I will be back in five minutes,' she said as she went through the door. How could she have forgotten about her other two guests? Had they heard the news? she wondered, as she hurried across the courtyard to the guesthouse.

Before she reached it Rhona with Peadar behind her came out through the door. One glance at the woman's face told Mara that the news had reached her.

'I wonder would you be kind enough to lend me a couple of ponies, Brehon,' she began as soon as she saw Mara. 'I must get back up there. I . . .' She left her sentence unfinished, but Mara understood her concern. The future of her son was at stake. Garrett had failed to turn up to Poulnabrone and now what was to happen to young Peadar. Something I must consider, thought Mara as she cordially invited Rhona to take her pick from the stable and called Cumhal to attend to the pair from Scotland. No word of sorrow was expressed by Rhona and Mara liked her all the more for that and busied herself with practical offers of help when Rhona would have decided what she wanted to do. The woman seemed dazed by the sudden change in her son's fortune and almost incapable of thinking until she returned to Carron and saw the position for herself. Mara waved a goodbye and then returned to her schoolhouse and her studious scholars.

The half hour had just finished when there was a commotion from outside. Several horses were rode straight onto the cobbled yard outside the schoolhouse, voices were raised. Turlough called to Brigid – something about being as hungry as a lion – his cousin, Teige O'Brien shouted out a joke to Cumhal, Mara's stablemen exchanged words with men-at-arms – and then the door burst open and in came Turlough.

'Mara,' he shouted. 'You'll never guess what has happened. Garrett MacNamara is dead.'

'We're before you with that news,' said Mara. 'Ardal O'Lochlainn dropped in on his way home – he was the one who found the body. It sounds as if it were a terrible accident, but I'll go up there tomorrow when you are off to Thomond.' She smiled at her scholars. 'You have worked well and silently,' she said always happy to praise when they deserved it. 'Now why don't you have a short break?'

When they had gone out, Fachtnan following them, she said to Turlough. 'Let's put it from our minds now and enjoy the rest of the day. Come into the house; you can have a rest. I don't suppose that you had much sleep last night. Brigid will bring the food across when the school is finished. Will you stay, Teige? We can give you a bed if you wish,' she ended, rather insincerely. She and Turlough had little time together and she did not want that time to be occupied by raucous jokes and reminiscences of the cattle raid. Since her visitors had all left, Mara and Turlough, once school was over, could visit their little son and then have a peaceful meal together. The duck and the special sauces had not been served last night, so no doubt Brigid had reserved them in the underground storeroom until Turlough should be there to appreciate them.

'No, I'm off home,' said Teige. 'They didn't steal any of my cows – they came across from the west. O'Donnell had the nerve to drop off men secretly at the same time as he dropped off Garrett's visitors. The plan was to pick up the cows in Galway Bay where he had more ships lying in wait, ready to bring all our good fat cattle back to his own sour land. Well, we foiled them – and they've had a few sore heads to take back to Donegal.'

Four

Críth Gablach
(Ranks in Society)

The riches of a man and his status in the kingdom depend on his cattle. For that reason it is illegal:
1. *To drive another's cattle in a way that causes them injury, even if they are on your land.*
2. *To drive another's cattle into the sea or into a marsh.*
3. *To drive another's cattle into a place frequented by wolves.*
4. *To drive another's cattle into a disease-ridden cow house, unless they came originally from that place.*
5. *To drive another's cattle in a way that would startle them with angry fierceness that would cause bones to be broken.*

Anyone who drives another's cattle without permission must also be liable for any damage that they cause, even after he has left them.

An awkward fact is like a thorn embedded in your finger, thought Mara. Unless you dig it out, it goes on making its presence felt. Garrett's broken body had been washed and tightly bound with a winding sheet by the time that she and her scholars had arrived at Carron Castle early in the morning. She had commanded that the sheet be undone, and had to force herself to gaze down at the remains of what had once been Garrett MacNamara. The body had been terribly mutilated though it still possessed the remains of its four limbs. But there had been no trace of a piece of chain around what had been a leg. The blood-soaked clothing had been burned or thrown out and presumably the chain had gone with everything else. No one seemed to know anything about it.

Slaney, Mara was interested to see when she arrived at the castle, was playing the part of a grief-stricken wife, sitting over a fire in the hall and sipping mead while various maids hovered around her. She accompanied Mara on her mission to see Garrett's body, crossing herself and issuing sighs that turned to gulps as she struggled to contain her emotions. Only when Mara mentioned the chain around the leg that Ardal had seen, did Slaney revert to her usual self and she snapped out the words, 'no such thing' with such rapidity that it was no wonder that the servants immediately denied having seen any such thing.

And what could be done? Mara asked herself. Nothing for the moment, was the answer. Against that solid bank of women who had cleaned and bound up the remains of the body, it was one man's word – and the word of a man who, moreover, had just seen the body lying in mounds of filth and dust and blood. And yet, thought Mara, I have known that man for the whole of my life, we were brought up as neighbours, I have never known Ardal to be inaccurate. He was not a talker; he said little, but that which he said was always carefully considered. Mara passed between her fingers the rosary beads which Slaney had handed to her and mechanically made the responses to the prayers while thinking hard.

From a distance she could hear sounds of merriment in the hall. It had been full of silent men and women when she had arrived, but the removal of Slaney's presence had unlocked tongues and probably the mead had been flowing. There had been no sign of Stephen Gardiner, the Englishman – perhaps he had retired to his room to write up his notes – but Jarlath had been there, moving among the clansmen and women, already, in their eyes, invested with the status of *taoiseach*. The man Tomás had been whispering in his ear and there was an eagerness on the faces of all as they looked at the handsome, amiable young man. Rhona and Peadar were still outsiders, though. Once again they had withdrawn to the seclusion of a window seat and Peadar's young face wore an expression of angry embarrassment which made Mara feel rather sorry for him. What would be his position now? The question must be troubling both, but it was not the most urgent problem to be solved at the moment so Mara turned her thoughts back to the terribly mutilated dead body in front of her.

A chain around the leg? Was there any possible reason why Garrett himself should tie a chain around his leg? She could think of none. Garrett was a pompous man, a man who always dressed well for his role as *taoiseach* of his clan. During his four years of office she had never seen him

71

engage in any work on his land – and even if he were dragging something, surely the chain would have been wound around his shoulders. She dismissed that thought from her mind and went back to Shane's suggestion. A lunatic, or a fierce dog, might be tied in order to prevent him from escaping. But a man in possession of his senses would not be detained long by a chain around his leg unless his hands also were bound. But Ardal had not mentioned a chain around the wrists – more shocking and more noticeable than one around the leg.

'The third sorrowful mystery: Jesus is crowned by thorns,' announced Slaney. 'Let us consider in silence for a moment the agonies of our saviour.'

Another thirty 'Hail Marys', not to mention the 'Our Fathers' and 'Glory be to the Fathers' and the other prayers that Slaney kept inserting, thought Mara, hearing an impatient sigh from Shane. She rose resolutely to her feet and beckoned to Slaney and withdrew to the window, waiting for the woman to follow. Let her servants go on praying; the Brehon had work to do. The scholars had not hesitated but had immediately got to their feet and clustered around her. She did not wave them away. This was law school business. She waited grimly until the sour-faced Slaney approached.

'I'm sorry that you cannot spare the time to pray for the soul of—' she was saying in a furious whisper, but Mara silenced her with an imperative gesture.

'Make no arrangements for the wake or the

burial at the moment, Slaney,' she said sternly. 'I am not satisfied that this was an accident. It may be that it was a secret and unlawful killing – one that I and my scholars must investigate. I want this body moved to a small room and the keys of it handed to me until my enquiries have finished.'

'What!' Stony-faced, Slaney glared at her, and then gulped and clutched at her heart. Mara ignored her. Maol the steward had just entered the room and she beckoned to him.

'Have the body of your *taoiseach* carried to a small wall chamber,' she said.

He stared at her and she stared back – all the authority of her eighteen years of office in her gaze. The light was poor in this north-facing room, but she had an impression that he had paled.

'Immediately,' she said in a peremptory way. 'This terrible death must be investigated.'

'I am to be nobody in my own house,' exclaimed Slaney bitterly.

'This is now a matter for the king and his officers,' said Mara. She spoke more gently than she had done to the steward. Though a tall, heavily-built woman Slaney seemed to shrink and there was a look of terror in her very blue eyes. She was clutching the back of a large oak chair for support and Mara thought she saw a slight tremor in the sturdily built piece of furniture.

Garrett's body lay on a wooden pallet and within minutes it was being carried to one of the small wall chambers that were slotted in, here and there, by the sides of the spiral staircase

73

in the old part of the castle. Its window was not much bigger than a loop hole for an arrow to pass through, but the place was small enough to be well lit by a couple of candles. Once the pallet had been placed on a pair of trestles, Mara ordered a double candlestick and positioned it in the deep sill of the tiny window. There would, she thought, be enough light. She nodded her thanks to the servant and then held out her hand for the key, waiting until Slaney summoned her housekeeper and handed over the second key, also. The room was freezing cold, but so much the better to preserve the corpse.

With a great air of ceremony Mara watched Fachtnan lock the door, melt in the flame of Maol's candle a piece of sealing wax from his satchel and then paste it over the lock. While it was still warm Mara scratched her initials into the wax with a quill pen from her own satchel. The pen would be ruined, but if anyone in the castle were guilty of having anything to do with Garrett's death, then these elaborate preparations should alarm them.

'I shall be back,' she said to Slaney. 'Do nothing about this death until I give permission.'

And with those words she went soberly down the wide staircase followed by Fachtnan and her scholars who were exchanging slightly over-awed looks. Mara said nothing to them until they were all outside the iron gates and then she spoke.

'Fachtnan,' she said. 'I want you to ride to Thomond as quickly as you can safely do so.

Tell the king about the death of Garrett MacNamara. He will want to attend the burial and conduct the inauguration ceremony for the new *taoiseach* as soon as possible. Oh, and Fachtnan, I have one other task for you. Bring back Nuala. Tell her I need her urgently. I want her to give an opinion on the cause of death, and on the time of death. Nuala will do that better than any other physician.' Her mind went with tolerant scorn to the young man at Caherconnell; he would not serve her purpose.

'Is Nuala a qualified physician now? She's only about my age, isn't she, or not much more?' asked Fiona rather sharply and Mara suppressed a grin as Aidan and Moylan informed her how talented Nuala was and how she had done so well in her final examinations that the king's own physician, Donogh O'Hickey, had spoken of her in Rome.

Fachtnan said nothing, just looked at Fiona with concern in his dark eyes. What a tangle that was, thought Mara impatiently. Nuala adored Fachtnan and, herself an heiress of valuable property on the Burren, was willing to share her considerable wealth with him in marriage, but Fachtnan worshipped Fiona who thought of him purely as an elder brother and comrade, though she enjoyed his homage. Still they would have to work matters out for themselves so Mara dissipated the slight atmosphere of embarrassment among her scholars by giving some crisp commands to Fachtnan and checking that he had silver with him and instructing him to request a meal when he arrived at Turlough's main castle in Thomond.

'Now,' she said to her scholars as he set off towards the west, 'I have a task for your young brains.' She looked around but there was no one on their road back to the law school; she could speak without being overheard. 'First question is this: why should that chain have been removed from Garrett's leg? The second question is: why was a chain tied to his leg? No, don't answer now, wait until we get back to the law school.'

And I must ride over to Baur North to see my little Cormac for a few minutes, she thought as they rode in silence. The next week or so would be busy. The life of a law enforcer and judge for the whole kingdom, as well as being the wife of the king, meant that her moments with this late-born second child of hers were rationed. She was grateful to his foster parents Cliona and Setanta O'Connor, but there were times when, secretly, she felt an angry jealousy rise up within her – especially when she heard Cormac address Cliona as 'Mam'.

And yet, she knew that she had done the right thing, and that her active, masculine little boy was having a wonderful time playing with his foster brother, only a few months older than he, helping on the farm, driving sheep to new pasture, guarding the newborn lambs with the aid of the long-tailed sheepdogs, scattering straw for beds for the lambing sheep and soon there would be all the excitement of the sheep shearing to look forward to. He was a strong-willed, happy boy and she would not have him different in any way.

Cliona, her son Art, and Cormac were nowhere

to be seen when Mara rode onto the small farm. Only Setanta, her fisherman husband, was there vigorously pulping some unsold fish into a smelly paste to put onto the land as a fertiliser. He did not know where Cliona and the two little boys were, but he was eager to go in search for them.

'No, no,' said Mara hurriedly. 'I can't stay long in any case – he's well?' she enquired trying to keep a wistful note from her voice.

Setanta grinned. 'Bursting with health, and mischief,' he added. 'Wait till you hear his latest. Cliona had shut some of the sheep into the cabin to wean the lambs who were born early in the year. The rest were out in that field on the top of the hill and what does young Cormac do, but put a cat on the neck of one of the sheep – "just being kind to it and giving it a ride" – that's what he told her, of course. Well, the sheep ran, the cat hung on, and would you believe it every single sheep in the place started running and that was not all; the sheep that Cliona had shut in the cabin – she mustn't have shot the latch through properly – well, they burst out of the cabin and joined their sisters and cousins. Took Cliona an hour to round them all up!'

'I hope she punished him,' said Mara, trying to stop a smile.

'Well, she told him that he would have no honey on his bread at suppertime, but he came out with so many arguments about not being anywhere near the sheep when they started running and being hundreds of miles away from the ones that burst from their cabin, that by the end of it all she told me she didn't know if she was standing on her head or her heels. "What do you expect?" I said to her. "His mother is a lawyer and his grandfather was a lawyer – bred in the bone it is for him to argue."'

'Tell him that anyone who drives another's cattle or sheep must also be liable for any damage that they cause, even after he has left them, and that is the law,' said Mara severely, but she chuckled to herself when she left him. Turlough, she thought, would enjoy that story.

When she arrived back at the schoolhouse it was to find the scholars, including Fiona, playing a game of hurling and Brigid, her housekeeper, standing at the door to the kitchen house and determined that Mara should eat something before settling back to work.

'I'll bring something across to your own house,' she began as soon as Mara dismounted and handed her horse over to the stable boy.

'No, no, I'll have something here,' said Mara hastily. The Brehon's house, a two-storey stone building, stood a couple of hundred yards away from the law school. It was nice to be able to retire there after school was finished and to leave the scholars to the care of Brigid and Cumhal, but now she was eager to get on with solving this mystery. Bran came across to greet her and she fondled him absent-mindedly. Garrett, she remembered, hated dogs. He was, she had often thought, actually frightened of Bran. Would a man who was nervous of a friendly, well-trained wolfhound, actually voluntarily go out on the road to confront a herd of stampeding cows?

78

Not in a thousand years, she told herself. Even glimpsed from the mountain there had been something terrifying about the look of them hurtling down the road, maddened by blows and shouts and by the primeval instinct to be first.

'Have something solid in you,' said Brigid firmly when Mara asked for a glass of milk. 'I've got some nice little goat's cheeses, just got them this morning from Tahra MacNamara.' Brigid's hands were busy as she stripped the green leaves from the succulently oozing fresh cheese, placed it on a slice of fresh soda bread and then slid it on to the hot griddle plate that hung over the kitchen fire. Her eyes, however, were on Mara as she repeated with emphasis, 'It was Tahra MacNamara that I got these from, Brehon.'

Mara roused herself from her thoughts. 'And what did she have to say about the death of her *taoiseach*?' she enquired obligingly.

'She had plenty to say.' Brigid's face bore the expression of one who has plenty to say herself and Mara waited. Tahra MacNamara was a gossipy old woman who carried tales from house to house as she bartered her excellent goat's cheese for food or firing.

'She said that the clan all guess what happened to the *taoiseach*,' hissed Brigid, giving a dramatic glance at the open doorway and then closing it rapidly. 'She says that it was that wife of his that pushed the poor man under the feet of the cattle and then went back into the castle and left him there.'

'Oh,' said Mara. She was rather taken aback at that.

79

'And they do say, according to Tahra, that the clan want revenge on her. Her being from Galway and English and all that, or so Tomás MacNamara says and he's a clever man; mind you, he is the grandson of that fellow Sean MacNamara who held the townlands up there at Creevagh and made a fortune from digging lead out of the ground. There used to be very strange tales about him and what he got up to at Creevagh – he was the one that dug out the sunken passageway to the dolmen. But Tahra says Tomás is good, steady man and Cait his wife is a hard-working woman. And she's birthed seventeen children and reared seven sons and three daughters from them.'

'Seventeen children, oh my goodness!' exclaimed Mara. 'And she's a little small woman, isn't she? If I were she, I would have felt like murdering my husband by the end of that.'

Not a sentiment to be uttered by a Brehon, she thought a minute later; and so Brigid told her immediately citing the example of a woman of Galway who was executed for killing her husband.

'And, mind you, Brehon,' said Brigid with emphasis, 'according to the man that told me, she only did it because he kept beating her and starving her and she couldn't get rid of him in any other way and she was forced into it . . . and . . .' Brigid paused to gulp in some breath and finished rapidly: 'And do you know what those *dúnmharfóirí* in Galway did to the poor woman? Well, they tied her to a stake and they burned her to death.'

80

'And do the clan want something like that to happen Slaney?' enquired Mara innocently.

Brigid nodded emphatically. 'Well, people think that she should be punished, Brehon. I'm not saying that is what the clan thinks should happen to the *ban taoiseach*. Tomás says that the clan want revenge; that's what Tahra said,' ended Brigid, dissociating herself, with the last words, from the bloodthirsty statements from the MacNamara clan.

'Revenge,' repeated Mara. The heated goat's cheese had begun to smell delicious, but she felt that she had lost her appetite for it. It was true that Slaney was not truly Gaelic. Her family was one of the merchant families in Galway, alien to Gaelic laws and customs, although they had spent hundreds of years in Ireland. Nevertheless, she was married to the *taoiseach* of the MacNamara clan and had spent four years in the kingdom of the Burren. A feeling of anger rose within her at the thought of the clever Tomás laying down the law. She would soon show him who was in charge of legal matters in the kingdom of the Burren, she thought and attacked her goat's cheese and bread with assumed relish.

'Delicious,' she said aloud, but she hardly tasted what she was swallowing rapidly. Her mind was busy. Murder of husbands or wives was a very rare occurrence in Gaelic Ireland because divorce, with an equitable division of property agreed between both, was so easily granted. It was, in fact, easier for a woman to get a divorce from a man, than the other way around. And as the woman was considered to be a partner to the man, her share of the property would usually amount to about half of what they jointly owned. Mara thought back through her years as Brehon, and through the incidents from her father's time, and could not remember a single case when a wife had murdered her husband.

'Do you think that you could call the scholars back into the schoolhouse, Brigid?' she asked after swallowing a gulp of milk and then cutting off another piece of bread and forcing herself to swallow it. She would need all of her energy if there was going to be trouble at the MacNamara castle.

'I've sent Fachtnan to Thomond to fetch Nuala,' she said as her housekeeper went to the door and watched Brigid's face turn back and then grow soft with affection. Nuala had no parents of her own, but she had been the daughter of Mara's cousin Malachy and of Mara's best friend Mór, a sister to Ardal O'Lochlainn. Nuala had been an only child, unhappy at home after the death of her mother and had spent much of her childhood and girlhood at the law school. Brigid had mothered her and the boys had been like brothers to her.

'I'll make up a bed for her in the guest house,' was all that Brigid said, but Mara could see the satisfaction on her face as she went out. She would be pleased, also, that Fachtnan had been sent to fetch the girl. It was her dearest wish that the two would be married.

One thing at a time, thought Mara as she finished her milk and handed the rest of the goat's cheese and bread to Bran. Resolutely she pushed the information from the gossiping Tahra to the back of her mind and focussed on the chain.

'The chain,' she said as soon as they were all seated; Hugh and Shane, the two youngest, directly in front of her, and Fiona, Moylan and Aidan on the table behind them. She had begun to think of a reason herself but she wanted to give them the opportunity of guessing. Shane's eyes were sparkling with excitement and Hugh was looking at him with a smile. The two older boys and Fiona looked annoyed when Shane's hand went up, so they were obviously not in on the secret.

'Yes, Shane,' said Mara. She was not surprised. At present, though the youngest, he was certainly the cleverest of her scholars. He rose politely to his feet and looked around at his fellow pupils.

'I thought it might have been possible that Garrett MacNamara was unconscious before the chain was tied around his leg and that he was dragged down and then left in the middle of road as the cattle were stampeding down the hill.'

'Put the case,' growled Aidan.

Fiona raised her hand, but Mara shook her head. 'Let Shane put the case, first, Fiona, and then you can debate.'

Shane passed a hand over his black hair and turned his dark blue eyes on her. 'If someone wanted to murder Garrett,' he said, 'he or she could knock him unconscious, tie a chain around his leg, drag him down onto the road and leave him there in the path of the cattle. In reality, then it would mean that it was the cattle who murdered the man.'

'Wouldn't stand up in a court of law,' muttered Aidan. 'Who ever set him down in the path of the cattle was guilty of murder. Anyone would know what would happen if that huge herd of cattle trampled an unconscious man.'

'If I may speak,' said Fiona sweetly, 'I would like to say that I don't think my learned and juvenile friend is quite correct in his surmise.'

'Well, go on then, if you're so clever, what's your guess?' Shane dropped back onto his stool and glared over his shoulder at the girl scholar.

'Well, use your brains,' snapped Fiona. 'The Brehon asked us to come up with a reason for the chain being tied around the dead man's leg. You haven't given a reason. Our murderer – let's call him or her OM – well OM could just as easily have grabbed Garrett by the legs or even by the hands and dragged his body down on to the road. The chain would just have been a nuisance.'

'But it was pretty clever of Shane to think of Garrett being probably unconscious before he was trampled down,' said Hugh in hot defence. Hugh and Shane were near in age and had been friends ever since Shane had joined the law school five years ago. Mara could never remember an occasion when this particular pair had fought with each other.

'I've got it,' said Moylan suddenly. 'The body was dragged down onto the road – we should go and see the exact spot, Brehon, shouldn't we? The O'Lochlainn could come with us and show us where he saw it – he was the one who brought news to the castle, wasn't he? – but from memory there are lots of rocks on the side of the road leading up to the castle, so the unconscious body was placed in the middle of the road and just in case the noise of the cattle hoofs roused him, then a chain was tied around his leg and the other end was tied to one of the rocks.'

'And then if he got to his feet, most likely feeling sick and giddy, and tried to run, then the chain would jerk and he'd fall down and a minute later he would be pulp,' said Fiona slowly. 'Moylan, you're a genius. I think that you've got it.'

'It was Shane's idea, first,' said Hugh hotly while Shane shrugged, but looked annoyed, more with himself for not thinking the idea through, than with Moylan for coming up with a more plausible solution, thought Mara. Shane had a formidable intellect and a calm disposition.

Aloud, she said, 'You've all helped, well done. That sounds a very plausible explanation and we will keep that as a working hypothesis for the moment.'

'So OM picks up something heavy, bangs Garrett over the head,' said Aidan. 'Then OM ties a piece of chain around his leg—'

'No, no, OM does that when Garrett is in the middle of the road!' interrupted Fiona.

'Perhaps Garrett groans or something and OM thinks, Oh my God, he's going to wake up,' put in Shane.

'Drags him down, with or without the chain, ties him to a stone, dashes away and then gets back into the castle or somewhere,' finished Aidan.

'So who is OM?' asked Hugh looking around at his fellow scholars.

'I don't think that we should speculate about that just yet,' said Shane. 'I do see a few problems in our hypothesis. If we knew the exact spot, then we'd know better, but I was thinking that OM took quite a risk What if someone looked out and saw someone dragging a body down the hill?'

'And then arranging it in the middle of the road and taking time to attach the chain to a rock.' Hugh looked at this friend and received a nod.

'There's a worse problem than that,' said Fiona suddenly. 'The O'Lochlainn said nothing about a chain being tied to a rock – he would surely have noticed it. The cows might have broken the chain, but they wouldn't have untied it from the rock. I think that we should go up there, Brehon, and search the spot where the body was found.'

'I agree,' said Mara. 'I was going to wait until Nuala came but now I think, like you, that we should search the area quickly before any evidence is moved.'

'Probably too late,' said Moylan gloomily. 'Shall I go and ask the O'Lochlainn whether he would accompany us to Carron, Brehon? We'll need him to show us the exact spot. I'll be very polite and say we will await his convenience,' he added quickly before she could reply.

Mara smiled at him. Moylan was growing up and turning from an awkward, silly schoolboy into a polished young man. He would, she thought, undoubtedly pass his final examination in June and then she would see if she could find a position for him. The Brehon of Beare, a kingdom in south-west Ireland, was looking for an assistant lawyer, she had heard. Aidan might perhaps have to have another year and then he and Fiona would graduate.

'Also we should check if any windows from the castle overlook the spot where the body was found,' said Fiona when Moylan had departed. 'Rhona, the Scottish woman, told me that most of the MacNamara clan were staying on at the castle for a few days after the funeral of the *tánaiste* because they thought there would be some sort of celebration after Peadar was declared to be the son of Garrett. And—' she paused for effect – 'she told me, too, that, when she and Peadar left the castle to come over to Poulnabrone, Garrett and his wife Slaney were in the bedroom shouting at each other at the tops of their voices. She decided not to wait for Garrett as it would be embarrassing if Slaney came out and shouted at her – it would upset Peadar and she'd had a hard job persuading him not to go back to Scotland. He hates Ireland; he wants to go back to Scotland where he was working in an abbey garden and learning about herbs and things' finished Fiona.

'Quarrelling?' queried Mara.

'Actually fighting,' confirmed Fiona. 'Rhona was laughing about it. She said that she heard what was probably a stool being thrown across the room and that she thought Garrett was getting

87

the worse of it. She could hear him cry out a couple of times as though he were hurt, but thought she shouldn't interfere.'

'I'd say that Slaney is heavier than the *taoiseach* is, *was* I mean,' said Hugh, correcting himself and suppressing the chuckle that had been in his voice when he began to speak. 'I was forgetting that he is dead,' he added in a subdued manner, looking rather ashamed of himself.

'I don't think that we can speculate anymore until we look at the place where the body was found. Perhaps, while you are waiting, you'd better see to your ponies,' said Mara. She guessed that Ardal, always the soul of politeness and helpfulness, would come straight back with Moylan. It would be just as well if they were all ready for him when he arrived. May was a busy time for him with lots of young foals being born. Especially with this very bad weather and the frequency of cold, wet showers, his valuable foals would be needing care and shelter.

Slaney, she thought, as she crossed the yard to have a word with Cumhal, was she perhaps a murder suspect? Well, that was an interesting thought. Mara examined the existing evidence with scrupulous care. The thought that she disliked Slaney made her take extra pains. Could the woman have been so full of anger against Garrett that she would go to the length of killing him? Mara considered the matter carefully. Divorce might not have seemed like a solution to Slaney. After all, Slaney was a Galway woman, brought up under English law. She would not regard a divorce as a possible solution to her fury and jealousy when her husband introduced another wife into his household. It would have no legality in the city of Galway so she would be merely a wife who had deserted her husband. And what if Garrett decided to divorce her for infertility? That would shame her dreadfully. Slaney was not a woman to flout conventions, definitely not an impulsive woman who would run off and turn up empty-handed at her relations. She was a shrewd woman who always knew how to turn matters to her own advantage.

And the trick of slipping the body onto the path of the marauders driving the herds of stolen cattle was a clever one.

Five

Maccslecheta
(Son Sections)

*A son by a woman other than the chief wife has
full rights of inheritance as long as his father
recognises him in public. If the father disputes
the claim, then such matters as family appearance,
voice and way of behaviour, as well as the sworn
oath of the wife, is taken into account by the
judge of the case.*

Ardal was already in the law school enclosure
by the time that Mara came out of the kitchen
house. He was tenderly helping Fiona onto her
pony, and enquiring whether her cloak was warm
enough for the cold wind. Mara surveyed the
two with interest. Ardal had reduced to despair
all of the mothers and their daughters of the
Burren and of the surrounding territories. He
was immensely rich, not just from his lands and
rental on the Burren, but from the successful
business which he ran, selling beautiful and
well-bred horses to the whole of Ireland and to
many people in England, including King Henry
VIII himself. He would be a splendid match for
Fiona, but did seventeen and forty-two go
together? Still, thought Mara, I married at
fourteen and I married a selfish, untalented and

90

loud-mouthed schoolboy and after the first few ecstatic months was extremely unhappy with him. She smiled to herself, remembering how shocked the people of the Burren had been when she had successfully conducted her own divorce using a little-known Brehon law that a wife may divorce a husband, who, in a public ale house, discusses details of their love-making. Ardal would make Fiona a wonderful husband, and with his copper-coloured hair and blue eyes and tall, broad-shouldered figure, he was a handsome man still. But, apart from the age difference, would it be right for a clever girl, like Fiona, to give up her studies and her chance to become a Brehon like her father? And if she wanted to continue on her path to become a Brehon, would Ardal be happy to allow her? With a sigh, Mara shook her head and urged her mare Brig to go faster. I have enough to do without match-making, she told herself severely, and turned her mind away from Ardal and Fiona.

This murder, if it were a murder – and Mara had a strong feeling that it was an intentional killing – had to be solved quickly before there were any repercussions from the MacNamara clan. The peace of the kingdom, and the peace of mind of her husband, Turlough Donn, depended now on her ability to solve this secret and unlawful killing as soon as possible. The people of the Burren and its four main clans, the O'Briens, the O'Lochlainns, the O'Connors, as well as the MacNamaras, depended upon her tact, her brains and her ability to unravel clues. And all of these abilities had to be brought into play in order to solve this secret and unlawful killing of Garrett MacNamara.

'Cold weather for the time of year.' Ardal had moved up beside her and was surveying the fields, dotted with cowslips and pale mauve cuckoo flowers. 'Very little growth in the grass, yet,' he said gloomily. 'Hard to realise that it is May. Not a butterfly to be seen. Usually those cuckoo flowers are covered in those orange-tipped butterflies at this time of year. And I've only heard the cuckoo once or twice. It's more like winter than late spring.'

'It will come in a rush when it does come,' prophesied Mara. Cumhal had made that remark this morning and Cumhal was a good weather prophet and Mara often found that repeating his forecasts gave her an undeserved reputation of knowing about the land and the problems of those who farmed it. While trotting out a few more of Cumhal's sayings her mind went back to that chain around Garrett's leg and she interrupted Ardal's account of a late spring when he was a young man to ask him about the length of the chain.

'How long, Brehon?' He was taken aback by her question.

'Yes,' said Mara. 'A foot, a yard, three yards . . .? What would your memory of it be, Ardal?' Her scholars, she noticed, had stopped chattering and teasing each other and had moved up close to them and were obviously listening to the conversation.

Ardal took his time before answering. It was one of the things that she liked about him. She could not have asked for a more accurate and careful witness.

'The foot was broken in half, twisted, but the upper half remained,' he said speaking slowly. 'And, of course, most of the flesh from the leg was gone, trampled. Just the bone, quite dislocated from the knee, but still attached by some sinews, I'd say. I would reckon that the chain had been originally tied to the poor man's ankle. It was quite a slender piece of chain,' he went on, his blue eyes not looking at her, but staring straight ahead. 'In fact, now that I come to recollect, it may well have been one of those short lengths of chain that are used to lead a bull, to tie through the ring at the end of his nose, these ones with long, flat links which can be threaded through to form a noose – so, to answer your question, Brehon, altogether about three feet.'

'Thank you, Ardal.' Mara's voice was sincere – certainly he was a good and careful witness, but inwardly she felt dismayed, and she heard a low murmur from the scholars behind them. There seemed to be no sensible explanation for a three-foot long piece of chain to be tied to a man's ankle. She stared ahead, noting the black cloud in the distance and calculating how long it would be before one of those downpours of sleety rain would occur. Three feet of chain – that did not seem enough to tie an unconscious man to a rock by the side of the road. She thought of something then and turned towards him.

'This is a lot to ask of your memory, Ardal,'

she said, 'but did the end of the chain look broken, look as though it had been snapped?'

He answered her very readily. 'No, Brehon, I could almost swear that it had not. That was probably why I thought of it as a bull chain – these chains, though short, are always strongly made to make sure that they will not break with the weight of the animal.'

Moylan, from behind them, cleared his throat in a diplomatic manner and Mara looked back.

'Yes, Moylan,' she said gravely, suppressing a grin at his tact and good manners. A year ago he would have impetuously joined into the conversation.

'Fintan MacNamara at the smithy makes chains like that, Brehon,' he said. 'I've seen them on the shelves up there – and they would be about a yard long.'

'That's right, Moylan.' Ardal nodded his approval. 'And these bull chains are always made from slender flat links because it is much easier to slot them through than if they are thick.'

'So a chain like this would be possessed by many people on the Burren,' put in Fiona and Ardal gave her a tender smile.

'You're right,' he said. 'I would say that there wouldn't be a cabin or a barn in the whole of the kingdom that would not have some of those chains stored in them. We're just coming near to the spot, now,' he added. With an air of relief, he said, 'It looks as though an effort has been made to clean the place up.'

Bother, thought Mara, feeling annoyed with herself. I should have sent orders for the place

94

to be left alone. It had, of course, at first seemed not to be a crime, but an unfortunate accident – in fact, it might still turn out to be that, but the more she thought of Ardal's strange story about a chain around the leg of the dead man, the more she felt that this death would turn out to be a secret and unlawful killing, something that she, as Brehon of the Burren, would have to investigate and allocate a punishment to the guilty person.

'Just about here,' said Ardal, checking his beautiful mare with a gentle shake of the reins. 'Yes, I remember that gorse bush was just in line with the body. You can see it is broken on the hillside edge of it. I reckoned that the herd of cows did that.' He jumped lightly from the back of his horse, looped her reins over a stump of a willow bush and went to the head of Mara's horse.

'There's a good stone here, Brehon,' he said leading her towards a large flat boulder by the side of the road and helping her to dismount and then carefully performing the same service for Fiona while the boys leaped athletically from their ponies and stood looking in dismayed silence at the spot where Garrett's body had lain.

About ten yards of roadway had been shovelled clean – had probably even been swabbed down with buckets of water from the nearby river – as the road seemed extraordinarily clean in comparison with the rest of the route. Mara compressed her lips, angry with herself for not being on the spot earlier, or at least not to have sent an urgent message.

'We'll search the sweepings, Brehon.' Fachtnan was at her side and seemed to know her thoughts. He spoke consolingly and then ordered Shane and Hugh to use their knives to cut some strong twigs from the goat willow bush so that the scholars could rake through the debris at the side of the road.

Mara looked around her. The spot where Garrett's body had lain was well chosen. It was on a small road that ran through a valley between the mountain sides. Looking around she realised that it would be completely hidden from the castle itself. Nothing but a small cabin could be glimpsed from that spot and on a day when most of the inhabitants of the Burren were up on the mountain getting ready to celebrate the festival of Bealtaine, there would be no one in the fields or attending to the calving cows.

'Search carefully for the chain,' she said coming over to her scholars and looking down at the cowpats that they were forking through with their sticks.

'At least the wind has dried them out,' said Ardal in a low voice. 'The stench was terrible when I came upon the body. I had just called in at the castle and was taking this route as a short cut back when I saw all the crows pecking at something. I thought it was some unfortunate cow or a calf and then realised . . .'

'A leather pouch with a broken strap, Brehon,' shouted Fiona, unconcernedly picking it out from the mess with her dainty fingers.

'The strap's broken,' said Shane. 'I'd say that once the man was down and lying on the ground, a cow probably caught its leg in it and then broke the strap loose.'

'A cow weighs about six hundredweight – that's what my father says – think of that; they're massive animals – about six times heavier than Fiona – well, they are massive!' said Moylan, and the other scholars, by their thoughtful faces, were picturing the scene when the cows swept over and across the prostrate body of Garrett MacNamara.

'Let's look in the pouch,' said Aidan impatiently and Fiona opened it.

'There's just this, Brehon,' she said and handed to Mara a folded and sealed roll of vellum. Her eyes widened as she read the inscription. 'It's to Cardinal Wolsey,' Fiona said. 'Perhaps it belongs to Stephen Gardiner, what do you think, Brehon?'

'He would just be the messenger, I believe,' said Mara examining the small neat letters. 'This is Garrett's handwriting,' she added as she broke the seal and unfolded the vellum. It only took her a minute to scan the words and then she rolled it up again and placed it within her own pouch. She would have read it aloud if only her scholars were present, but in front of Ardal, although he was discreet, she felt that she could not betray Garrett's secrets to him. Back at the law school they would discuss the implications. For now she would keep in mind that Garrett had been a traitor to his king and to his clan; that he was planning to do service to King Henry VIII in return for the title of earl; that he would follow English customs, would wear English clothing and that his eldest and only son Peadar would be given the title of Lord Mount Carron and would, without any election, succeed his father to the title of earl and to the extensive property formerly belonging to the MacNamara clan and ruled over by an elected *taoiseach*. No mention, thought Mara, that this son had only just been discovered and that he was not the son of Garrett's lawfully wedded wife, Slaney. The English minded about things like that, mused Mara, but Garrett had probably decided that nothing should be said on that score, and Stephen Gardiner had been too pleased at securing a convert to the English way of life to bother about a small matter like that. That would be Stephen. An ambitious man, a man with a twinkle in his eye and probably his feet set firmly on the first rung of the ladder to success.

'I think, Brehon, if you have no further tasks for me, I will leave you now. I must have a word with my steward.' Ardal's voice broke into Mara's thoughts and she smiled gratefully at him. He was such a well-mannered, sensitive man; he had immediately picked up on her slight hesitation and was now making haste to remove himself from the scene and leave her to consult with her scholars on business, which, for the moment, would have to be private. Mara thanked him warmly for giving up his time and when he was gone turned to her scholars who were looking at her expectantly. Briefly she summarized Garrett's letter to Cardinal Wolsey, chief advisor to the English king, Henry VIII.

'What would that have meant for the kingdom,

Brehon?' asked Moylan after a minute of stunned silence when the scholars looked at each other with horror. It was one thing to hear that the O'Donnell of Donegal had bent the knee to the king of England, but another that one of the four chieftains in the kingdom of the Burren was proposing to do the same thing.

'It's a very good question, Moylan, and I'm not sure of the answer,' she said honestly. 'However,' she went on slowly and with a feeling of pain in her heart, 'it may have caused war and many deaths. I don't think that the MacNamara clan would have been happy to give up all their ancient rights and to become mere peasants and slaves to their overlord.' As she spoke, Mara was aware of the many tangled threads that might have led to the possible killing of Garrett MacNamara, the man who was willing to betray his clan for the position of earl and for the heritage of his recently acknowledged heir.

'It was, perhaps, a sad thing for Peadar, that he was killed before Garrett had formally recognised him at Poulnabrone—' began Moylan and then he was interrupted by Fiona.

'But a good thing for Jarlath,' she said quickly. 'If Garrett had lived, and had surrendered his birthright to Henry VIII, then Jarlath would have had no place on the Burren and would have had to go back to his life as a merchant.'

'Stephen Gardiner told me that under the English system the position of *tánaiste* does not exist – the inheritance goes purely by primogeniture,' said Moylan. 'That means that the eldest son inherits,' he added to the two younger boys with a trace of condescension.

'We know that,' said Shane impatiently. 'We know Latin, you know, Moylan – first born . . . And that's interesting, isn't it, Brehon? Jarlath's position as *tánaiste* would have had no relevance, whereas now—'

'Whereas now, and as I was about to say before I was rudely interrupted, he is the heir and will, I suppose, definitely be elected as *taoiseach*.' Fiona looked sternly at Moylan and he threw up his hand in apology.

The scholars looked at each other and heads were nodded in acknowledgement of Fiona's assessment.

'Perhaps,' said Mara with a look of approbation at Fiona, 'we should now speculate on whether Garrett could, somehow or other, have been placed in the path of the marauding cattle, without danger to the murderer. In other words, was Garrett murdered by someone—'

'OM,' reminded Hugh.

'OM,' corrected Mara. This was a good approach for the scholars to take to a murder. There was no point in trying to put a name to the criminal too early. The facts had to be gathered and the motives explored before they moved forward in this investigation.

'No way could it have been seen from the castle,' said Aidan, looking back up the hill.

It was true. There was a sharp, small hill in front of them and nothing to be seen there, except a small cattle cabin and the remains of an old mill. They would have to go about

100

another five hundred yards, decided Mara, before they reached a spot which would have been visible from the castle. Was this spot chosen for that reason? Did the murderer – OM, amended Mara – drag the unconscious Garrett to this spot because it was shielded from the view of the castle by the intervening hill, or was this just a fortunate occurrence, an accident? Would, she speculated, Jarlath have had time to do something like this before the cattle arrived at Carron? Perhaps it was the impulse of a moment, a crime born of impatience. Perhaps he struck his brother and then left the body in the path of the marauders?

But that did not explain the chain.

'There's no sign of the other end of the chain, Brehon,' said Aidan. While busy with her thoughts, Mara had been conscious that he and Moylan had walked the length of the road, checking each roadside rock.

'You've checked thoroughly, haven't you?' she asked. It was strange, she thought, not to find the other end of the chain. Or was it, as Ardal had surmised, just a short chain for leading a bull in safety? In which case it would not have been long enough to be tied to a rock.

'There are no fence posts on this stretch of the road, Brehon,' said Hugh breaking into her thoughts.

'Perhaps the O'Lochlainn made a mistake,' said Shane, scanning the roadside.

'I doubt it,' said Moylan fervently.

'Is it important?' asked Fiona and Mara was not sure how to answer her.

It was a good question. What role had the chain around Garrett's leg played? Or was it possible that Ardal O'Lochlainn had made a mistake? Mara looked up the hill and then began to walk up the steep road until she was far up enough to see the tall, grey limestone tower house. 'We saw the cows running down the road from the south of the kingdom,' she said, recollecting the scene. 'They had a few steep hills to scale which would have slowed them down after that . . .'

'There would still have been an unbelievable amount of noise, though, and Garrett's own cattle would have been running to join – cows do that,' said Moylan, a farmer's son.

'And Garrett came running out to stop them,' supplemented Hugh with a note of doubt in his voice.

'Doesn't sound like him,' said Moylan dismissively.

'I've got it,' said Aidan triumphantly. 'Slaney beat him up and told him he was a lunatic and tied him by the leg to a post . . .' His voice tailed away as Mara eyed him severely. Her scholars had to be trained to take law business seriously, however much they could joke and laugh in their own private time.

'Aidan is right, though,' said Fiona, rather unexpectedly taking his part. 'I think there is something very strange about this death and we can't just shut our eyes and say that it is a great mystery. We have to speculate on what might have happened – and even if some of the guesses are wide of the mark—' she smiled sweetly at Aidan – 'they might lead some more intelligent member of the school into hitting on the truth.'

'Well, make the case, then,' said Mara. Fiona had a clear mind and a confidence in her judgement which would serve her well when she became Brehon. Scotland would be proud of their first woman Brehon. She remembered her thoughts about Ardal and decided that it would be a shame for Fiona to throw up her future and become a wife and mother too early in her life. She would play no part in furthering that romance, she decided.

Fiona took a cautious look around and then said decisively, 'We have a death – a death which looks like a terrible accident and would have undoubtedly been considered as an accident if it were not for the evidence that a chain had been around the dead man's leg when his body was first discovered – by the O'Lochlainn. Unfortunately by the time that we reach the castle then there might be no sign of the chain – they'll have cleaned him up . . .'

That was probably true, thought Mara. Brigid had mentioned nothing about a chain. Her informant, the woman with the goat's cheese, would have undoubtedly mentioned that strange fact if she had been aware of it. She stared across at the valley still flooded from the heavy and unseasonal rains. Ardal was right. This was going to be a difficult time for the farmers. The grass still had a bleached appearance, though the thrushes were trilling as melodiously as ever.

'We'll have to question the maidservants who

burned the clothing,' Moylan's eager voice interrupted Mara's thoughts. 'I'll do that, Brehon, if you wish.' He flicked back his hair with careless fingers, his expression showing his belief in his ability to get the truth from impressionable young girls.

'If I may continue . . .' said Fiona amiably but with a warning glint in her eye, 'I was just about to say, Brehon, that I don't think that we should concentrate so heavily on this affair of the chain, because it is too puzzling, but we should investigate the case as though it is an ordinary secret and unlawful killing and find out who had motive and opportunity.'

'That makes very good sense,' said Mara with a nod of approbation. At the same time, she thought, there is something so puzzling about the idea of a short chain, probably a narrow bull chain, tied to a man's leg and probably, according to Ardal, not broken in any way. It was like a chess puzzle, she thought and turned her eyes towards Shane, the best chess player in her school. His dark blue eyes were inward looking and thoughtful. She would not question him now, but allow him to reflect.

'We'd better go up to the castle,' she said. No doubt she and her scholars had been spotted by now and all would be wondering about the purpose of her search.

The hall was full of members of the MacNamara clan and the noise of voices was high as a servant escorted them up the stairs. There was a sudden silence when Mara came through the door and all heads turned towards her. Jarlath was there, standing by the window talking to Stephen Gardiner and to the man Tomás and it was Tomás who came across to her instantly.

'Brehon,' he said courteously. 'Let me get you a goblet of mead.'

'No, thank you,' said Mara instantly. She hated mead, that intoxicating drink, made from honey. It always tasted unpleasantly sweet to her. She sent a warning glance at her scholars and relied on Moylan to make sure that they refused also. This was not a social occasion, although the clan seemed to be treating it as such. This was official business about the death of their *taoiseach* who even if he were not particularly mourned still had to have justice granted to him and his terrible death investigated.

'Where is Slaney?' she asked and saw an expression of satisfaction pass over his face. He was a handsome man in the dark-skinned, brown-eyed manner of the MacNamara clan and he had an air of command about him. He had been a cousin of Garrett and Jarlath and was probably, apart from young Peadar, their nearest male relative. She wondered whether he would be elected as *tánaiste* of the MacNamara clan when Jarlath was confirmed in the office of *taoiseach*. Behind him was what looked like his son, a boy whom he introduced briefly as Adair and seemed to think that she must know who he was.

'She is available for your questioning, Brehon,' he said promptly. 'My own wife and several of the other women are with her in her bedroom.'

'I should wish to pay my respects and to explain to her my plans for the investigation of the untimely and terrible death of her husband,' said Mara blandly. She did not like his manner. It was for her to investigate – it almost sounded as though Slaney were being watched and kept immured. 'But first I had better have a word with Jarlath.'

'There's just one thing, Brehon,' he said weightily. 'We, as a clan, wonder what is the position now of the two people from Scotland.' He indicated with a nod of his head, Rhona and her son. 'We should, of course, wish to treat them with all courtesy and make sure that they have a safe passage back to their home.'

So the clan wanted to be rid of this newly discovered son of Garrett; that was interesting. Mara pursed her lips and examined Tomás and his handsome young son, Adair.

'This, I suppose, is a matter for Peadar to decide,' she said firmly. 'As the only son of his father, there will be a considerable property for him to inherit and, I should imagine, that he will want to see to that.'

'But, I understand that the case was never heard at Poulnabrone.' Tomás fixed his dark eyes on her and widened his shoulders as he gazed down at her. Mara looked severely at him, conscious that Moylan had taken a step forward and was now by her side.

'My eldest scholar will perhaps enlighten you on that subject,' she said and listened with satisfaction as Moylan explained clearly and tactfully about the rights to an inheritance of any son, no matter who was his mother, if he had been recognised by his father.

'Yes, yes, I know all that,' said Tomás impatiently. 'And I do know that Garrett had the intention of recognising him, but it didn't happen, did it? Obviously Garrett had second thoughts about the matter as he did not turn up at Poulnabrone.'

'That's an interesting point,' said Stephen Gardiner from behind Mara. 'Certainly under English law an intention to bequeath can never be taken as the deed itself. And the man did not meet his death until several hours at least after the court was held. He could indeed be deemed to have changed his intentions. That's how my teachers of law would have seen it, in any case . . .' He tailed off rather apologetically as Mara raised her eyebrows. She gazed at him stonily.

'But we are not talking about English law,' she reminded him. 'Under Brehon law if a man makes public his acceptance of a son, then that son has inheritance rights. And, Garrett did speak in public on this matter. I heard him myself. Shane, you have a good memory. Can you quote to us the words of Garrett MacNamara on the subject of his son Peadar when we attended the wake of his *tánaiste*? God have mercy on his soul,' she added hastily.

Shane shut his eyes for a second and then opened them. A crowd had now gathered around them, listening intently, but Shane was unperturbed and his dark blue eyes gazed steadily at Mara.

'He said, Brehon: "This is my choice for

tánaiste. My son, Peadar, bred of my bone and acknowledged by me." These were his words.'

'That is my memory, also,' said Mara, but there was no confirming murmur from the MacNamara clan. They would prefer that Rhona and her son would go back to Scotland; that Slaney would retreat to her family in Galway. Then the clan could start again with a young and popular leader, in the form of Jarlath and perhaps a steady, experienced man like Tomás as his *tánaiste* and assistant in clan matters. Peadar, she noticed, as though he felt the atmosphere, was staying at a distance, but Rhona had approached and Mara saw a gleam of gratitude and relief in the woman's grey eyes. There was something else to be said, though, and Mara decided that it should be said in public. There was a slightly unpleasant atmosphere here in the hall and there was no doubt that the pair from Scotland was unwelcome amongst the MacNamara clan.

'Peadar was acknowledged in my presence, and in the presence of the clan as his father's son, and is, unless any other sons appear, the inheritor of his personal lands and property, other than that wealth accumulated personally by Garrett which he was allowed, under the law, to bequeath as he wished.' Mara paused and then went on: 'The position of Rhona, his mother is different. Although Garrett did declare his intention of taking Rhona as a wife of the second degree, this should have been brought before the court and the words of the chief wife, Slaney, should have had the opportunity of being heard. But for some reason, neither Garrett, nor Slaney, attended the hearing at Poulnabrone on the eve of Bealtaine, therefore Rhona was not declared a wife of the second degree and so has no rights over his property.'

Slaney, she knew, benefitted considerably under Garrett's will made after the first month of his marriage, but that was not a matter for the clan. Garrett had personal wealth from his enterprises as a sea-merchant, and that wealth had been his to do with as he pleased. Who knows whether, if he had lived, that he might not have changed this will and given that silver to his newly discovered son, or, indeed, to the mother of that son. For a moment Mara speculated about Slaney. Had she, indeed, played a part in urging her husband to confront the herd of cows?

Rhona was looking indifferent to her pronouncement. She appeared an intelligent woman and she was acquainted with a Brehon in the Highlands of Scotland where the law was the same, so, no doubt, she was prepared for Mara's announcement. She showed no particular signs of sorrow at Garrett's death; in all probability she had just come to seek him out in order to give her young son his rights.

'And,' said Mara loudly and clearly, 'I now need to ask the clan, and as I know that at least one member of each branch of the *derbh-fine* is present here today, whether you are satisfied that the *tánaiste,* Jarlath, be declared to be your *taoiseach.*'

There was a full-throated shout of 'ay' at that and several exuberant members of the clan drummed their feet on the ground. Mara held up a hand for silence. She had not liked Garrett particularly, but she found the lack of sorrow for his terrible death and the lack of sympathy for the widow to be slightly distasteful.

'I shall speak to the king of your wish and, if he approves, the ceremony will take place within the next week if possible, at the ancient burial place outside the tower house and all members of the clan will be invited to attend,' she said curtly. It would be, of course, unknown for the king to go against the wishes of the clan in such an important matter of the election of a *taoiseach*, but she was pleased to see the slightly startled look in the eyes of Tomás.

Mara beckoned to Jarlath. 'Where can we speak alone?' she asked. Until, and not until, Tomás was elected by the clan as *tánaiste* he had, in her view, no special place, so Jarlath the inheritor of his brother's position was the one to talk to.

He led the way in silence to a small room leading off the hall. He did not, she thought – as she beckoned her scholars to follow her – have the elated look of a man who had suddenly, and unexpectedly succeeded to high office at a young age. It must have come as a shock to him – and perhaps not a pleasant shock. There had been just a matter of about ten years between the brothers and Jarlath had been leading an adventurous life on the high seas where death could come at any moment, either from attacks by pirates or from storm-force winds and tumultuous seas, while Garrett cosseted himself in the

110

warmth and comfort of his newly furnished castle. There would have been no guarantee that Jarlath would have ever been *taoiseach* of the clan. In any case, he had been so recently elected as *tánaiste* that he had hardly had time to reflect on the future.

'I just wanted to ask you about yesterday, Jarlath,' Mara said as soon as the door was closed by Fachtnan. 'I seem to remember when you left us on the mountain you had determined to go down to Carron – you used some such words as "root Garrett out". Did you, in fact, see your brother?'

'I didn't, Brehon,' said Jarlath, his tone sounding sad. 'There wasn't a sign of him anywhere. I suppose he was already dead.'

'But you didn't see the body, did you?'

He looked startled at that. 'No, of course not,' he said indignantly. 'You don't think that I would go off on a hunt after cattle thieves and leave my only brother lying dead on a mountainside road. No, I came from the easterly direction – I came by way of Knockanes and then down; the cattle had passed – I could hear them thundering down the road at a distance so I went straight to the stable and got my horse and followed instantly. By that stage, I suppose, poor Garrett was dead on the Castletown road and I could have done nothing for him.'

'And all was quiet at the castle when you arrived,' suggested Mara.

Jarlath stared at her with an expression of astonishment.

'What? Quiet!' he exploded. 'You can't know

much about cattlemen, Brehon, if you think that. The whole place was in uproar. They had been in the middle of their supper when the news came. The women were dashing around like headless chickens and the men were pelting down the road, which was just plain stupidity, because any man that got in the way of that herd would end up like poor Garrett.'

Mara suppressed a smile. She liked him for his frank indignation and his youthful energy. He was on his feet now, striding around the room energetically.

'What did you do?' she asked.

'Sent them through the fields to get ahead if possible,' he replied impatiently, 'told them that if they couldn't get ahead, then to be on hand to get as many of them back as possible. Of course it didn't help that Garrett, silly id— . . . that Garrett had quarrelled with his chief cowman and dismissed him so that there was no one on hand to give orders to the others. For a moment I thought he might be going to help but when he saw me there he just went back into his cottage and shut the door – can't blame him really. By all accounts, Garrett had no right to dismiss him from his position. They lost a few cows because Garrett refused to rebuild a cattle cabin that had blown down and so there was nothing but that rickety old place on the hill which only held one calving cow at a time.'

'And had Garrett's body been discovered by the time that you got back?' Mara guessed the answer before he nodded in agreement. Ardal would have been ahead of him. Ardal was a solitary man who had little interest in cattle – his main livestock were either sheep or most importantly horses. He had left as soon as the cattle had been recovered and rode on ahead of the crowd. Jarlath was a more convivial type who would have enjoyed the company of the other men and would, no doubt, have jogged along, exchanging tall stories and jokes with Turlough, Teige O'Brien and Finn O'Connor, *taoiseach* of the O'Connor clan. Ardal would have been the first back and the first to discover the body.

'That's right,' he said. 'Slaney—' he wrinkled his nose with distaste – 'well, she was useless, prostrate with grief, according to herself. She had told the maids to clean him up and—'

'And to burn his clothing,' interrupted Mara.

'It had to be done,' he said. 'The body – well, I've seen some terrible sights at sea, but never anything as bad as this.' For a moment, he almost looked sick and then shook off the memory. 'It had to be done,' he said firmly. 'When I arrived, they had got as far as removing him from the road and putting the remains onto a pallet and carrying it into an empty cabin to keep the dogs and pigs away. He was lying there when I arrived and I told them to carry him into the house.'

Mara's heart sank. So the body had been left unattended for probably about an hour. Before Jarlath arrived, there would have been opportunity and time for anyone to have removed the chain

– if indeed there was anything suspicious about its presence. However, she asked the question and he stared at her blankly.

'A chain, Brehon, why, on earth, would anyone tie a chain around Garrett's leg?'

And so the question was still left unanswered.

Six

Berrad Airechta
(Oaths at the Courts)

A witness must be sensible, honest, conscientious and of good memory. A person who gives evidence in court can only give that evidence on matters seen or heard and has to swear that his words are true. No evidence can be accepted which has not been seen, personally, by the witness. If possible there should be two or three witnesses, but the evidence of one trustworthy witness is superior to the evidence of several untrustworthy witnesses.

Mara had a practical mind and seldom spent too long on questions that could not be answered. Jarlath's evidence, she told herself, had neither confirmed nor denied the presence of a chain. She had, she admitted to herself, puzzled over the evidence of Ardal O'Lochlainn that he had seen a chain around the leg of the trampled body of Garrett MacNamara. But that had been denied by his wife Slaney and by the maidservants who had stripped and washed the body and burned the remnants of clothing. And Jarlath seemed to have no knowledge of it, either.

And why should they lie?

Mara moved the affair to a back shelf in her

mind as she returned to the great hall and sought out Tomás. She watched him unobtrusively for a moment. Jarlath was on friendly terms with all, popular and unassuming, slapping a back of one man, bestowing a warm smile on another and then cracking a joke with a group who were gathered around a large flask of mead. Tomás, on the other hand, appeared to have taken over the position of host, of master of the house, directing one servant to refill the almost empty wood basket and another to light the candelabra on the wall, a third to pull across the heavy velvet curtains. A fourth servant, who had just entered the room, made straight for him and whispered something into his ear. He it was who seemed to be in charge at the moment and Mara approached him.

'I need to speak with Slaney, now,' she said firmly.

He frowned slightly. 'I feel that you may be wasting your time, Brehon. I have just received a poor account of her state of mind.'

'I shall be judge of that,' snapped Mara. 'Please summon a servant to show me the way.'

'I had better go with you myself, to make sure that you are admitted,' he said weightily after a moment's pause

And this was another puzzle, thought Mara as, followed by her scholars, she was ushered ceremoniously by Tomás up the stairs, past several men-at-arms who were lounging on window seats and who straightened abruptly at the sight of Tomás. Why was Slaney being confined to her bedroom? How could she be under suspicion,

116

in any sensible mind, of having a hand in her husband's death beneath the hoofs of the cattle? After all, at the moment, only the tiniest suspicion that Garrett's death might not have been an accident existed in Mara's mind alone, and none but her own scholars were aware of her thoughts on this matter.

And yet it did appear that Slaney was confined and under guard.

Tomás tapped on a richly carved door. Almost immediately there was a loud click in the door lock and then it was opened to him by a woman with a key in her hand. Mara acted quickly, took the key and then instead of entering the room, she pushed the door shut again, right in the face of an astonished woman.

'Why is Slaney locked in her bedroom?' she asked Tomás calmly, suppressing the anger that she felt. She placed her back against the door and kept her voice down to a low level so that none other than Tomás could hear her. Facts before feelings, was what she always told her scholars and she was continuously aware of her duty to give them the best of examples in dealing with the people of the kingdom. She would deal with this matter coolly and sensibly.

Tomás hesitated. He looked at her scholars with a frown and she gestured to Moylan to move them back to the window. She would not give this man any excuse not to tell the truth, she thought.

'There's an ugly rumour that Slaney is responsible for the death of her husband,' he said eventually in a low tone. 'The clan are very angry about this. She is locked in for her own safety.'

'A rumour,' she repeated. 'What is the rumour?'

'It is said that she goaded and shamed the man into going out and trying to stop the cows,' he said eventually.

'A man is responsible for his own deeds,' Mara retorted. 'Even if this is true, and I have heard that there were quarrels between them on that day, no sane man would face a herd of stampeding cows. If your cousin Garrett did do this, did go down and face the stampede, then the responsibility was his and the consequences, God have mercy on him, had to be borne by him.'

'The clan don't think like that.' Tomas was stiff-necked and hostile. 'They feel that his wife is responsible. It was not like him to do a thing like that. He must have been forced to do it. That is what the clan believe, Brehon,' he added.

'The clan, like all other clans in the kingdom, will keep within the letter of the law,' snapped back Mara. She was losing her patience with this man. Quickly she twisted open the handle of the door and once inside did not return the elaborate key to the door, but brushed past the woman with the outstretched hand.

'Slaney,' she said in loud clear tones, as she approached the carved and curtained bed, followed by her scholars. 'Slaney, I am very sorry for your trouble.'

The traditional greeting to those in mourning had no effect and there was no reply.

A woman who was sitting beside the bed stood

up quickly, looking uncertainly at Tomás, and without a glance at her Mara took her place and bent over the statuesque figure lying inside the elaborate draperies.

She had been drugged or deliberately fed too much mead, Mara guessed as she looked into the very black centres of the woman's prominent blue eyes that stared at the draperies overhead. It was ridiculous to say that sorrow had reduced her to this. Mara had seen her a few hours after the discovery of her husband's body and Slaney had been her usual authoritative self, bullying people into saying rosaries and very much in command of her household.

'Slaney,' she said. Her voice was low, but pitched to the woman's ear and Slaney turned her eyes on her. For a moment there was a flicker in them and then the eyelids shut.

I wish Nuala was here, thought Mara as she reached over and took the woman's hand in hers, her finger on that spot in her wrist where, according to Nuala, the heartbeat could be counted. If that was true, Slaney's heartbeat was very slow, not agitated in the way that a bereaved wife's should be.

'She's not well,' said a servant on the other side of the bed. Her voice was low and she cast a quick, almost guilty look at Tomás. She spoke Gaelic but with a strong English accent. Mara recognised her. She had come from Galway with Slaney, and unlike the rest of the servants at Carron Castle, appeared to be devoted to her mistress.

'She's had nothing but what she has brewed

119

herself,' said the voice of Tomás from behind her. 'My wife, Cait,' he indicated a small thin woman with mild blue eyes who looked up in a fearful manner at him. She bobbed a quick acknowledgement of Mara's greeting and Tomás smiled at her in a kindly fashion. 'Cait,' he continued, 'was worried about how agitated and sleepless Slaney seemed to be – she couldn't seem to relax, just kept pacing up and down the floor of her bedroom and twisting her hands together and sobbing.'

'Wondering what was to become of her, poor soul.' Cait heaved a sigh and cast her eyes piously in the direction of heaven.

'I don't think she would need to worry about that,' said Mara in bracing tones. She thought about the likelihood of Slaney worrying about the future while Tomás was explaining that Cait had just given Slaney some medicine she normally took – a jar beside her bed, apparently. But why had the bereaved wife suddenly become so distraught? Slaney, she guessed, unless Garrett had gone to another lawyer to make a later will, would be very well endowed and would be able to go back to Galway, her native city and live there in comfort, if not luxury. Mara cast her mind back to the time, a few years ago, when Garrett had made his will. Yes, Slaney had been present, had interrupted so often and had reminded Garrett of various bequests in such an authoritative manner that her scholars had been helpless with giggles as they all rode away from the castle at Carron.

Slaney, in her right mind, could have had no

doubt that she had been left extremely well provided for.

In the meantime, though, the woman seemed to be locked into some stupor – not a quiet sleep, either. She continuously tossed and turned and muttered as though haunted by nightmares. Mara looked across at Slaney's personal maid.

'Fetch me this medicine that your mistress brewed for her personal usage – the one that was given to her today.'

The woman gave a quick glance at Tomás, but he said nothing, so after a pause she went out of the room slowly as though reluctant or worried in some way. Mara waited impassively, her eyes on Slaney. The woman did dabble in various remedies; she knew that. And on many occasions, her fits of rage and her lack of self-control were deeply embarrassing to Garrett. Perhaps she had concocted something to calm her, or something to change her mood. Slaney's pride would not allow her to consult a physician on the Burren as she had imbibed the Galway attitude: Galway people, who spoke the English language and lived by English laws and English customs, had contempt for the ways of the Gaelic Ireland, referring to the people as 'mere Irish'.

There was silence after the maid had left the room and it was broken only by the mutterings of the woman on the bed. There was a feeling of tension in the air, thought Mara. It did not emanate from Tomás, who seemed perfectly at ease and in command of the situation. From his wife perhaps, who appeared fearful of him, or perhaps from the other women servants?

What were all these women doing in the room, anyway? wondered Mara. One woman, Slaney's personal maid, should be enough. A suspicion crossed her mind that Tomás had them there to emphasise how Slaney was no longer – and could not be – mistress of the house, but was now a prisoner. And, perhaps, that he was now in command. This last thought angered her so much that she turned towards the woman who had been housekeeper of Carron Castle from right back to the time of Garrett's father.

'Have you been given orders to remain here?' she asked, her eyes going to the other three maidservants who were standing around doing nothing.

The housekeeper's eyes went to Tomás and then back to Mara.

'Because, if not,' said Mara pleasantly, but with a note of authority in her voice, 'I'm sure that you have a lot to do with all of your visitors. Your presence here, and that of your maids, is probably unnecessary.'

Jarlath will need to take the reins of this household firmly into his own hands, was her thought. What a pity that Jarlath did not have a capable wife. Mara's mind ran over suitable girls in the Burren as she waited for the housekeeper to finally leave the room. She was gesturing to the maids to go to the door but at the same time casting nervous glances over her shoulder at Tomás. I'll find Jarlath a wife as soon as possible, thought Mara. A *taoiseach* needed a wife. Ardal O'Lochlainn, it was true, had no wife, but Ardal had a capable steward, an intelligent young man who managed everything for him. This house-keeper did not look too bright.

Once again there was that odd look from the housekeeper towards Tomás, almost as though she were asking for his permission, but he said nothing so the woman dropped a curtsey and jerked her head at the other servants indicating that they should follow her.

It seemed a relief when they were gone. Despite the cold weather the room was unpleasantly warm with a roaring fire in the chimney and several braziers, burning charcoal, dotted around the room which was hung with dust-laden tapestries and strong-smelling sheets of painted leather. Aidan wiped his brow and Hugh looked a little pale, his freckles standing out against his white skin. Mara was sorry for them.

'Wait for me outside,' she said and they went instantly, Moylan holding the door open for Fiona and then continuing to hold it as Slaney's personal maid came back in with a small jar in her hand.

'What is in it?' asked Mara, holding the jar up to the light of the lamp above the bed and regret-ting her ignorance of herbs. Still, she thought, Nuala will be here soon and there was little that Nuala, even as a child, did not know about the properties of medicinal plants.

'Cowbane and some other things; I'm not sure,' said the woman hesitantly.

'Cowbane!' Mara's voice rose with surprise. She knew nothing about the medicinal use of the plant but remembered clearly how Cumhal, her farm manager, scoured the marshy land on the edge of her property for traces of the tall white flowers and uprooted and burned every vestige of them – especially the roots. He had warned her and told her to warn the scholars never to touch the plant.

'Some of the young ones might think to make whistles from the hollow stems,' he had said. 'They need to be told of its dangers. I've seen a cow die ten minutes after swallowing an uprooted plant.'

'Are you sure that Slaney made a medicine using cowbane?' she asked the maid.

'Probably only used it in tiny quantities,' said Tomás reassuringly and his miniature wife nervously nodded an agreement.

'Better sure than sorry,' said Mara weightily. 'I'll keep this and ask a physician about it.'

'If you think that it would be best,' he said with a note of indifference in his voice.

'And there should be no question of locking the door; I shall speak to Jarlath about the proper courtesies due to the widow of his brother.'

'Even if she were guilty of that terrible death—'

'At the moment,' said Mara firmly, 'God alone knows why the poor man went down there alone and unarmed and faced the terrible stampede of cattle.'

She bent over the woman's bed and took the wrist in her hand again. Slaney had shut her eyes now, but Mara was still not convinced that this was a normal sleep. Perhaps there was some level where she was conscious of those around her.

'Don't worry, Slaney,' Mara said, replacing the

wrist on the linen sheet, and deliberately speaking with a raised voice, 'I shall make it my duty to find out what happened to your husband.' She straightened and looked around at the assembled women and at Tomás's brown eyes. Cait had moved over beside him, standing on tiptoe, and he was whispering in her ear. Had Cait been placed here as a jailor by the efficient Tomás; had his own wife been given the task of imprisoning the wife who was going to be blamed for her husband's death? A feeling of anger came over her. Who was Tomás MacNamara to appoint himself as judge of this matter?

'You may safely leave all investigation into this sad death to me and my scholars,' she assured him, allowing a patronising note to creep into her voice and then turned towards the door as an elaborate triple knock from a fingernail came from it.

'Yes, Moylan,' she said opening it.

'I'm sorry to disturb you, Brehon,' said Moylan suavely, 'but—'

But Mara had already seen the tall, broad-shouldered form of Jarlath behind him and she turned herself towards him with concern. Only the threat of the man bursting into Slaney's bedchamber would have made Moylan disturb her. Something was wrong. Jarlath's sea-browned face had a yellowish tinge to it and his lips were compressed. His voice, though, was steady when he spoke.

'I need to speak to you about something very important, Brehon,' he said and she moved towards him instantly, concerned for him and braced for more bad news. She waved back her scholars and Tomás who had followed her out of the room, and withdrew into the privacy of a window embrasure. The walls were about twenty-foot thick in this old part of the castle and they had complete privacy there, but Jarlath looked unable to come to the point. He moistened his lips, looked over her shoulder as though he feared that they would be followed, and when he did speak, his voice cracked uncertainly.

'One of the maidservants told me that you were enquiring about a chain tied around Garrett's leg, Brehon,' he said eventually. 'So you are sure that there was such a chain. I couldn't understand it when you asked me about it, but I have been thinking of it since then.'

'I did hear from someone that was the case, but it appeared, from what Slaney and the maids said, that they felt my information was incorrect,' said Mara carefully.

'Could it be that someone tied him up there in the path of the marauders?' he muttered.

'It doesn't seem likely,' she replied calmly, looking closely into his face by the light from the tiny window. 'Remember that the report said that the chain was around one leg. Now, if it had been around both legs, and if the arms, also, had been bound, well then—'

'Yes, but he could have worked loose from his bonds before the herd came. One could hear them from miles; everyone at the castle heard them apparently; all the clan members from Thomond were at the windows and some were on the roof when I arrived,' he interrupted, his voice shaking.

'So Tomás was on the roof, was he?' asked Mara quickly.

'No, no, Tomás went hunting for Garrett – he thought he was in Slaney's bedroom but she shouted out that she had not seen Garrett for hours. By the time he got outside, it was too late to do anything. The MacNamara cows were already breaking out of the fields and running down the hills. Cows do that, you know. They will always join a herd.'

'That's right,' said Mara. Cumhal had told her that. But what was bothering Jarlath? Why had he interrupted her? Why had he wanted to see her so urgently? What was there in the maid's information to have upset a tough young man who had little acquaintance, little affection, probably, for a brother that he had not seen for years?

'So you think this affair about a chain around Garrett's leg was just a fancy, is that it?' he asked. 'Could have been a piece of torn material from his trews or from his jerkin?' he added and she was sure that she heard a note of hope in his voice.

'I don't think that my witness would make a mistake like that,' said Mara.

He stared at her for a moment. 'So you believe that someone caused his death, do you?' he asked and when she didn't reply, he said hurriedly, 'but who would have a motive to do something like that? I certainly could be held to . . .' He stopped and when he spoke again his voice had changed.

'That's not really what I wanted to see you about, Brehon,' he said. He straightened himself and moved back out towards the passageway outside Slaney's bedroom and when he next spoke it was in a clear, fairly loud tone of voice.

'All of the clan are assembled in the hall, Brehon,' he said politely. 'There is something that I wish to say and I would like you to be there to hear me say it. Would you come down, also, Tomás, and anyone else that can be spared from caring for Slaney, poor woman?'

Saying no more, he turned and began to go back down the staircase. Mara followed him without a word, though she was conscious that Tomás had uttered a startled question. Her scholars were behind her and she was glad to observe that none of them spoke and that they trooped down in a sober manner. Jarlath, she noticed as she turned the twist of the spiral staircase, was in the rear. She did not look at him. Soon she would know why she had been summoned. Could there have been another death? Or could it be a terrible revelation about the strange death of Garrett?

'What is it?' whispered Fiona to Moylan as they passed through the doorway into the hall.

Mara did not look at them. She, like they, was in the dark. The room was full of people including the tall, dark-haired figure of Stephen Gardiner, the emissary from Cardinal Wolsey in London. Apart from him, the hall held only the MacNamara clan as Rhona and her son Peadar were absent. All of the members of the *derbh fine,* the descendents of a single great-grandfather of royal

128

blood, were present and several other members of the clan, also. Many of them were unknown, or only known slightly by her as the majority of the higher levels of the MacNamara clan lived in Thomond, south-east of the Burren. As she looked at them a door at the back of the hall opened and Cait, Tomás's diminutive wife, came in with her tall son Adair and they both took their place beside Stephen Gardiner.

It was obvious that they were all puzzled by the summons. Several of them, by their wind-flushed faces, had been called in from the out-of-doors. Others looked as though they had been dozing in their chambers, awaiting the call to the evening meal. But there was no food or drink laid for them, just Jarlath standing by the great fireplace and looking very tense. He waited until all were inside and until the doors were closed and his relations seated or standing beside the walls, or ensconced into window seats.

'Brethren,' he said, and it was obvious from the effort that he put into the words that this, the traditional way of addressing the clan, came uneasily to his tongue. 'In your presence earlier I accepted your desire that I should be your new *taoiseach*. However, since then, I have thought long and hard and I feel that I am not the man that you are looking for. I have been a wanderer for many years and the wandering is in my blood and I don't think that it is something that I can easily shake off. You have done me great honour in selecting me; but I don't think that I am worthy of that honour. Tomás here—' and with a gesture he signalled to his cousin from the kingdom of

Thomond to come forward – 'Tomás is the man who has the clan's interest at heart. He will make you a wonderful *taoiseach* – I feel sure of that . . .'

Jarlath stopped talking and looked appealingly at his cousin. Tomás bowed his head gravely.

'If I can serve the clan,' he said graciously and with a deep note of sincerity in his voice, 'then my life's dearest wish will be granted.'

Mara caught a glimpse of the diminutive wife, Cait, clasp her hands together and raise them to her mouth as though to stop the words in praise of her husband flowing out. His tall son had flushed a deep red, but the man himself stood modestly and quietly by Jarlath's side, looking only at him. She, herself, had to admit that Tomás had handled Jarlath's surprise announcement with dignity and adroitness. The clan, of course, had no doubts. They had been through an uncertain and difficult time – Garrett had been deeply unpopular. He had begun his reign over them by raising the tribute of goods and silver expected from them to an unprecedented level and he had proved to have a poor understanding of the people that he ruled over. Perhaps there may have been some fears that Jarlath would follow in his footsteps. There was no doubt that Tomás knew every one of them, knew their desires, their needs, their resources and their expectations. He would probably make a good *taoiseach*. At any rate, he had the sense to make his speech short and then to step back, signalling to Jarlath to come and stand beside him.

Mara looked around the hall. The majority

of the clan of MacNamara were definitely present. There was no doubt that representatives of all main branches were there. She would take a vote, she thought. The people would have their say.

'All those in favour of Tomás MacNamara for *taoiseach* say ay,' she said unemotionally, and the hall rang with the acclamations. 'Against,' she said and not a person raised their voice.

'I hereby declare that Tomás MacNamara is the true choice of the clan for the position of *taoiseach* and I shall ask the king if he is willing to ratify your decision,' she said and after a moment all cheered.

Tomás slipped out of the room and a few minutes later, the housekeeper followed by men and women servants came in, bearing platters of honey cakes and other fine food and flagons of mead.

It was almost, thought Mara, as if all were already prepared for a feast this evening.

Turning a blind eye to her scholars, who were enthusiastically sampling some pastries and hopefully eyeing the mead, she strolled across to Jarlath.

'Any regrets?' she asked.

He turned a smiling face towards her. His eyes blazed with emotion – relief, perhaps, jubilation certainly, the face of a man who had made the right decision.

'No regrets,' he said with a short laugh, 'but a strong desire to get out of here before they start toasting my own corpse.'

'Come home with us,' she invited. 'Spend the night at Cahermacnaghten. In the morning you can think of what to do. I'd say that you've made the right decision,' she added, looking at his worried face. 'What do you want for your life – settling disputes, worrying about leases, thinking of your tribute? No, you're a young man, brave and adventurous; you've enjoyed life on the high seas – enjoy it for a few more years.'

Mara looked around her. A big group were around Tomás; various women were gathered in a smiling throng listening to Cait simpering, her eldest son's hand firmly clasped within two of her own tiny hands; the mead was flowing with a generosity that almost seemed as though this eventuality had been foreseen. Mara approached Tomás, murmured her congratulations and promised to speak to King Turlough on his behalf and made her excuses. Moylan, nobly resisting a refill of mead, immediately answered the message from her beckoning hand by gathering up his fellow scholars and, accompanied by Jarlath, they all left the castle.

'So that's all settled,' said Aidan as they mounted and rode down the empty road in group, Moylan going ahead with Jarlath and the two younger boys while Fiona and Aidan were riding one on either side of Mara.

'Bird brain,' said Fiona scathingly. 'How can the matter be settled when we don't know what happened to Garrett? Haven't you got any intellectual curiosity?'

'Not really,' said Aidan with his usual

frankness. 'I couldn't stand Garrett MacNamara.' He lowered his voice slightly at the last words, but they penetrated through the worry about Slaney that was going through Mara's head. It was a dangerous sentiment, she thought, though a boy's heedless words.

' "To no one will we deny justice",' she quoted aloud. 'The law is the same for all people in the kingdom. We owe it not just to Garrett MacNamara, but to everyone on the Burren, to find out the truth about his death.'

'So we start to investigate the death,' said Fiona briskly. 'I am making a list in my mind,' she added.

Aidan looked at her with curiosity. 'But if the O'Lochlainn had not seen a chain around the leg of the corpse then there would be no further bother – what if he has made a mistake? And you're a birdbrain if you can't see that.'

Fiona gave him a disdainful look, snorted something under her breath and urged her pony ahead. Jarlath glanced over his shoulder and dropped back to ride by her side.

Mara roused herself from her worry about Slaney. Aidan's point was a valid one and it needed answering.

'I always evaluate evidence, not just for what it contains, but also I evaluate the character of the person bringing the evidence,' she told him. A moment later she added, 'What is your opinion of Ardal O'Lochlainn, Aidan?'

She thought he might make a joke; he was the school's clown, but he seemed flattered to have his opinion asked.

133

'Careful sort of fellow,' he said after a minute.

Mara waited. It would be good for him to formulate his ideas and to learn to trust his judgement.

'I was listening to Muiris O'Hynes talking to Diarmuid O'Connor about a mare that he bought for breeding purposes,' he said after a pause for thought. 'And he said: "I paid a good price for her because the O'Lochlainn said he liked the look of her and he never speaks until he knows what he's talking about." That's what Muiris said and he's pretty shrewd himself,' added Aidan with a wise air that she found rather endearing. He was growing up, the little boy who liked jokes and funny stories in preference to work. Soon he would be gone from her and she would have a new generation of children to train up in the intricacies of Brehon law.

'That's a very good point,' she said, allowing a note of admiration to enter her voice. 'I'll remember that, Aidan. I think that is an excellent example of how a man's reputation should influence what weight is given to his evidence.'

Her mind went to Jarlath's words. Was it possible that Garrett had been bound hand and foot – and presumably gagged – and then had managed to free himself, just too late, of all chains except one? Or had there just been one chain which had knotted both ankles together? A man might be able to unpick a knot, but it took time; and time, with a herd of maddened cows thundering down the road, was not available to anyone in that particular situation.

But she and her scholars had searched the roadway soon afterwards and there were no signs of any chains on the paving or in the ditches on either side. She wondered whether Nuala would be able to discover any signs of the second ankle or leg being tied. Or was it possible that Garrett's wrist had been secured to his ankle by a piece of twine threaded through the links and then he was slung down into the pathway of the cows, the second knot slipping free as he was thrown. It would take an immensely strong man to throw a heavy-weight like Garrett down the hill.

Her eyes went thoughtfully to the tall figure of Jarlath. The two young boys, Shane and Hugh, had gone ahead with Moylan. He and Fiona had fallen behind and were joking and laughing about something. Jarlath showed no signs now of the almost panic with which he faced her in the window embrasure and spoke of his dead brother. Why had he sought her out so urgently and cross-questioned her about Garrett's death before coming to the decision to give up the leadership of the clan?

Had he been determined to show that he had no reason to murder his brother for the position of *taoiseach* since he had been so quick to give it up?

And yet, he would not have been under much suspicion as he had been on top of the mountain when the marauders had started the cows on their stampede through the Burren. Yes, he had reached Carron before the marauders, but probably not that long ahead of them; it was unlikely that he would have had time to stage an accident.

And why had Stephen Gardiner looked like a man with a great problem to solve when he heard that Jarlath was declining the post of *taoiseach* to the MacNamara clan? After all, though Jarlath had been his companion and friend on the journey from Donegal in the north of Ireland, the affairs of a tiny kingdom on the Atlantic fringe could not have been of such great interest to an emissary from the great king of England.

And what did Stephen Gardiner think of the fact that Tomás, a man of small importance until today, was now to be the leader of the MacNamara clan?

Seven

Bretha Crólinge
(Judgements of Blood-Letting)

A person found guilty of murder must pay a fine to the relatives of the dead.

If, however, the murder has been committed by one of the near kin, such as a son or a brother this is classified as fingal *and then no fine is big enough. The guilty person must be placed in a boat without oars and abandoned to the sea and to the vengeance of Almighty God.*

Mara slept well that night, forbidding her mind to range over the puzzle until more of the facts about the strange death could be ascertained. She needed Nuala's knowledge before coming to any conclusions, she decided. The party from Thomond would not be expected to reach the law school of Cahermacnaghten before noon and in the meantime there was much work to be done since study had been interrupted by the unexpected events of the last few days. The scholars had, after a few groans, accepted her dictate that they should not talk about the death of Garrett MacNamara until after Nuala had arrived and had had a chance to examine the body. They had worked well that morning, conning passages of Latin, turning out their own versions of poems

137

in that tongue, memorising tens and twenties of the wise sayings of Fithail, examining the laws of inheritance and referring to *Miadslechta* (sections dealing with rank and status) about the procedure for the election of a new *taoiseach*. With the example of the MacNamara procedure fresh in their minds, this would make the dull triads and heptads easier to memorize, Mara thought. She owed a lot of her success as a teacher to her practice of seizing on any real-life examples to illuminate the dry facts of the laws of Ireland.

After almost three hours of work, they had looked tired and Mara had relented. It might be, she thought, there would be little that Nuala could tell them. It had been impressive on one occasion when she was able to tell whether a wound had been inflicted before death, or after. However, on this occasion the body of Garret would be days old before Nuala could look at it. And the blood had been washed from it before even Mara and her scholars had seen it.

'I suppose we could speculate a little about the death of Garrett MacNamara,' she said cautiously when her hour glass showed her that they had now worked for a good, solid three hours.

'A secret and unlawful killing,' said Aidan with relish.

'Motive and opportunity,' said Moylan smartly, almost as if he had waiting for this moment.

'Let's look at motive first,' said Fiona thoughtfully. 'Opportunity is difficult when we are not exactly sure of when he was killed.'

'Should Hugh write on the board, Brehon, since Fachtnan is always saying that his handwriting is the best in the school?' asked Shane and Mara nodded with a feeling of pleasure. She had been right to choose Fachtnan as an assistant. She had had many clever scholars that had qualified at her school and then passed on. Quite a few of these would have been pleased to work under her and learn how to conduct a successful law school, but Fachtnan, despite problems with memory, had always had those special qualities of understanding and sensitivity. Hugh, they both knew, had little confidence in himself, but Fachtnan had obviously been quick to praise him and to emphasise his strong points to the other scholars.

'The usual categories, Hugh,' called out Moylan as soon as the fifteen-year-old was in position in front of the board with the charcoal stick in one hand and the damp sponge beside him. The board had been recently lime-washed by Cumhal, the farm manager, and the black strokes of Hugh's neat script stood out starkly against the white as he wrote: 'GREED; FEAR; ANGER; REVENGE' across the top and then turned enquiringly towards his fellow pupils.

'Greed is probably going to be the most important category,' said Shane thoughtfully. 'It's not as if Garrett was a poor man without possessions. He had a lot – plenty that someone else could have wanted.'

'Office of *taoiseach*,' said Aidan said instantly.

'Inherited by Jarlath,' said Aidan. 'But . . .'

'Let's finish this category,' said Hugh with unusual firmness.

'Personal wealth,' said Moylan with an interrogatory glance at Mara.

'Fairly considerable,' said Mara. 'There's his rental for a start: his tributes bring in about fourteen pieces of silver or its equivalent in cows, leather, wool or food stuff, from each of his sixty tenants.' She had always been open and honest with her scholars and relied on their oath which they took at the beginning of Michaelmas term every year to keep secret any knowledge they had of the affairs of the people of the kingdom. Ignoring Moylan's exclamation about the worth of eight hundred cows if Garrett chose to be paid like that, she picked out a small key from her pouch, unlocked the large wooden press in the corner of the room, took down a box labelled 'MACNAMARA' and carried it back over to her table. The will had been made four years ago and she doubted that any of her scholars would remember it. Four years was a lifetime at that age.

'Garrett's will leaves to his wife Slaney the entire contents of his castle. This was fair enough,' she explained when Moylan made a stifled exclamation of surprise. 'The old lord, Garrett's father, had allowed affairs to go to rack and ruin in the castle. There was very little furniture and what was there was mostly ruined by beetles and by damp – no hangings, no curtains, nothing that is there now. Garrett and Slaney made that castle what it is and I did feel that it was quite fair that he should bequeath its contents to her.'

'And what about the merchant sailing

140

business?' enquired Moylan. 'Jarlath told me that Garrett owned half of the ships. Will those be Slaney's also?'

'There's no mention of them in the will,' said Mara with a slight frown and then she nodded in a slightly exasperated manner. 'How could I have forgotten?' Quickly she found another scroll and opened it. 'Of course,' she said, 'the old lord left an equal portion of his ships between the two brothers with the proviso that if one brother died the whole was to revert to the surviving brother. That means that Jarlath inherits Garrett's ships. I seem to remember that he had some notion that a woman would not be able to run the business, so a widow with a young son—'

'You shouldn't have allowed him to make a will like that; it's not fair to the widow,' said Fiona fiercely, while Moylan, used from his earliest days of being under the rule of a woman in a man's world, looked at her with an ironic smile.

'A lawyer is the mouthpiece of the client,' said Mara, but she understood what Fiona meant. Slaney, she thought, would have been a better merchant than Garrett who was irresolute and disorganised. Still the woman had enough left to her as it was. Thoughtfully Mara's eyes went to the words on the board. Greed, she thought. Yes, that would be a feature of Slaney's character. A lot of the trouble between Garrett and his clansmen originated from his wife because Slaney was continually urging him to demand more in the way of tribute from the men who held farms under him.

'So write up Slaney's name under "greed",' ordered Moylan. 'Everyone agrees, don't they?' He gave a perfunctory glance around at his fellow scholars before going on.

'What about Jarlath? Do we put him up under that heading, too? After all he could have reasoned that if he murdered Garrett, then he would be *taoiseach*.'

'He turned it down, birdbrain,' said Fiona hotly.

Moylan shrugged. 'That doesn't say anything. I might desperately want yet another one of Brigid's honey cakes, but then when I got it, I might find that I was too full after all. He changed his mind. So? In any case he has inherited all those ships and they bring in quite a sum, I'd say.'

'I still think it's wrong to write Jarlath's name,' said Fiona emphatically. 'I think that a man who turned down the position of *taoiseach* is a man that silver doesn't matter that much to. In order to murder someone out of greed you need to be the sort of person who covets and lusts after possessions.'

A good point, thought Mara, but she said nothing. She tried to stay out of these discussions as much as possible and allow her scholars to argue the case amongst themselves. This was an important facet of her teaching.

'I agree with Fiona,' said Shane.

'Let's have a show of hands; all those in favour of adding Jarlath's name to the list under "greed" please raise your right hand.' Moylan looked around in a challenging fashion. Aidan responded instantly and, after a moment, so did Hugh.

'I think he is a possibility,' he said with an apologetic glance at Shane. 'I was thinking that he might have done the deed, thinking that no one would ever reckon it to be anything other than a terrible accident, and then when he realised that the Brehon was taking the matter seriously and had not allowed the body to be buried until a physician had the opportunity to examine it, well—' Hugh spread his hands in a deprecatory fashion – 'he just might have panicked and declared that he did not want the office of *taoiseach* – he might give quite a good explanation about it, about liking the sea and things like that and might appear in company as though a weight had been taken off his shoulders, but that might not be the whole truth; he may just have panicked. After all if he killed his own brother it wouldn't be just a case of a fine to be paid. It would be classed as *fingal* and that is a terrible end for any one in their sane senses.'

'That's true,' said Shane. 'Funnily enough I was explaining about *fingal* to Stephen Gardiner. I was telling him about how a man who has murdered someone of his blood – a father or brother – then he is banished from the kingdom and set adrift on the ocean in a boat with no oars. He was laughing at that and saying he didn't think it much of a punishment and that in England anyone who committed a crime like that would be hanged, then while he was still alive would be cut down and his entrails and private parts stuffed into his mouth and that he would die in agony,' finished Shane airily as Moylan eyed Fiona teasingly to see whether she was embarrassed.

143

'In fact,' went on Shane, 'Stephen Gardiner was saying to Jarlath that soon English law would be in Ireland and then penalties like that would be happening, here. Funny, really, because he's not stupid, Stephen Gardiner, but he really does seem to think that it would be a great advance for Ireland if English law were to prevail.' He smiled in the superior fashion of one who was calmly sure of his own intelligence and judgement.

'What did Jarlath say?' enquired Hugh with interest.

'He said that to die a slow death from thirst adrift on the sea would be worse than any other punishment, including hanging, drawing and quartering,' said Shane, thoughtfully. 'That's why I've changed my vote. He sounded very genuine when he said it. There was a sort of sound of horror in his voice at the notion if being accused of *fingal*.'

'So you're out-voted, Fiona, put Jarlath's name under "greed", young Hugh,' said Moylan briskly and Hugh wrote the letters neatly.

'Anger?' he queried.

'The funny thing is that we could put Slaney there, as well,' said Fiona. 'I was telling you, wasn't I, how Rhona overheard them quarrelling and how something like a stool had been thrown at Garrett. Perhaps Slaney hit him so hard over the head that she killed him and then she dragged his body out and then threw it down the hill right onto the road in front of the stampeding cattle. What do you think, Brehon?'

'I think that you've made the point well, Fiona, and there is no reason why one name should not

144

appear under two categories. Most people have mixed motives for their actions.' Mara thought briefly about Rhona, but opportunity was lacking so she did not waste much time in her thoughts and waited for her scholars to give their suspects.

'What about Rhona and Peadar – they've both got motives which would put them in the "greed" category – or, at least, Peadar has,' said Shane as if he read her thoughts and the others stared at him.

'They were on top of the mountain and came home with us, birdbrain,' exclaimed Moylan spacing out his words and speaking as though to one who was half-witted.

Mara frowned at him. She disliked this habit of scornful abuse and words like 'birdbrain', but Shane did not appear bothered. He had a quiet confidence in his own brains and ability and took little notice of Moylan's airs of superiority.

'We haven't moved onto "opportunity" yet,' said Hugh, backing up his friend and looking enquiringly at Mara.

'Does everyone agree that Rhona and Peadar should be entered under "greed" for the moment?' she asked and all heads nodded. 'I've thought of a couple for "anger or revenge",' she continued. 'There was Maol, the steward – he told me that Garrett was threatening to remove him from his position and there was also Brennan the cowman who had already, according to Jarlath, been dismissed. Do you all agree that Hugh should write up those names?' she asked politely, biting back a smile as heads were eagerly and vigorously nodded.

'Brennan the cowman is a particularly good one,' said Aidan enthusiastically. 'He'd know all about cows and he'd know how quickly they would run and everything about them. I heard someone say, when we were on the mountain for the Bealtaine celebrations, that the MacNamara had made a terrible mistake to dismiss him – "he'll rue it all his born days", that's what Lorcan was saying.'

'Any names for the "fear" column?' asked Shane.

'Don't think anyone would really fear him, would they? He was a bit of a fool, really, wasn't he?' said Aidan looking from face to face and then adding hastily, 'not that I wish to speak evil of the dead, or anything . . .'

'I think,' said Mara rising to her feet, 'that we have done as much as we can usefully do at the moment. Fachtnan, would you ask Brigid if you can all have an early lunch and then we'll be ready to go up to Carron in the afternoon.'

She concealed a smile until they had disappeared through the doorway. Garrett MacNamara had been a pompous man with an inflated idea of his own importance, but he had not deceived her scholars. They knew him for what he was: a man of straw. But why had he been killed, murdered, if Ardal was right? She wiped the names from the board with the damp sponge that lay in front of it and then went to talk to Cumhal. If anyone could tell her about a cowman, it would be her farm manager.

'He's a slow sort of man, Brehon. Got something wrong with his speech – his tongue doesn't seem to be hung in the right place and he's got a strange lip – split in the middle – more like the lip of a hare, than the lip of a human,' said Cumhal. 'You can't beat him with cows, though,' he added. 'The beasts seem to trust him. He's saved the MacNamara *taoiseach* a power of silver. Not a calf lost during all his time and then what does my lord do? Only turned him off because he interrupted the *ban tighernae*, the MacNamara's wife, when she was telling him what to do with the cows. Telling him! Her! I ask you!' said Cumhal with a snort of laughter.

'Would he bear a grudge, this man, Brennan, what do you think, Cumhal?' asked Mara, her tone light and her eye fixed on the apple tree overhead. It was interesting, she thought, that Cumhal had given one explanation for Brennan's dismissal and Jarlath another. She reached up her hand and felt for the tiny hard embryonic apple inside the faded blossom. The harvest this year would not be good with this severe weather in April and May, but the orchard at Cahermacnaghten law school was very sheltered by the twenty-foot wall all around it so she could hope that there would be the usual abundance of apples for their festival of *Samhain* at the end of October. Her scholars always celebrated that feast day with vim and Brigid turned out a wonderful supper with a groaning table laden with the fruits of the season. Four great feast days in the Celtic year and now one of them was marred by a possible murder, she thought as she waited for her farm manager to reply.

Cumhal paused. His face bore the look of one

147

who had been checked mid-stream. The strange death of Garrett MacNamara under the feet of the cows would, he knew, have to be accounted for by his mistress.

'I couldn't tell you, Brehon,' he said carefully. 'I suppose any man would regret leaving a job that he did well. In fact, you could have a word with Brennan now if you wish. I've given him a few days' work since we are busy with calving. I meant to mention it to you, but you were busy – a man with small children . . .'

'I'm glad you did,' said Mara decisively. 'And you know I always trust you to do what is best. Hire whom you will and whenever you need help.' Cumhal, in fact, took the whole management of the lands left to her in her father's will, onto his own shoulders. She had no wish to be consulted about any part of his work which he did so efficiently.

'I'll fetch him to you.' Cumhal was a man of few words and Mara waited by the apple tree. She had handed her scholars over to Brigid for a nourishing snack and told Moylan that in the absence of Fachtnan that he was in charge and could permit the scholars to have a half-hour break with a game of hurling if they wished.

In a moment Cumhal was back with a tall broad-shouldered man. His face, with its heavy jowls, was quite pleasant with its apple-coloured cheeks and shrewd blue eyes, but was marred by the strange mouth with its split upper lip. Mara went to meet him.

'Thank you for helping us, Brennan,' she said. 'Cumhal tells me that you are an excellent cattleman so I hope that you can stay for as long as he needs you.'

'Oh, aye,' he said. A man of few words, she thought and wondered how much he could understand.

'How long have you worked as a cattleman for the MacNamara?' she asked, deciding to confine her conversation to cattle as much as possible.

'Ole lor,' he said, forcing the words out.

'And you worked for his father before him,' Mara nodded her head. Garrett's father was always known as the 'old lord'. Brennan looked about thirty, she thought, though it was difficult to be sure. 'About twenty years?' she hazarded.

He nodded but didn't say anything, smiling amiably.

'You've heard all about the death of the *taoiseach*,' she stated and he nodded again.

'Why do you think that he ran out in front of the cattle?' she asked innocently.

He grinned and then a low chuckle escaped him. Suddenly he looked younger with a smile showing two large, slightly protruding teeth. 'Din't,' he said forcing out the word. 'Frit of cahle,' he volunteered and then laughed again.

'Why would he have had a chain around his leg?' asked Mara and he looked startled, glancing over at Cumhal for an explanation.

'Chain,' said Cumhal, twisting his hands to mime the word.

'No goo,' said Brennan. 'Wdne stop 'em.'

Mara gave him a friendly smile. 'Well, enjoy your time with us, Brennan,' she said and Cumhal pointed with his head towards the field. Brennan looked glad to go, but Mara waited until he disappeared before saying to Cumhal, 'Did he understand, do you think?'

'Understands a lot more than he pretends,' said Cumhal briefly. 'Get's a bit worried though, about talking to someone new.' He didn't ask her any questions but he looked puzzled. He was an intelligent man with a great knowledge of farming so she decided to try her question on him, though by now she was fairly sure that she knew the answer to that particular puzzle. But who had tied the fateful knot?

'Cumhal, can you think of any reason why the body of Garrett MacNamara might have had a chain looped around his ankle?' she asked and was not surprised when he shook his head the puzzlement fading from his face as he understood the purpose of the question. Cumhal had been puzzled, but, thought Mara, as she walked the short length of road between the Brehon's house and the law school, the inarticulate Brennan had shown no surprise at her question. If he had understood her – as Cumhal seemed to think – then why had he not looked surprised? Why had he evaded her question and pretended to think that she had asked him whether Garrett had taken a chain to stop the cattle stampeding.

Mara's mind was whirring with ideas when the party from Thomond arrived. She felt stale and she was tired and she was worried and when that happened she usually took her rest and recreation in her flower garden in front of her house. Despite the poor weather and the cold winds that still blew, her flowerbed, shaped like a stream, of dark blue gentians all in flower was a glorious sight as they threaded their curving path through the centre of her garden. The warm weather earlier in the year had advanced the growth of the roses and several pale pink buds appeared on the rambling branches just at the entrance to the little piece of woodland that sheltered her garden from strong westerly winds. The lilies in the baskets of woven purple willow were growing tall but the recent cold weather had held them back and this year, she thought, they would not flower until June. She bent down to pull out a weed from the paved pathway that led to her front door and then straightened. The sound that she had been awaiting – the noise of several iron-shod horses on the limestone road – rose above the lowing of the cows and the anxious twittering of the nesting swallows. With a smile she went to the gate and waited for the party from Thomond.

Nuala had changed. Once released from Turlough's bear-like hug, Mara studied her young cousin. Nuala had always been grown-up for her age and now, at eighteen, she was a woman, tall, brown-eyed, assured, her glossy, jet-black hair braided and coiled behind her head. Mara felt tears sting her eyes when she thought how proud Nuala's mother would have been of her daughter. The beautiful, talented poet, red-haired Mór O'Lochlainn, sister to Ardal, Mara's best friend, had died of a malady in her breast when Nuala had been only twelve and the girl had a difficult time growing up with an indifferent father, the physician Malachy O'Davoren, who had not acknowledged the girl's intelligence and interest in the profession of her father and grandfather.

'I need your help and your brains,' Mara assured her, throwing her arms around Nuala. 'But first come in all of you, come in and rest and hear the story, as Brigid says.'

'I'll just go across to see the other boys with Fachtnan, first, and let you talk to my lord,' said Nuala. 'I'm not tired in the least.' The boys at the law school had been like brothers to the solitary girl when she was growing up and perhaps it had been inevitable, thought Mara, that the kind, handsome Fachtnan should have been adored by Nuala. She would have enjoyed her ride from Thomond in his company. Her olive skin was glowing and her dark eyes smiling.

'Brigid,' she shrieked as she saw the sandy-haired housekeeper come out from the kitchen house and begin to run down the road. Nuala was a huge favourite with Brigid who could never quite forgive the pretty Scots girl Fiona, for distracting Fachtnan's attention from the girl who had worshipped him from the time that she was twelve years old. Mara watched the meeting with a smile and then turned back to her husband.

'So Garrett is dead,' said Turlough. 'Well, I'm sorry about it, but I can't say that I'm too sorry. Not a man for the post. God have mercy on his soul,' he added hastily.

'Come inside,' said Mara, taking her royal husband's arm and leading him rapidly inside the Brehon's house. Turlough, despite almost fourteen years of kingship, was terribly indiscreet and was quite liable to bellow out his opinions in the hearing of all.

Brigid had lit a fire of beech logs in the parlour and the clear bright flames lent a glow to the lime-washed walls. Mara escorted her husband to the cushioned bench beside the fire and poured some wine from a flagon that had been warming gently on the hearth.

'Your Venetian glasses,' said Turlough holding it up to the light of the window. 'The ones your father brought home from Rome. Is this a special occasion?'

'It's always a special occasion for me when you come,' said Mara with sincerity. She would not have her life be different, but it was true that she and Turlough, he as king of the three king-doms of Thomond, Corcomroe and Burren, she as Brehon of the Burren and *ollamh* (professor) of Cahermacnaghten law school and mother of a three-year-old boy, saw too little of each other. Still, snatched moments were precious. She swallowed a mouthful of her own wine and smiled.

'How very decadent to be drinking wine at this time of the morning,' she said with appreciation. The wine was a full-bodied Burgundy imported to the city of Galway and sent across to her by her son-in-law Oisín who was a trader in that city.

'Tell me about Garrett,' said Turlough after a minute while he, too, savoured the wine and nibbled one of the buttered griddle scones that Brigid had left, wrapped in a clean linen cloth, on the iron rack to the side of the glowing logs.

Mara told him of the terrible death, trampled

153

to death beneath the hoofs of the cattle stampede, but he, no more than anyone else, had any idea why the late *taoiseach* should have had a chain tied around his leg.

'If it was anyone other than Ardal . . .' began Mara and he nodded.

'Hard to see Ardal making a mistake,' he agreed. He took another sip of wine and said, lowering his voice a little, 'To be honest, I'm not that sorry about the death, God be good to the man, but he was . . . well, I was never sure of him. Young Jarlath will make a much better *taoiseach*. I'll deal with him very well.'

'I'm afraid that you won't be dealing with him at all,' said Mara with a grimace. 'Jarlath accepted the position and then, I don't know whether it was because he felt that he might be under suspicion, but subsequently he declined it in the presence of all the clan. A man called Tomás from Thomond is now their choice.' She would say no more about Tomás, she decided. Turlough was impulsive and emotional. If he took a dislike to Tomás and felt that he was usurping the place that should have been Jarlath's, then it might be hard to talk him out of it.

'Let me tell you about Stephen Gardiner,' she said rapidly.

'Seemed a nice fellow,' he said idly. 'A lawyer, isn't he? You and he should get on well.'

Mara pressed her lips together. 'I'm glad you liked him,' she said demurely, lowering her eyes over her glass and taking a sip to conceal the smile that she could feel tugging at the corners of her mouth. 'He came over here from Cardinal Wolsey, chancellor to your fellow king, Henry VIII.'

'That's right; one of your lads was telling me. Writing a book, so young Shane said . . . Clever fellow I'll be bound. More your type than mine.' Turlough was no scholar and seldom looked at a book, but regarded Mara's collection, most of which had been handed down to her by her father, with great respect.

'As a matter of fact, he came to the Burren, on the advice of O'Donnell, the Earl of Tirconnell, to inveigle Garrett MacNamara into giving up his loyalty to you and bowing the knee before the king of England. In return, Garrett would, too, have been an earl – the Earl of Castletown, and his son Peadar would have been Lord Mount Carron and the automatic inheritor of earldom from the moment of his father's death,' said Mara and then sat back and waited for the explosion.

'There's one thing that puzzles and worries me,' she said when he had run out of steam and vented his feelings on the treachery of the late *taoiseach* and had consoled himself with another glass of wine. He looked at her enquiringly.

'I'm just wondering about Stephen Gardiner,' she said. 'I think that Garrett's death came as a nasty shock to him – and that is understandable. After all, the work that he had put in was now come to nothing – and even if Peadar, or rather Rhona, his mother, had been part of the plot, Peadar was now discarded by the clan and Jarlath, I imagine, would not have been interested

155

in being an Englishman and an earl. But I'm just wondering about Stephen. You see when he heard the news that Jarlath had refused the position, he looked odd, you know, Turlough; he looked to me like . . . Well, I keep wondering why did he look like a man who was thinking intensely . . .' She hesitated and then went on: 'Really like a man who sees an opportunity opening up – I could see his eyes flying from Tomás to the other clan members and then to Jarlath . . .'

'Troublemaker, they're all troublemakers,' said Turlough in an agitated tone of voice. He never liked the feeling of being betrayed, of his vision of Gaelic society being disturbed. 'I remember my father, Teige of Coad, God have mercy on him,' he continued. 'I remember him talking about the time that the Duke of York came over to Ireland – the duke was fighting with the king of England at the time – one of the Henrys – the sixth one, I think – and he tried stirring up trouble over here in Ireland. Putting father against son; that was what he spent his time doing while he was over here. Pretended to care about Ireland, but his thoughts were all for England and how he could get an army together and get rid of whichever Henry was on the throne then. Sooner we get rid of that Stephen Gardiner, the better, if that is his sort.'

'We'll do that,' said Mara calmly. She was suddenly conscious of receiving a huge insight and she smiled at him gratefully. He might not be reckoned to be very clever, but he had a sensitivity, an almost animal instinct, that scented out trouble. She hated to see him disturbed out of his normal routine. He was, she thought, looking at him dispassionately, one of the ancient race; one of the Irish kings of gone-by ages. Times had changed; she knew that, but she hoped, intensely, that this husband of hers would be able to live out his life according to the simple and honest rules that he had set up for himself.

'Don't worry,' she said aloud. 'I'll handle Stephen Gardiner. I know his sort. I'll leave you now for a little while – perhaps you would go and see Cormac and then have a rest – or the other way around. But I do want Nuala to see the body as soon as possible and tell me what she thinks.'

Nuala, she thought, had advanced hugely in confidence. She was, according to Turlough, the prize pupil and then assistant of the chief physician in Thomond – O'Hickey, the healer. He had a son, Mara knew, a son who was winning himself the renown that had previously been his father's, but Nuala spoke little of the young Donough O'Hickey and when she did so it was in tones that revealed to Mara that her interest in the young man was professional only. From time to time, her dark brown eyes wandered towards Fachtnan; however, she was no longer a child, wearing her heart on her sleeve, as Brigid would phrase it, but a controlled, thoughtful young woman.

'What do you think?' asked Mara and Nuala smiled at her impatience.

'I can't tell until I see the body, Mara,' she

said. 'At least,' she amended, 'I can't tell you anything other than what your own commonsense and experience will already have told you.'

And with that they all had to be content.

'I'll tell you everything I can once I have examined the body,' was all that she would say to the eager questions from the scholars as they rode in a group across the valley and then up the steep slope towards the castle which had been the pride and joy of Garrett MacNamara and his wife Slaney.

'No one around,' called Moylan as they breasted the last slope.

'I suppose everyone is waiting for the burial to take place,' remarked Shane, looking around at the empty roads and the quiet fields.

'They can't be still holding the wake,' muttered Shane. 'They'd all be as drunk as March hares by now if they were still at it in the castle.'

Nevertheless, they were all still there. As the party from the law school dismounted they could see that the stables were still full of horses and many strange grooms, who did not seem to recognise the Brehon, came to help her dismount with a surly air.

'Heavy drinkers these men from Thomond,' said Aidan. 'Not the ladies, of course,' he added with a quick look at Fiona who tossed her head and was unsure of whether to be pleased, or whether to assert that ladies could drink as much as men.

'You'd think that they'd have gone back home to see to their farms, by now,' said Moylan disapprovingly. 'I don't think many of the clan that we saw the last time we came here were from this kingdom.

Moylan is right, thought Mara as they stood in the small entry passage. In fact, I hardly recognise anyone. The man who took the message to Tomás was definitely a stranger and the guards' chamber normally occupied by one man, was now full of about ten war-like looking individuals, dressed in quilted leather jerkins who were all engaged in sharpening their throwing knives under the eye of one authoritative-looking man who barely acknowledged her greeting.

From Thomond, definitely, she thought.

But why had Tomás seen fit to bring men-at-arms over from Thomond to his new residence in the kingdom of the Burren?

Eight

A Statute of the Fortieth Year of King Edward III, enacted in a parliament held in Kilkenny, A.D. 1367, before Lionel Duke of Clarence, Lord Lieutenant of Ireland

XV. Also, whereas the Irish agents who come amongst the English, spy out the secrets, plans, and policies of the English, whereby great evils have often resulted; it is agreed and forbidden, that any Irish agents, that is to say, pipers, story-tellers, bablers, rimers, mowers, nor any other Irish agent shall come amongst the English, and that no English shall receive or make gift to such; and such that shall do so, and be attainted, shall be taken, and imprisoned, as well the Irish agents as the English who receive or give them anything, and after that they shall make fine at the king's will; and the instruments of their agency shall forfeit to our lord the king.

The man servant who took the message to Tomás did not reappear for a long time. Mara sighed impatiently. It happened so often that she was detained while the master, or mistress, of the house went to change their clothing for something more suitable for receiving an important guest such as herself. Or a hasty order might be sent to the kitchen for refreshments to be supplied and laid out ready for her when she entered the room, or else a treasured cushion disinterred from the darkness of a wooden press and placed ceremoniously on the best chair in the house.

Aidan and Moylan had begun to shuffle their feet; Hugh and Shane had retired to the window seat and Fachtnan had gone in search of stools for Fiona and Nuala by the time that the man came back. He came down the stairs so slowly that, impatiently, Mara was already on her feet and had actually placed her foot on the lowest step by the time that he spoke.

'The *taoiseach* is very busy at the moment,' he said without any note of apology in his voice. 'He asks if you would wait for some time, mistress, and then he will attend to you.'

'Brehon,' said Mara with a note of steel in her voice. 'You address me as Brehon, not mistress. I am the king's representative in this kingdom and am here on the king's business. Kindly conduct me to the presence of Tomás MacNamara.'

She would not give Tomás the title of *taoiseach* – that was for the king to grant and for her to ratify at the ancient place of judgement at Poulnabrone.

'I have been told to see to it that refreshments are brought to you and to your young friends,' he said nervously.

'Unnecessary,' she said tersely. She gave a glance around at the startled faces of her law school and the amusement in Nuala's eyes.

'Wait here,' she said to them all and brushed

past the servant and was halfway up the stairs before he recovered himself.

'Mistress,' he said imploringly and then as she continued to climb, 'I mean, Brehon. I meant no disrespect. I'm just not used to a woman being a . . .'

Mara ignored the agitated voice and rounded the corner, continuing to climb until she reached the large wooden door leading to the great hall. The whole company was in there, she reckoned by the murmur of voices. By the time that she had her hand on the door latch, however, that murmur had ceased and only one voice prevailed. A strong voice, a voice that was trained to reach to the furthest corner of a hall or a court . . . a voice speaking, not in Gaelic, but in English.

'About this question of the murder of your former chieftain, or captain, as we English prefer to call him, well, according to the law in England, which, according to the Statutes of Kilkenny in 1366, the fortieth year of the reign of Edward III, is also the law of Ireland—'

Mara pushed open the door and strode into the hall. A trestle table, the length of the hall, had been set up and every seat on either side of it was occupied. At the head of the table stood Stephen Gardiner, emissary of the court of London and by his side stood Tomás MacNamara, no doubt ready to translate the words into Gaelic. The table was laden with platters of food – large dishes of smoking beef, pork and mutton, intersected with tall flagons of foaming beer and dark red wine. No one was eating or drinking, though. At her entrance all heads had been turned towards Stephen, but now they swivelled around to watch her with astonished eyes. Mara looked back coldly. Most were unknown to her. She did not pause, but walked resolutely forward until she had reached the head of the table. Then she turned to face them, holding her hands straight out on each side of her and gesturing to the two men to step back.

'The law of Ireland,' she said in Gaelic, 'existed when England was ruled by the Romans and long before that. When the blessed St Patrick came to this country he saw the wisdom and nobility of our Brehon law and he confirmed them as is written in *Seanchus Mór.*' She half-shut her eyes and recited: ' "And nine people were appointed to arrange this book of ancient laws. These were the three bishops: Patrick, Benen and Cairnech; the three kings: Laeghaire and Corcthe and the three learned men: Rósa MacTrechim and Dubhthach, both doctors of Brehon law and Fergus a poet. And the name of the book is Nófis because it was arranged by nine people." And,' Mara opened her eyes fixing them sternly on the men and women seated around the table, 'and,' she repeated, 'its laws have been the laws of the people of Ireland ever since. Your king, Turlough Donn O'Brien, rules the three kingdoms of Thomond, Corcomroe and Burren by Brehon law and I am his representative here in the Burren. Any talk of law in this kingdom,' she continued emphatically, 'is to be spoken by me or by the king. No one else has the right.'

And then she turned to Stephen and translated her last sentence to him, finishing with the words: 'We have extended hospitality to you, young man, but do not confuse hospitality and good manners with a licence to disrupt our society.'

She gave him a moment to absorb this before she turned to Tomás. 'You have not thought fit to invite the MacNamaras from the Burren to your gathering,' she mentioned mildly. 'Several names come to my mind: Fintan MacNamara, the blacksmith; Niall MacNamara, the miller; Eoin MacNamara, the sheep farmer – I could name many more,' she told and watched for a guilty flush.

It did not come, however, and the brown eyes that met hers were hard and opaque so she continued on.

'Perhaps you should give orders for your followers to eat their meal or else it will be cold,' she said watching the fat congeal on the wooden platters. She deliberately walked away from him and touched Stephen on the sleeve.

'A word with you, Stephen, if I may,' she said. Probably few people there understood English, but she took the precaution of withdrawing into a window embrasure with him. Not too much older than Jarlath, she guessed, as she looked at the smooth cheeks above his neatly trimmed beard and tiny moustache. Ambitious, though, she reckoned. There was a sharp look in his grey-blue eyes.

'You were talking about the law of England,' she reminded him.

'Just spreading the gospel,' he said lightly, but she did not smile.

'I am the law enforcer in this kingdom; I will have no other law uttered in this place.' She gazed at him sternly and he essayed a small smile.

'"I am the lord thy God; thou shalt not place strange gods before me",' he murmured.

'Tell me your message now, before I call the king's soldiers to usher you straight out of this kingdom,' she said fiercely and purposely looked over her shoulder at the window behind her.

He cast a quick glance through the window, but she did not bother to try to ascertain what he could see. These windows were tiny; for all that he knew she might have a whole troop of men, standing outside the castle, at her call.

'It's Tomás,' he said, spreading his hands in a deprecating way. 'He feels that his honour is concerned in punishing the killer of his cousin, Garrett.'

'I see. And why are you involved in this? You may be a lawyer, but you have no jurisdiction in this country, and certainly not in this kingdom.'

He made no reply to this.

'Take care,' she said warningly. 'I have found the letter that Garrett wrote, at your dictation, no doubt. Perhaps you wish to make a convert of Tomás, also. You have appealed to the dark side of his nature. You have dangled before his eyes the false gold of an English earldom and automatic succession to the title for his fine

165

young son and his son after him. In return for this he follows your bidding to try to establish English law here in the Burren. I will not have it. I am Brehon of the Burren and I am the king's representative and I speak in his name. You are no longer welcome here in this kingdom. I give you forty-eight hours in which to leave. You may go to Dublin and join your fellow Englishmen who still occupy that part of Ireland, though century by century their presence here in Ireland has diminished. You may go to Donegal and tell the O'Donnell that you have failed, or you may go to Galway and find a ship that will take you back to England. The choice is yours, Stephen, but the decision is mine. Go.'

And with that she turned her back on him and went across to where Tomás sat, not eating, but whispering into the ear of his tall son who bent down to hear him. About eighteen, the boy was, she thought. Just the right age for ennoblement, Tomás must have thought. He, not Peadar as Garrett had planned, would wear the title of Lord Mount Carron, if Stephen persuaded Tomás to give up his allegiance to King Turlough Donn and to bend the knee in front of the English King Henry VIII. And the price would be the rejection of Brehon law and the establishment of laws of England.

'I'm sorry to interrupt your meal,' she said once she had compelled him to stand up by gazing at him in stony silence until he did so. 'I presume that this meal is part of your wake ceremonies and I come to tell you that, once my physician has finished the examination of the body, the burial can take place tomorrow morning. Indeed, it should not be left any later,' she added when she saw him open his mouth. 'I shall send messages to those of the MacNamara clan in the Burren who will want to pay their last respects to Garrett, God have mercy on him. I propose to read the will this morning so perhaps after the physician has made the examination then you could make sure that as many people as are concerned in that matter will be present for that ceremony, including, of course, the son of Garrett and his mother, and also Jarlath MacNamara.'

He bowed stiffly, but a glint of interest was in his eye and he offered no objection. People always love to listen to a will, reflected Mara.

'You do not need to send a servant with me to the room where the body of Garrett lies,' she informed him in kindly tones. 'I remember the way and I possess the key.'

And that seal had better be unbroken, she thought as she made her way alone back down the stairs to the entrance hallway.

It was more crowded than when she had left it. Rhona was chattering about the highlands of Scotland to Fiona while her son Peadar, the silent, awkward fifteen year old, was interrogating Nuala with eyes blazing with excitement and a slight flush on his freckled face. As Mara drew near she could hear him say, 'I acted as a servant boy to the monk who was the physician to the Maclean. I am skilled in herbs and

167

I wanted . . . I wanted . . .' He stumbled over his words.

'You wanted to study, was that it?' asked Nuala looking at him with interest.

'Yes, that's it. But—'

'But we had no silver to pay for fees.' Rhona shrugged.

So that was it, thought Mara. So that was why she had tracked Garrett down. She touched Rhona on the arm and withdrew out of hearing of the others.

'Did you always know where Garrett lived?' she asked the woman with a sudden curiosity. How long had the liaison lasted, or was it a one-off occasion that had resulted in a boy who bore a strong likeness to his father?

Rhona shook her head. 'A sailor landed at the Mull of Kintyre where we lived and spoke of a certain Jarlath MacNamara, told me that Jarlath's ship was following his into the harbour. I was curious when I heard the name . . .'

'So you hadn't known Garrett very well,' said Mara with a friendly smile.

Rhona smiled and spread her hands, but her eyes were anxious. She must be wondering whether there was anything for her son in the tangled affairs of the last few days. Her eyes went to Peadar, but she said nothing.

'Do you want to come and examine the body with me?' Nuala was asking the boy. 'It's been dead for days – you won't turn squeamish on me, will you?' she added in a casual way.

'No,' said Peadar firmly. 'I want to learn.'

'I wouldn't go if I were you,' said Moylan

frankly. 'Still, there's no accounting for tastes. I'd be sick as a dog. Fiona, shall we two do a bit of nosing around while our young friends tangle with dead flesh?'

'Excuse me, Brehon, the master sent to know if you would like any refreshments.' Mara was about to refuse curtly, but then stopped herself. The young maidservant who appeared from the back door had a familiar look.

'You're Eoin MacNamara's eldest daughter, aren't you?' she enquired. 'Goodness, how you've grown. It's Caelyn, isn't it? I haven't seen you for a while – I suppose you've been working here. Moylan,' she continued with a flash of inspiration, 'perhaps you would help Caelyn with the refreshments – you remember Caelyn, don't you, Moylan? – in about twenty minutes, Nuala, will that suit you?'

'She won't have any appetite after standing over that stinking body,' muttered Aidan to Hugh, but Nuala ignored him. In fact, she ignored Mara also. Having requested water, soap and towels from young Caelyn MacNamara, she had turned all of her attention to Peadar and she was busy instructing him – instructions which he absorbed with a look of bliss on his plain face. He seized her bag and preceded her up the stairs with a confident air, very different to his usual round-shouldered, shambling walk.

'Have some fresh air,' Mara advised her remaining scholars. 'Rhona, perhaps you could show them around outside the castle. I will be reading the will of the late *taoiseach* in the great hall in about an hour's time.' She glanced at the clock on the wall. Trust Garrett to have a clock for the benefit of his men-at-arms and visitors. There was probably one in every room. Garrett and his wife Slaney had certainly furnished this place with the most modern of comforts and conveniences.

'Shall we say meet back here in twenty minutes and then that will give us time to have our refreshments before the reading of the will?'

She wasn't sure what the four scholars would discover in their tour around outside the castle but any information at the moment would be useful in solving this extremely puzzling case. Her mind ran down the list of suspects and then she paused on the corner of the stairs. Tomás MacNamara was one person that neither she nor the others had thought of when assessing who might have profited from the death of Garrett and yet he, ultimately, was the one who had gained the most from that. Motive, yes, she thought; opportunity, certainly. But how could he have guessed that Jarlath would have decided to reject the office of *taoiseach* and that he would be the one to profit? Deep in thought she went on to where Nuala and Peadar were waiting for her outside the locked and sealed door of the wall chamber where Garrett's body lay.

'I can't tell you a lot, but I do know that he was dead when he was trampled by the cattle,' said Nuala eventually. 'See,' she said, answering the question in Peadar's eyes, 'if you look there at the arm, Peadar, you'll see that though the flesh has been battered and torn from the bone, just here, yet there is no sign of black bruises under the skin – something you would expect if the man had been alive when he was trampled.'

'Why is that?' breathed Peadar. He had an ecstatic look about him and appeared to take little notice of the smell or the revolting appearance of the body.

'I'm not quite certain,' confessed Nuala, 'but it does seem to me that after death the blood no longer moves in the body. I wish I understood more myself. There is great work going on in Italy. I might go there for a while.' She had a reflective look. Mara guessed that she was thinking of Fachtnan. If he had no interest in marrying her then Nuala might be lost to the Burren and Mara desperately wanted her to return and to take up her heritage of a farm and a beautiful house at Rathborney.

'Nuala,' she said, 'would you examine Garrett's ankles, both of them, please, and tell me what you think.'

'I noticed that,' said Nuala. 'There is a ridge there, see, Peadar, on the right ankle. Something was tied around this ankle. Something quite thick – the ridge is broad, but it was pulled tightly, whatever it was. The flesh still bears a mark.' She looked at the boy and said, 'Do you think that you could tell the Brehon whether it was tied onto the man before death or after death, Peadar?'

'After death,' said Peadar without hesitation. 'I can see that there is no bruising under the skin, just this hollow ridge.'

'I would say, also, that the chain was tied to the ankle immediately after death. If there had been a lapse of time then the skin would have lost its elasticity. Interesting, isn't it, Peadar?'

'And what about the other ankle, or the wrists?' asked Mara thinking of the theories that had been advanced at the law school.

'Nothing there,' said Nuala after making another quick examination of the body.

'That tells me what I want to know,' said Mara rising from her place. 'Is there anything else that you can tell me?'

'Only this . . .' said Nuala. She took from her bag a long, wickedly sharp knife and without hesitation slit the stomach of the corpse with one neat slash. The stench was appalling but Nuala regarded her handiwork with satisfaction and Peadar did not flinch.

'I saw this done in Italy,' said Nuala as she bent over and peered into the stomach. Then she leaned back and said, 'I can tell you something else about Garrett: he had not eaten for several hours before he died.'

Odd, thought Mara. She remembered Jarlath's words about everyone rushing out from their supper. So Garrett was killed before that meal – and yet the fact that he had not been present had not been mentioned.

'This, I think,' she said, more to Peadar than to Nuala, 'is a fact that should be kept to ourselves for the moment.' She surveyed the two, rapt in their medical secrets and smiled humorously.

'Come on,' she said to Nuala, 'I want you to look at Slaney. I'm not happy about her.'

'I'll just sew up the stomach first,' said Nuala calmly. She produced a large needle already threaded with fine linen thread, rapidly sewed up the incision and then wrapped the body again in its winding sheet.

'Wash your hands very carefully,' she said to Peadar and stood over him while he scrubbed with a brush which she produced from her medical bag. 'Now let's see the live patient,' she said when they both had washed.

Slaney was still in bed, but this time none, other than her maid from Galway, was with her. Mara gained instant access to her bedroom after a quick rap on the door.

'She's no better, is she?' she said after a moment, looking down at the woman on the bed. Slaney almost seemed to have lost weight since her last visit. She was lying there, quite inert, previously an opulent figure, now subtly shrunken. She appeared to be fast asleep and snores broke from her once aristocratic nose. Nuala crossed the room and without ceremony snapped open one eyelid.

'Drugged,' she said tersely. And put her finger on the wrist of the flaccid woman.

'What has she been taking?' she asked and Mara, silently, produced the jar from her pouch.

'Cowbane,' she answered and saw a flicker of anger in Nuala's dark brown eyes. Peadar, beside her, drew in his breath in a gasp of horror. 'I took this jar away but there must be another source, somewhere,' said Mara with a glance at the maid.

'Cowbane,' said Nuala. 'No wonder that she is like this.' She glared angrily at the servant. 'Why have you given her this?' she said, spacing the words out, as one who is controlling her temper with difficulty.

'It's her medicine; she brewed it herself.' The woman was half-paralysed with fright and Mara held up a hand to Nuala.

'Yes, yes,' she said soothingly. 'But did she ask for this medicine just now? And has she had the usual dose?'

The woman's eyes were shuttered. She took a long moment before replying. 'As to that, Brehon,' she said hesitantly, 'it was not I who gave her the dose.'

'I see,' said Mara soothingly. 'It was . . .' She hesitated for a moment. What was that woman's name? It was probably the wife of Tomás, who gave the dose to her. 'So someone else gave the dose to her,' she said, watching the woman's face. 'Is that right?'

The nod was enough, though the woman repeated with the same hesitation. 'It was not I who gave her the dose.'

'I see,' said Mara soothingly. 'It was . . .' She hesitated for a moment. What was that woman's name? 'It was Cait, the wife of Tomás that gave the dose to her. Is that right?'

A tiny nod told her what she wanted to know. Without waiting for an answer, Mara continued, 'The physician here—' she indicated Nuala with a world of confidence in her voice and in

174

her gesture – 'she will see to your mistress. Do all that she asks of you without question. She has had experience in cases like this and will soon be able to restore your mistress to her usual self. Peadar, you will remain here to assist the physician for the moment. I will send for you shortly.'

No time for refreshments, she thought. The meal was being cleared away from the great hall when she returned. Without asking permission from Tomás, she sent a servant to find her law school scholars and also Rhona, and to request them all to return to the hall. Stephen Gardiner was missing, now, she noticed as she stood in impassive silence awaiting the arrival of her scholars and of Peadar. It might be that Stephen had retired to his room when he saw her once more approach the great hall, but she hoped that it meant that he had taken his leave. Despite the poor weather, it still was the season of May and if he rode fast he could be in the city of Galway before night fell.

At that moment Peadar, accompanied by his mother Rhona, entered the room. The scholars, ushered in by Fachtnan, followed. Mara raised a hand to quell the low-voiced conversation and spoke out clearly.

'I would have wished that the wife of the deceased man could be present, but that, I feel, given her condition, is not possible. Rest assured, though,' she said making her voice as emphatic as possible, 'rest assured,' she repeated, 'that I shall make sure that this woman has her rights.'

And then she took up the will, reading out the

various bequests to Slaney in clear, unemotional tones, ignoring the gasps as the clan realised quite how much had been left to the woman from Galway.

'And now we come to another matter,' she said as she rolled the will and slipped the knot of pink tape around it. She paused. Every eye was upon on her. 'Under our law,' she said, 'any son of a father is entitled to succeed to his portion. In this case, Garrett MacNamara had no son by his chief and only wife Slaney. However, days ago, when all here were present at the wake for the late *tánaiste*, Garrett MacNamara publically recognised this boy.' With one forefinger she beckoned to Peadar and when he came to her side she placed one hand lightly on his shoulder and then continued, 'This boy here, from Scotland, was, in my hearing and in yours, recognised by Garrett as his son – "bred of my bone" was the expression that he used, if I remember rightly.' She turned, picked up a branch of candles from a nearby table and held it in front of Peadar's face. 'I ask all here to attest that this boy has, in the words of the Brehon law, "the family face and the family manner". Indeed,' she resumed, replacing the candles, 'it seems to be that likeness is remarkable and there can be no question about the matter.' She paused, but none spoke, so then she resumed. 'This means,' she said briskly, 'that Peadar MacNamara inherits the property which was Garrett's own personal possession; that is the farm at Castletown. All other property, with the exception of the personal silver and possessions bequeathed to his wife Slaney, will go to the new *taoiseach*.' Mara eyed Tomás sternly before finishing, 'Whoever he may be.'

There was a thoughtful look on the face of Tomás but he did not argue with her verdict and after a moment of waiting for queries, Mara said decisively, 'And this is the position about the last will and testament of Garrett MacNamara; may God have mercy on his soul and grant him everlasting peace.'

There is nothing like a tag from the Bible or the prayer book with which to end an awkward moment, she thought, as she moved away from the centre of the room and carelessly helped herself to a honey cake from the table now pushed against the wall. Not as good as Brigid's cooking, she thought critically as she munched through its sticky texture, nevertheless it gave her something to do while she waited to see whether any would approach her with a question.

It was Peadar, however, whom she found by her side, his mother, Rhona hovering anxiously behind him.

'How much is that farm worth?' he asked abruptly.

'Are you thinking of selling it?' asked Mara with interest. He could probably get a good price for it, she thought. It was very good limestone land with fields on the high plateau as well as in the fertile valley. Muiris O'Hynes, always on the look-out to increase his land, might well be interested in it. 'I wouldn't know how much it is worth,' she went on when he didn't answer her question. She looked across at Rhona and added, 'But I do know that it would bring in enough for you and your mother to live on in comfort.'

'Oh, Mother wants to go back to Scotland; she has nothing to keep her here,' he said with a grin. 'And I have no interest in farming,' he added impatiently. 'I want to go to one of those schools for medicine in Italy. There are none in this country, Nuala says . . .'

For Peadar everything came back to Nuala. That had been a fortuitous meeting for the young man. Mara left him to his dreams after promising to ask her farm manager about how much silver he might be able to get for the farm. Possibly Ardal O'Lochlainn might be interested – he was one of the few people in the kingdom of the Burren who was reputed to own boxes of silver. He sold horses to England and to Spain; unlike others such as Muiris who traded locally, mainly with bartered goods. Muiris would probably prefer to rent the farm and to pay in goods rather than with silver. If Peadar did want to go to Italy, goods were of no use to him. However, she had another idea and immediately went over to Nuala.

'Do you remember how much you wished that there was a school for physicians in Ireland?' she asked. 'I recollect how you envied my scholars when they were discussing law cases with each and sharpening their wits on their fellow pupils.'

Nuala looked at her in a puzzled way. 'Yes, but . . .'

'But you no longer need a school,' Mara finished. 'But what would you say to the idea that you should open a school? You are eighteen years old now – the very same age as I was when I took over the law school at Cahermacnaghten. All here on the Burren respect you greatly – and have done since you were a child of twelve or thirteen. You could start with Peadar over there and then by the time you had taught him, other pupils would follow. That house that was willed to you in Rathborney is lying empty and you remember what Toin said in his will and testament. I read it to you the night that he died.' Mara had an excellent memory and she found the words had come to her mind and she quoted them softly, ' "This testator would like to express a hope that the gift will enable the said Nuala, daughter of Malachy O'Davoren, to fulfil her ambition to have a school of medicine and also to enable her to pursue her studies in that subject." Of course,' she continued, 'the revenues from the farm have fed and clothed you, paid your fees when you were an apprentice and enabled you to visit Italy in pursuit of knowledge. Perhaps now is the time to fulfil the second part of your ambition . . .'

With that she left Nuala and sent a glance across to Fachtnan who was sitting beside Fiona. Fiona was taking no notice of him and was exchanging whispers with Moylan. Mara sighed and went up to Tomás.

179

'I understand that there is a suspicion in your mind that the death of Garrett was not due to an accident,' she said bluntly.

He looked at her through narrowed eyelids, but said nothing.

'This is a suspicion that you should have brought to me first before talking to any of your guests,' she said forcibly. 'In these cases the truth can only be ascertained by a careful sifting of the evidence. However, since it has been spoken of to the people assembled here, then I must deal with it now. Please ask everyone to sit down and I will address them in five minutes. And if any are missing from the room, summon them and summon all of your servants who were present here in the castle on the evening of Bealtaine – with the exception of Slaney's personal maid who will need to remain with her mistress.'

She left him to bustle around and beckoned to her scholars, withdrawing into a window embrasure where they could talk unheard. Nuala was busy talking with Peadar and she did not disturb her. Nuala had given her information and Mara knew that everything she had said seemed to point to a deliberate murder.

'Well, Moylan,' she said quietly. 'How did you get on with Caelyn?'

'Very well,' teased Aidan. 'He . . .'

Mara gave him a stern look and Aidan flushed uncomfortably and fixed his eyes on his friend's face with an attentive face.

'I obtained the information that you were interested in, Brehon,' said Moylan demurely. 'The girl was one of those who were deputed to wash

180

the body and to burn the clothing. But she first asserted that she had no memory of a chain around the ankle. When I asked her if she were sure, she pretended to be annoyed that I doubted her word. First she got another maid to agree with her and then she dragged me out to the stables. Apparently Ardal sent two grooms to carry the body to the castle. I'd reckon that one of those grooms is a sweetheart of Caelyn . . .'

'And?' Mara tried to keep the impatience from her voice.

'And she was making faces at him, but this man said that there was a chain. He and Caelyn had an argument about it, but he stuck to what he said. He said that it was all trampled and covered in cow filth, but he did think it was a chain. I don't think he's too bright. He didn't seem to have wondered why a chain was there in the first place, but he was positive.'

'Did you ask him whether the chain was broken?' demanded Shane.

Moylan nodded. 'I did. For a while he couldn't think – in the end he said that he thought it was not. He said it was a short chain.'

'And Caelyn didn't see it,' stated Aidan with a nod.

'That's what she said,' agreed Moylan. 'But that's not the end of the story.' He gave a self-conscious flick to his hair and a slight smile parted his lips.

'Go on,' said Mara. She was beginning to guess what came next.

'Well, she was trying to make the groom jealous, I think,' said Moylan trying to sound

181

modest, 'but she was flirting with me and I—' his eyes slid across to Fiona's and he grinned – 'well, I gave her a kiss and told her that I swore she would not get into trouble so . . . in the end she told me that they, the maids, got rid of everything including the piece of chain, but they were scared to say it in case their mistress would turn them out of the house. She had screamed at them that there had been no such thing. You remember, Brehon, Slaney was very loud in swearing to us that there had not been a chain.'

'I do, indeed, Moylan, and you have done very well,' said Mara deciding to ignore the dubious methods that he had used. 'And you know what this means, all of you?'

Fachtnan nodded. 'The death of Garrett MacNamara was no accident, but a secret and unlawful killing,' he said thoughtfully.

Nine

An Seanchas Mór
(the Great Ancient Tradition)

The fine for killing a person is fixed at forty-two séts, *or twenty-one ounces of silver or twenty-one milch cows.*

To this is added the honour price of the victim.

An unacknowledged killing is classified as duinethaoide *and this doubles the fine to be paid making it forty-two ounces of silver or forty-one milch cows.*

Críth Gablach
(Ranks in Society)

The honour price for a taoiseach *is ten séts or five ounces of silver or five cows. A secret and unlawful killing of a* taoiseach *would bring a fine of forty-six ounces of silver or forty-six cows.*

By the time that Moylan had finished telling his story the hall was full. Mara stepped forward and stood in front of the fire, allowing the members of the MacNamara clan, and their servants, to gather in front of her. Her law school, Fachtnan, Moylan, Aidan, Fiona, Hugh and Shane flanked her on one side, standing neatly in height order and gazing impassively at the crowd.

183

Mara waited until the murmurs ceased and then took one step forward, greeting them all in a pleasant manner and telling them that she had something important to say. 'The death of your *taoiseach* Garrett MacNamara may not have been an accident, but may have been a deliberate killing,' she said decisively. 'I as Brehon of the Burren, the representative of King Turlough Donn in this kingdom, will investigate the killing and if I find that it was a deliberate act of violence, and not a terrible accident, I will impose a penalty on the guilty person who will have to answer for this crime before God and before me at the ancient judgement place of Poulnabrone,' she said now speaking slowly and deliberately, her eyes wandering from one face to another. 'It appears from what my physician has discovered that the victim had not eaten for hours before his death, although you were all at supper when the marauders drove the cattle along the Carron. Perhaps, Tomás, you could tell me whether Garrett had joined you at supper?'

'He did not, Brehon,' said Tomás.

Mara frowned. 'Does anyone know why? It seems strange that guests should eat without the presence of their host.'

'Neither Garrett, nor his wife, was present at the supper, Brehon, nor had they been present at the midday meal.' He had answered readily but there was something about his eyes, a sly gleam that she mistrusted. Still she obliged him by asking whether he knew why.

'The wife of the *taoiseach* had not graced the table since the announcement about taking a second wife and recognising a son,' he said drily. 'Several reports had been heard of violent quarrels between them so no one was surprised when we ate alone.'

'I was there at midday, Brehon,' said Jarlath readily. 'My brother was not there so I took the head of the table. As for the evening meal, I was absent as I had gone to Poulnabrone and afterwards had begun the climb up Mullaghmore Mountain when the news came of the cattle raid. As you know I returned here as soon as possible and found all were agitated about the loss of the cows. By then my brother must have been dead.'

There was an indifferent note in his voice, thought Mara. The brothers had had little affection for each other.

'I saw the late *taoiseach* just before the midday meal,' volunteered one woman.

'That's very useful,' said Mara enthusiastically. 'Where was he?'

'Going up the stairs towards the main bedrooms,' said the woman colouring slightly and looking across at Tomás's wife, Cait.

Mara surveyed the crowd. A few of them had gone to Poulnabrone out of curiosity, but the majority would not have bothered and would have stayed within the castle or outside in its grounds. They were people from Thomond and they had no interest in the legal affairs or ceremonies of Burren. The MacNamara clan on the Burren would not have been guests at the castle, though they should have been invited to any ceremony, such as a wake or an inauguration. They would, of course, be staying in their

185

own houses on their farms. If Garrett MacNamara had been killed just before the cattle stampeded through Carron, then it was almost certain that he had been killed by someone present at the MacNamara castle at that time.

'I would now ask all who were not present either in the castle, or in the grounds of the castle near to the time the marauders herded the stolen cattle through Carron, to please leave this hall now. Fachtnan, would you go to the doorway and write down the names of all who leave; Hugh, would you assist him?' Mara waited until Fachtnan and Hugh were in position before waving a hand to give those not involved permission to withdraw. Nuala was the first to leave, bestowing a warm smile on Fachtnan as she went unhesitatingly through the door. She was closely followed by Peadar, who was beginning to remind Mara of an overgrown, but devoted puppy, and then Rhona in conversation with Jarlath and then a couple of men and their wives from Thomond. Mara vaguely remembered seeing them at Poulnabrone, but reminded herself to check these names rigorously later on.

Soon the small crowd had left and Mara allowed her face to become very serious. She knew what had been happening before she had interrupted Stephen Gardiner. The MacNamara clan had wanted this crime solved and the person responsible punished. It was odd that they had immediately believed that it was a murder. After all, she had only gradually become sure of that fact herself.

Or was it that a scapegoat had been found

186

almost immediately and the instinct which makes a pack of dogs dangerous, though individual dogs within it may be mild, that instinct had taken over and the crowd had scented blood?

I must be very open in this investigation, thought Mara, thoughts flashing rapidly through her head as she waited for everyone to settle down. This was not like the usual cases of law-breaking among the people of the Burren. Those of her own kingdom, where she had been Brehon for almost twenty years, trusted her implicitly. Among these people from Thomond, the same trust would not be forthcoming. For a moment she considered sending for Brehon MacClancy from their own kingdom, but then her pride stiffened her back. She would work this one out carefully, share her findings with those concerned and would leave all those people who had been involved satisfied that justice had been done.

'According to the physician, Garrett MacNamara was dead when his body was trampled by the stampeding cattle,' she said in a low, clear voice, which she knew from experience would reach the outer corners of the large hall. 'The question is, how did the body of a man get placed on the roadway in front of the herd?' She looked around, inviting replies or speculation.

There was no answer to her question. Several people glanced at Tomás who stood to one side, as though physically separating himself from them.

'Another matter is puzzling,' continued Mara riding over the hostile silence as smoothly as she could. She smiled on the crowd and hoped that she sounded totally at ease. 'This,' she said in a conversational tone of voice, 'is very strange, because it appears that when the body was first discovered there was a chain, a short length of chain tied around the ankle of the dead man. My informant,' she said looking well away from the corner where the servants clustered in an uneasy group, 'was Ardal O'Lochlainn, *taoiseach* of the O'Lochlainn clan here in the Burren. He is an intelligent and reliable man and I have complete faith in him and am as certain as I possibly can be that a chain had been tied to the ankle of Garrett MacNamara – and I do believe that this chain played some part in his death. Would anyone like to comment on this?' She waited for a few minutes, but the silence was complete and the people sat eerily still.

'Has a piece of chain been missed from anywhere?' This time Mara looked directly at the grooms, but heads were shaken. 'I shall question any not present afterwards,' she continued imperturbably. From what she could see there was no sign of Brennan the dismissed cowherd. 'Now, I would like to ask you all to bring to your minds the last occasion on which you saw Garrett MacNamara. This is a castle full of clocks,' she went on. 'I can see one here in the hall, and there is one downstairs near to—'

'Brehon,' interrupted Tomás, 'it seems to me that you may be wasting your valuable time on chains and clocks and such things. I think that all here are sure of what happened on that terrible day when our *taoiseach* met his death beneath the hoofs of a thousand cows.' His voice rose up, powerful and compelling and Mara found that it drowned out her words. 'We know what happened,' he boomed, each word like the stroke of a brass drum. 'You would say, wouldn't you, that a man must be mad to go down and face that stampede. You would say that no man could hope to stop them; could hope to control them. And you would be right.' He paused and then raised his voice even higher, pointing a dramatic finger at her. 'But what if the man was not in his senses? What if he had been driven out of his senses? We have all heard, have we not, of spells being cast, of incantations being chanted, of shape-shifting, of magic-wielding women; of herbal mixtures that make men have strange dreams, of—'

'That's enough,' snapped Mara. 'It is for me to talk and for you to listen. I warn you, Tomás, that the king is already in the Burren and soon will be on his way up here. I should be sorry to tell him that I find the clan's choice of a new *taoiseach* to be an unacceptable one.' She waited for a moment for the threat to sink in and then said in a calmer voice, 'I will ask my five scholars to seat themselves over there by the wall at the trestle table. Please form into six lines and give to one of them your name, where you were when the cattle came into Carron, and when you last saw your *taoiseach,* Garrett MacNamara. Fachtnan, perhaps you could assist in the formation of the lines.' She felt slightly shaken. There had been a strange hypnotic quality about Tomás's voice which for a moment had seemed to rob her of speech. Her commonsense

189

re-asserted itself; though. She held the whip hand. To her as Brehon of the Burren he might feel that he owed no allegiance, but as wife of his king, he had to recognise that her influence might be sufficient to deny him a position which he obviously so badly wanted.

'Come here, Tomás' she said to him curtly and led him over to a small wall table beside the ornately carved fireplace. She seated herself, allowing him to remain standing beside her.

'Your name is Tomás MacNamara,' she said, reading aloud as she added the words '*taoiseach* elect of the MacNamara clan' inside two brackets, a new form of punctuation that she had recently picked up from the Latin works of Erasmus of Rotterdam.

'And where were you when the cows stampeded through Carron?' she asked with an air of polite indifference, pen in hand and her eyes fixed on the lines that were being efficiently marshalled by Fachtnan.

'At supper,' he replied, 'entertaining the guests that had been abandoned by their host and hostess. Even young Jarlath had left us.'

'And before that?'

His eyes narrowed. 'Before that I walked around the hillside.'

'Alone?' she queried. It was an odd place to walk, she thought. The hillside around the MacNamara castle was no gentle slope but a vertiginous, perpendicular outcrop of limestone.

'Alone,' he repeated, staring at her belligerently. 'And no, I had nothing to do with Garrett's death. How could it have benefited me at the

190

time? I was not the one who had been left a fortune in goods and possessions.'

Mara ignored this clear reference to Slaney. 'And when did you last see Garrett alive?' she asked.

'At breakfast time,' he said curtly and made as though to rise.

'And what did you talk about?' she asked with genuine interest. Tomás had been such a shadowy and anonymous figure up to now. She found she could hardly recollect him from before the night of the wake and even then he had just seemed sensible and level-headed.

He hesitated and she said swiftly, 'I can always ask that question of someone else. No doubt there were others around.'

He shrugged. 'Nothing of importance,' he said. 'We spoke only of Jarlath and his love of the sea.'

That, however, might be of importance, thought Mara. Her lively mind began to picture the conversation. *'I can't believe that Jarlath will settle down as* tánaiste *or* taoiseach *here in this little backward kingdom,'* Garrett might have said in his pompous way. And Tomás, what would he have said? What would he had thought? Would dreams of a bright future have come to him? A future where, he, not Garrett, not Jarlath, would rule the powerful clan of the MacNamaras – spread over two kingdoms? There had been a time when the MacNamara clan had been almost as important as the O'Brien clan, when they had tried to take the kingship of Thomond into their own hands. Did that vision of Tomás's lead him into murder? A subtle and clever murder. Stephen Gardiner had made no secret of the fact that he knew all about this planned cattle raid; that he knew that O'Donnell's men had been ready for the moment when the men from the Burren were, like their ancestors before them, climbing the sacred mountain in order to celebrate the feast of Bealtaine? Had he passed on that information to Tomás? The two men seemed extremely friendly at the moment. Was there a pact or an alliance between them? Mara looked at Tomás speculatively. Was he clever enough to plan a murder that looked like an accident? She thought that he probably was.

But was he unscrupulous enough to murder his cousin on the guess that Jarlath might, if prompted, decline the office of *taoiseach*? Now, of that she was not sure. Tomás was a clear-headed, practical man. He would know the terrible consequences of his deed and the unlikelihood of its success. But ambition was a very potent force and she had met murderers who had taken greater risks.

'Thank you, that is sufficient for the moment,' she said coldly. Let him guess what her thoughts were. 'Now, on another matter, my physician tells me that Slaney, poor woman, still appears to be drugged by some herbal mixture. She is not in her right senses. I thought I forbade giving her anything of the sort so I questioned her personal maid servant who tells me – what was it she said?' Mara pretended to think for a moment and then when she saw an uneasy look come to his eye, she finished with: 'She said:

"It was not I who gave her the dose, Brehon."
Now who do you think did administer a dose of
this herb which is robbing her of her wits and
keeping her in sleep?'

'I don't know, Brehon.' His voice was stiff,
but he had called her Brehon and she felt that
she was beginning to get ascendancy over him.
Quickly she pushed her advantage home. 'See
that no more is given to her; I will hold you
personally responsible for her health and safety.
We may have to move her from here in order to
restore her to herself. Now are all arrangements
in place for the burial? My lord, the king, will
attend – at this moment he is at Cahermacnaghten
and has travelled here from Thomond for this
purpose.'

'The clan wishes the inauguration of the new
taoiseach take place first,' he said. 'This is the
custom.'

He was right about that. It was customary to
perform the inauguration ceremony before the
burial – probably so that the clan never felt that
they were left without a leader. In England, she
had heard, the saying was: 'the king is dead;
long live the king' as power automatically
descended from father to eldest son. Nevertheless
this case was different as Tomás had not been
tánaiste. Garrett's death and then Jarlath's
surprising refusal of the position had suddenly
left two offices open. Mara's mind scanned
through her books. Yes, she thought reluctantly,
she did own a book, a prize possession of her
father's, written by Maghus O'Duigenan, a
student at the MacEgan law school in East

193

Galway, which did describe such an incident, where in battle with the O'Rourkes, the *taoiseach* and *tánaiste* and their uncles and brothers had all been killed. No burial could take place; she remembered that the scribe had written, until the clan had elected a new leader.

'The body has waited long enough; it can wait another day,' said Tomás breaking into her thoughts.

'I shall consult with the king,' said Mara haughtily, but she knew that Turlough, in his easy-going way, would be happy to leave it to the clan to make their own arrangements and he would turn up and do his part. This was her husband's way of ruling over his territory and no one could say that it was a bad one since there had been peace within the three kingdoms since the year of 1499 when he had succeeded to that position after the death of his uncle. She stood up and nodded at him coolly. She walked across to where Fachtnan stood, supervising the scholars.

'Anything interesting turn up yet?' she asked.

'Shane suggested asking who they were with, so I told them all to do that,' he said in a low voice. 'This means that we can double-check on their statements. So far no one has said that they were with Tomás; his wife, Cait, was with their son. I checked the cowherds myself. No one had anything to say. The raid occurred just when they were all having their supper.' He looked over her shoulder and his face brightened. 'Here's Nuala,' he said.

Nuala was followed by Peadar, carrying the

battered old medical bag as though it were some sort of holy relic. The case had belonged to Nuala's grandfather, a highly esteemed physician whose notes had been used by the child Nuala as she struggled to attain her dream of being a physician. Nuala was a rich young woman who could buy the finest leather bag but she chose to retain her grandfather's possession.

'Just thought that you might like to have a word with Slaney,' she said. 'I've managed to purge her and get a lot of the poison out of her system. She's in a pretty strange state still. That cowbane gives strange dreams and visions – terrible nightmares if too much is taken. Come and see her.'

'I'll leave you here in charge,' Mara told Fachtnan. She lowered her voice and added, 'And give a sharp answer to Tomás if he tries to impede you in any way.'

He nodded with a half smile and when they were outside the door Nuala chuckled. 'Can you imagine Fachtnan giving sharp answers?'

'Nevertheless, in his own quiet way he gets what he wants,' said Mara.

'You don't need to tell me about Fachtnan's good points,' said Nuala quietly. Then she raised her voice a little. 'Peadar,' she said, 'go ahead to the patient's room. Announce that I am coming and that I am bringing the Brehon with me. Try to see if you can get her as alert as possible. It's not good for her to sleep so we must keep on preventing her doing that. Her maid is scared of her,' she added when Peadar had gone bounding up the stairs, and then in a different tone of voice she continued, 'I wanted to have you to myself for a minute to talk about Fachtnan,' she said and Mara's heart sank. Nuala was as beloved to her as was her own married daughter Sorcha. If she could have bought her what her heart desired she would not have grudged a box of silver. But life was not that simple. Fachtnan showed no signs of tiring of his love for Fiona who still treated him with friendly affability. He had never, Mara now realised, shown the same intensity for Nuala. He was fond of her; that was all.

And yet the match would be ideal and it would restore Nuala to the Burren.

'What do you want me to say?' she asked looking at the girl affectionately. Nuala had not the perfection of looks that Fiona owned. She was tall; Fiona was tiny. Nuala had the dark eyes and the glossy black hair of the O'Davorens, whereas Fiona was primrose fair with eyes of cornflower blue. Nuala was respected; Fiona was adored by all who met her.

Nuala did not speak for a moment. A thoughtful girl, considered Mara; a girl who had had an unhappy childhood with a father who was indifferent and then hostile to her ambition to become a physician and a mother who had been ill of a malady in the breast for years and then had died before Nuala was eleven.

'I suppose I just want you to tell me whether I might have a chance,' she said eventually. 'Or is he heart and soul belonging to Fiona?' she added in a tone which she endeavoured to make light.

'Not that; certainly.' Mara was prompt with her reply. 'Fiona doesn't want him. She'll flirt and amuse herself, but she's just as happy joking with Moylan and Aidan. Fiona will qualify – possibly next year, certainly the year after that, and then, I hope, she will go back to Scotland. Her father would be broken-hearted if she were to stay here in Ireland. I would not want an Irish match for her and I think she has no plans whatsoever for anything like that.' Once again she thought of Ardal O'Lochlainn and his tender expression and resolved to discourage this as much as possible. It would bring little happiness to either, she told herself and rejected the notion that it was none of her business. Fiona is my business, she thought.

She turned to the girl beside her. 'I almost feel like a soothsayer, now,' she said impulsively, 'but I have an odd feeling that things will work out eventually between you and Fachtnan. Remember men grow up slowly – some of them never become adult, but I don't think that Fachtnan is like that. He is mature, but not very confident. He may well feel that he is not good enough for you.' She stopped and said no more. They had rounded the corner in the stairs and Slaney's maid stood there, holding the door open for them.

'How is she?' Nuala frowned to see Slaney sleeping. 'I thought I asked you to keep her awake,' she said to the maid. She leaned over and pulled up an eyelid and then straightened with an angry frown. 'She's had some more of that stuff. How did she get it?'

'She's had n . . . n . . . nothing but spring water to drink . . .' The woman stuttered in her alarm at Nuala's expression.

'Nothing else?' Nuala looked puzzled and then pounced on a plate of sweetmeats by the bedside. 'Where did these come from?'

The maid looked at her guiltily. 'My lord Jarlath sent these up. He said that they had come all the way from Spain. I thought a few would not hurt her. She was awake, but depressed and weeping. She does love sweet morsels like these.'

Rapidly Nuala picked one of them up and sniffed it. 'Smell that,' she ordered the maid, fiercely thrusting the sweetmeat under the woman's nose. The servant flinched and looked at her appealingly.

'Let me smell,' said Mara, feeling rather sorry for the servant. Slaney had always treated her abominably and the woman had become cowed over the years. 'Hmm,' she said, 'there's a dust on them.' She cautiously licked a finger tip. 'Sugar, isn't it? I tasted that when I was in Galway some time ago. They grow it on an island in the middle of the ocean near Spain, I was told – the sugar is inside a cane, like a stout reed, I seem to remember.' She talked on, giving the woman time to recover.

'I just didn't think,' said the maid apologetic- ally. 'My mistress did enjoy them. She seemed so much better, but then those terrible dreams and visions came back again.'

'Do you think something was put into the sweets?' Mara queried and saw Nuala take out a tweezers and pull out some coarse fibres from the centre of the paste. Now that she sniffed again, there was something else, something slightly unpleasant.

'Mice!' she exclaimed. 'Yes, you're right, Nuala. There is a smell of cowbane from it. I remember Cumhal giving a crushed stem to the boys to smell and getting them to notice the smell of mice. He was warning them that they should keep away from cowbane unless they wanted to be like mice and to disappear underground.'

'Now I'll have to purge her again! It's fortunate that she has plenty of flesh to spare,' muttered Nuala. 'No good you staying, Mara; it will be useless trying to talk to her tonight. Peadar, we have more work to do; let's hope this time is the last time.'

'I think,' said Mara, 'that I will have a word with Jarlath and find out about those sweets.'

She went down the stairs meditatively and the first servant that she met she sent in quest of Jarlath. He came to her almost immediately.

'Was out looking at that property of mine,' he said when she met him in the entrance hall. There was an air of buoyancy about him and his white teeth flashed in his sea-browned face.

'Are you going to sell?' she enquired, leading the way outside onto the flat piece of garden in front of the castle where they could talk without being overheard. A splendid view, she thought looking straight down the almost perpendicular slope. The castle and its small area of pleasure grounds were perched like an eagle's nest on the slope and far below it was the flooded valley floor.

They were strange things those winter lakes, *tuar-lach*s they were called. Once the summer weather came the water would drain back into the limestone caves below and grass would spring up, fresh, and luscious, more nourishing to cows than anything from the higher fields. But at the moment small waves rippled its surface where swans rocked happily. Her eyes went toward the west where the farm that was Jarlath's portion was perched on a similar hill. Good limestone land, she thought. If he were to sell it and Peadar were to sell the farm that had been Garrett's portion from the old lord, then the place of the MacNamaras in the Burren was going to be even more diminished. Already they were the smallest of the four clans. Perhaps, after another few years, their main seat of residence would no longer be in Burren, but would have shifted to Thomond. And, of course, she thought with a slight chill, the next *taoiseach* of the MacNamara clan may decide to give up the allegiance of his forebears and bend the knee to the English king. In that case she would prefer that there were no MacNamaras left in any of the three kingdoms ruled over by her husband. The O'Donnell clan, she had heard, were not happy that part of their ancient lands were now owned by Henry VIII of London.

'I think so,' Jarlath said with a slight hesitation, carefully considering her enquiry, 'but I won't rush into anything. I would prefer to sell it to a MacNamara, of course. Perhaps Tomás would buy it for his son. But I am certain that I want to go back to the sea. I'm going to Galway tomorrow to look for a new ship and to buy

200

some new sails for Garrett's big ship; Ardal O'Lochlainn has told me of a place which has sails of all sorts for sale. I know I could get some made here, but I have a feeling that I want to be out of this place as soon as possible. You don't mind if I go to Galway for a day, do you, Brehon?'

Mara thought about that. Until the murder case was solved she did not care to have anyone involved go outside the kingdom. On the other hand, Jarlath had, by all accounts, arrived at about the same time as the stampeding herd, which had been slowed by the very steep hill going up to Carron. Even if it were a little earlier than was known, he would hardly have had time to quarrel with his brother and to hurl the dead body down the hillside into the path of the cattle. Nuala had been fairly sure that Garrett had been dead for some time before being trampled on by the hoofs.

'I wanted to talk to you about something, Jarlath,' she said, not answering his question. 'You sent some sweetmeats from Spain up to Slaney earlier this afternoon . . .'

He frowned in puzzlement. 'Not today,' he said emphatically. 'I brought some boxes of these sweets home with me and gave them to Garrett and Slaney the day that I arrived.' A grin twitched at the corners of his mouth. 'Slaney ate quite a few – they weren't to Garrett's taste, nor to mine, either, though I had a few to be polite; so then she decided to put them away in her stillroom, so that the crowd coming for the wake would not get their dirty paws on them. That was her

201

expression, not mine,' he added, the grin spreading.

So that was it, thought Mara. Another puzzle. Presumably most of the household would have access to the still room; there would be no reason to have it locked. Anyone could have inserted these fibres from the root of the cowbane plant into the sweetmeats. Despite the efforts of farmers, the plant grew everywhere on swampy ground and after a wet spring like this it would be flourishing; its frilly leaves and tall, lacy, faintly pink flowers decorating every ditch.

Mara looked thoughtfully at Jarlath. There was no real reason to suspect him, she thought. She appreciated Fiona's point that a man who voluntarily gave up the position of *taoiseach,* and that yearly tribute of eighty ounces of silver or equivalent which Garrett had been exacting from his clan, was unlikely to be the sort of person who would murder from a desire to gain more possessions.

'Well, I hope you have a pleasant day in Galway, and that you find what you are looking for, but of course you must wait until after the inauguration of the new *taoiseach* and the burial of your brother, and then a day away should be fine. Don't make any arrangements for a permanent departure, though, will you? I think that I would prefer you to wait until I have solved the puzzle of your brother's death.' She said the last words firmly and saw his eyes move from hers and look over her shoulder at something behind her. She turned and saw the tall, broad-shouldered shape of Rhona standing above them outlined against the grey sky. She was standing with her side turned facing north as if she were looking towards Scotland. Mara looked at her thoughtfully.

'Rhona is coming with me into Galway,' said Jarlath casually. 'She wants to get back to Scotland as soon as possible and there are a few goods that she wants to buy for Peadar to have him settled into the house on Garrett's farm before she leaves. He is determined to stay and she wants to go home, so they will have to part. I'll let her know that she must delay her departure, but that we may have our day in Galway once Garrett's funeral and the inauguration have taken place.'

'I'm sure that you will be of immense help to her,' said Mara. Rhona would miss her son, she thought, but it was the way of the world. Her own daughter, Sorcha, had been married when she was not too much older than Peadar was now.

Ten

Berrad Airecht
(Court Procedure)

All facets of a case must be considered before finding a person guilty; grounds for suspicion may be:
  1. *If the person is known to have been out on the night of a crime.*
  2. *If he sleeps in very heavily the next day.*
  3. *If he claims to be in a house of a friend or relative and it is proved that this is false.*
  4. *If it is known that he has uttered threats.*
  5. *If he trembles, blushes, turns pale or seems thirsty.*
  6. *If his footprint is found at the scene of the crime.*
  7. *If a shoe or an article of clothing belonging to him is found there.*

However, all judgements must bear in mind the character of the accused and the history of his life.

'Shane has a brilliant idea, Brehon,' said Hugh over his shoulder as soon as they had mounted their horses and cantered away from the castle.

'Oh, yes, what is it, Shane?' Mara had been riding beside Nuala, but the girl was silent and

204

unresponsive so she abandoned her and moved up to join Hugh and Shane.

'Well, it's this, Brehon,' Shane cast a glance around and waited until Mara was quite close before saying, 'I kept thinking about how could the body of Garrett be thrown down in front of the cows. He must have weighed at least a couple of hundredweight. No man, and certainly no woman, could lift a weight like that and hurl it down the mountain. And I considered the possibility of the murderer putting the body on some sort of cart and tying it loosely with a chain and shooting it down. But then I thought that couldn't have been the way, as the cart would have broken up into bits and the O'Lochlainn would have mentioned seeing something like that – and someone would have missed a cart – they're valuable, these things.'

'And you threw out a few questions, did you?' Mara had noticed that most of the servants had been chosen by Fachtnan to stand in the line leading to Shane and that he had taken longer than his fellow scholars over the questioning.

'Well, I thought I would use my initiative, Brehon,' said Shane demurely. 'I had a word with Fachtnan. Don't worry; I cloaked the questions well. But after a while I began to despair of my idea. There certainly were no pieces of a cart, no wood at all when we searched the road and that is quite a high and well-built wall on the far side of it so it could not have gone on tumbling down the other side of the road, but then I had another idea. Could we stop here, Brehon, and I'll explain to you?'

By this time they had come to the length of road where Garrett's body had been found. Mara called out to Fachtnan to stop and the others joined them, dismounting and holding the reins of the restive horses.

'Are we going to have another search?' Aidan was glancing around. 'I'm sure we didn't miss anything the last time, Brehon. We went over it really carefully.'

'I've got an idea and I think it's quite a good one,' said Shane with his usual air of quiet confidence. 'What if someone murdered Garrett earlier on in the day? After all no one had seen him since midday when Rhona heard the shouting match between him and Slaney – anyway, they murdered him and concealed the body and was wondering about burying him or throwing him in the lake after everyone had gone to bed. And then, the word comes about the cattle raid so – and here is the clever bit – our murderer – OM – slips out here with the body on a cart or something, and then gets an old millstone – there are quite a few cracked ones up there near to the old mill building – ties the body to it with the length of chain and sets it to roll down the hill, right into the path of the stampeding cattle. And what, my friends,' demanded Shane rhetorically, 'what happens to a millstone, when it tumbles down from a height and hits the road at high speed?'

'It smashes,' said Hugh beaming with pleasure at his friend's cleverness. 'And,' he added, 'that is why we found no sign of anything strange. There's stone everywhere – and lots of it is broken – loose boulders are always tumbling down those steep hills.'

'Not bad,' said Moylan. 'Well done, young fellow. I never thought of that. Let's search. These ditches are full of stone.'

'It might be the case,' admitted Mara, but somehow she did not believe it. Still, it was clever of Shane to think of it and it did fit in with the idea at the back of her mind. She would have a word with Cumhal, she thought. He was the man who would be able to visualize the effect of hysterical cattle being driven at high speed.

In the meantime, she encouraged her scholars to search the ditch and the hillside above and was as pleased as Shane when two pieces of stone turned up, each bearing the unmistakable rounded profiles of an old millstone.

'Let me make the case,' said Shane standing very tall and suddenly appearing older. 'Our murderer, OM, killed Garrett, probably with a blow to the head, laid him on the hillside above him – or her, for that matter.' With a quick gesture he indicated a space above where they stood. 'He laid the body on the slope, head at the top, looped a chain around Garrett's ankle – he could easily have got one from that cabin there – and then he found an old millstone – you know they will never reuse one that has the smallest crack in it – tied the chain loosely to it with a piece of twine – through the centre, a single knot, not a double one – just a loose knot that would unravel easily. Then, when the thunder of hoofs came to his ears, he rolled the millstone down the hill – the millstone cracked into dozens of fragments – and then a few minutes later the marauders arrived with the cattle running ahead of them. Garrett's body was trampled and they went on.'

'Very well argued,' said Mara with a smile at her youngest scholar. 'A very possible picture, isn't it? Has anyone else anything to say?'

'It's just so difficult, isn't it, to see whether this is a premeditated murder, or whether it just happened, quite suddenly on the spur of the moment,' complained Fiona. 'I suppose it has to be the spur of the moment, but it does seem complicated. All this finding a handy millstone and tying of a chain to the ankle . . .'

'I think,' said Mara, 'that when we get back to Cahermacnaghten, our first task will be to examine the question of opportunity for our suspects.'

'I believe that Shane has done jolly well,' said Moylan taking up his position as head of the law school and bestowing unusual praise on a junior.

'Thank you.' Shane was quite pink with pleasure and Mara gave Moylan an approving smile.

'I think so, too,' she said and then mounted her mare again. The few days ahead of her promised to be of great complexity, but first of all, she needed to consult with Turlough.

However, when they reached the law school, Turlough was missing. His men-at-arms happily feeding in Brigid's kitchen house were bemused when she enquired and jumped to attention instantly.

'We thought he was at your house, Brehon,' said Fergal guiltily.

'He's probably gone down the road to see Cormac,' said Mara. 'Bran is missing too.' Her giant wolfhound would never miss the opportunity of visiting Cormac in his foster home. He seemed to know that this little boy should really be part of his own household and always looked mournful when Cormac was returned to his foster parents.

Mara had hardly said the words when the bodyguards, red with embarrassment, shot out. She did not blame them for taking their eye off their lord, though she knew that they were consumed with guilt; Turlough was always trying to escape from them, complaining that it got on his nerves to be shadowed wherever he went. At the moment there was peace with his old enemy, the O'Flaherty, whose kingdom bordered that of the Burren but this cattle raid had shown that O'Flaherty and his clan were glad to lend a hand in facilitating the raiders.

'I shouldn't have kept them eating and talking but I thought that the king was lying on his bed in your house.' Brigid sounded anxious and guilty.

Mara was not particularly worried about Turlough so she went into the schoolhouse, sat down and began to think about the murder of Garrett MacNamara. She sat there for a long time until the scholars, followed by Nuala and Fachtnan, all refreshed by their meal, trooped in. They took their usual seats, Shane and Hugh at the table in front of hers and the three older scholars, Fiona, Aidan and Moylan, just behind them. Nuala perched on the broad windowsill and for a moment Mara wondered whether Fachtnan would join her there, but he went to his stool beside Mara's chair and did not glance in Nuala's direction. Mara sighed inwardly. Was there anything that she could do to bring about this marriage? she thought. Fachtnan was an adequate lawyer, but his poor memory made it most unlikely that he would ever be able to pass the stringent examinations that would qualify him as a Brehon. He was having a struggle with the body of knowledge needed to qualify him as an *ollamh* or professor, but she was determined that he should achieve that. He was, to her mind, a gifted teacher with a patience and a mature understanding that made her want to keep him permanently at her school. Next year, she thought, when Aidan and Moylan have moved on, I shall expand my school, take in a whole class of young children and train them up as future Brehons. Fachtnan will be ideal for them, and for Hugh; while I can give Fiona and Shane the fast pace and attention that their brains deserve.

'You look as though your mind is working as fast as that clock at Carron, Brehon,' said Fiona with a twinkle. 'I can hear it ticking,' she added daringly, while Moylan raised an eyebrow and Aidan tightened his mouth and shot a glance at his audacious classmate.

Mara laughed. 'You're right,' she admitted. 'My mind is active.' She looked mischievously at her scholars. 'Think of a chessboard,' she advised. 'The pawns are the cows, battling their way up the hill towards Carron. Let's make them white pawns. Now where is everybody else?'

'Well the *taoiseach*, Garrett, has to be the black king,' said Shane entering into her idea with zest. 'I'd say that he is already dead. And lying on the hillside above the road.'

'And the white queen, that is Slaney,' said Moylan. 'She is possibly beside him and is tying the chain around his—'

'That's going too far,' interrupted Shane. 'That's solving the chess puzzle before the pieces are set up. Who else have we got on the Brehon's chess board at Carron?'

'Tomás,' said Fiona. 'I wouldn't be surprised if he were the one that delivered the fatal stroke. He had opportunity, didn't he, Brehon?'

'Yes,' said Mara readily. 'He was walking on the hillside when he heard the cattle . . . saw the pawn formation . . .'

'I'll make him a knight; I'm lethal with my knights, and Tomás is a tricky type,' said Fiona decidedly. 'Now who else was around?'

'Brennan, the cowman,' said Fachtnan. 'What shall he be, Fiona?'

'A rook,' said Fiona. 'He's that shape, even if he isn't that important.'

'All pieces, all people, are important,' said Mara firmly. 'This is a murder enquiry and the guilty person is the focus of our debate. What about Maol, the steward?'

'He was with the cook for most of the day,' said Shane. 'And he was definitely with him when the cattle thundered past. They were down in the cellar, and both said that they heard the hoofs echo on the roof – I'd say that old cellar was originally a cave.'

'Like the one at my uncle's, at Ardal O'Lochlainn's place,' said Nuala. 'Could there be an underground passageway going from the cave to the hillside, just as there is in Lissylisheen?'

'That's a good idea, Nuala,' said Fachtnan admiringly and she flushed with pleasure.

'How many people knew that there was to be a cattle raid; that's the question, isn't it, Brehon?' asked Shane shrewdly.

'I've been asking myself that, also, Shane,' said Mara. 'I had a strong feeling that Stephen Gardiner knew all about it when he came down the mountain as everyone was exclaiming and shouting. After all, he did come from O'Donnell's place on a boat and that must have been a big cattle boat – and had lots of drovers, of cattlemen with large sticks, going on the boat, also. I'm fairly sure that he knew all about it – he certainly didn't deny it when I challenged him.'

'And that means that Rhona, and Peadar, probably knew about it, also,' said Aidan.

'And Jarlath – don't forget that Jarlath travelled down with them,' said Moylan.

'Wouldn't he warn his brother, though?' asked Hugh diffidently.

'That's a good point,' praised Mara. 'Wouldn't he? What does everyone think?'

'I'm not sure,' said Fiona. 'He didn't seem too fond of him and he may have thought it would

212

be a bit of a joke. I don't think that he wanted to be elected as *tánaiste*.'

'In that case, he can't be a suspect,' pointed out Shane. 'Why kill his brother if he didn't want power?'

'Well, I think we should have him on the board,' said Fiona. 'He can be a bishop; he's tall and slim. And a bishop moves long distances rapidly and Jarlath must have done that if he got from Mullaghmore to Carron just ahead of the raiders.'

'So, to sum up,' said Moylan taking charge, 'we have a board with a black king who is in deadly danger, a herd of white pawns, a white queen – and . . .' He stopped and then said, 'I've just thought of something. You remember the letter that Garrett had in his pouch, the one where Garrett promised to bend the knee to King Henry VIII, surely, in return for that, he would—'

'You think that he told Garrett about the cattle raid so that he could lock up his cattle or something . . .' interrupted Shane. 'And Garrett told Slaney, and Slaney took the opportunity of getting rid of Garrett. You've all heard the will. And you've heard that Slaney, according to Rhona, was having a huge row with Garrett on that day. Well, he might have gone out to the hillside to see whether he could see if anything was happening and she followed him and she hit him over the head – she's a strong woman; we know that – and then she tied the chain to the millstone and waited.'

'Could be,' said Nuala with interest. 'I was saying to Peadar, when we examined the body, that I thought, since there was quite a groove on the ankle, the skin must have still retained some elasticity so the tying of the chain must have taken place shortly after death.'

'So what do you think about your chess board, now, Brehon?' asked Shane. 'It's a pity that Peadar was on the mountain and then came home with us. Otherwise he might have been a pawn that becomes the young prince – you remember, Brehon, you told us once that some people from the east had the queen as a prince and heir to the throne?'

'Yes, Peadar and – or – his mother Rhona, would have been the chief suspects if they hadn't been under our eye all the time – but they did come back to Cahermacnaghten with us,' said Aidan in disappointed tones.

'Back to my chessboard,' said Mara. 'On it I have – as well as the stampeding pawns, of course – well, there is the unfortunate and doomed black king, Garrett MacNamara; the queen, Slaney; the rook, Brennan; the bishop, Jarlath; and the knight, Tomás.'

'Four suspects, but do they all have motives?' asked Moylan, 'May I write on the board, Brehon?' He hardly waited for the nod before he strode forward and seized the stick of charred wood.

'Let's give them marks out of ten for both motive and opportunity,' said Aidan.

'When we last wrote on this board we looked for motives,' said Moylan rapidly. 'Now we are looking to combine opportunity with motives. The first one is Brennan. His motive is anger and revenge because he had been dismissed, unfairly he thought, from his position as chief cowherd. He was around – he came out of his cottage when Jarlath arrived back from the mountain.'

'Jarlath said that he was sulky-looking,' remarked Hugh.

'His cottage isn't far from the road where the body of Garrett was found,' said Moylan. 'Shall we give him eight out of ten for opportunity and, say, five out of ten for motive?'

'Give him six out of ten for motive,' suggested Shane. 'This crime, if we are right, might have been a spur-of-the-moment fit of anger – Garrett was hit over the head with a stick, that's right, isn't it, Nuala? All this business with the cows might be just something that occurred to him. He's a cattleman. He would know that the cows would slow at that steep hill. He might just have a cool nerve enough to have dragged the body down onto the road and just got clear before the cows breasted the hill.'

'You're forgetting about the chain. How do you account for that?'

Shane shrugged; his blue eyes dark with thought and then his eyes lit up. 'I know,' he said triumphantly, 'no one has thought of this, but you know how some of these people are always afraid of bad luck coming to them, like picking May blossom or touching a lone tree. Well, perhaps, Brennan believed that it was bad luck to touch a body that you had killed – that it would bleed or something – so he had a chain with him – might have been a bull chain like

215

the O'Lochlainn suggested – and he tied the chain around Garrett's ankle and . . .' He shrugged again as he watched the expressions of his fellow scholars and said, 'Well, it's possible.'

'It's ingenious,' commented Mara.

'Let's give him six out of ten for motive,' suggested Hugh.

Mara watched as her scholars debated allocating three for motive and four for opportunity to Jarlath and a massive nine out of ten to Slaney for both motive and opportunity.

And then in large firm strokes Moylan wrote the name 'TOMÁS'.

'He, or his wife, is certainly very keen to keep Slaney in a state where she can say nothing to the Brehon,' remarked Nuala and Shane's eyes sparkled with interest.

'If Tomás was the murderer then a reason to keep Slaney drugged might be . . . Let me think . . . How about Slaney noticing Tomás coming back from the hillside above the road where Garrett's body was discovered; she mightn't have taken any notice at the time, but later on when she realized that the Brehon was making enquiries she might have tackled him and asked him what he had been doing.'

'That would be like Slaney,' said Mara thoughtfully. 'Whatever her faults, she does not lack courage.'

'Or tackled his wife,' suggested Hugh. 'Cait would have run immediately to Tomás; she's that kind of woman,' he ended with an air of a man of the world.

'Quite possibly,' said Mara, concealing her amusement.

'So Tomás has, say, eight out of ten for opportunity, but motive I would only give him three out of ten as he could not have been sure that Jarlath would have declined the position,' said Fiona.

'He'd guess that he would be elected *tánaiste* though and then he could always dispose of Jarlath in some clever way – or Jarlath might get lost at sea or something. I propose that we raise that to five,' suggested Shane and even Fiona nodded at that so Moylan wrote it on the board.

'What about Tomás's son?' asked Aidan suddenly. 'If Tomás is *taoiseach,* there's a chance that Adair will become *taoiseach* later on. He's a man grown; he must be at least my age. What about Adair for the murderer? No one has mentioned him yet.'

'Not much of a man,' said Fiona disdainfully. 'I don't mean you, Aidan. But that Adair is a doe-eyed little mother's boy. Cait is always popping choice pieces of food on his plate as though he were five years old.'

'A man will do a lot for an inheritance,' said Aidan wisely. 'A woman like you would not understand that.'

And a woman who is a devoted mother, thought Mara, will do a lot to gain an inheritance for her son. Her eye went to the door. Heavy, tramping feet, a hasty knock and the door was pushed open before she could call out permission to enter.

'Brehon,' said Fergal, thrusting his head into the schoolhouse. His fellow bodyguard was behind him and he took up the story, saying in alarmed tones, 'The king is not at his son's foster home and there are two strange horses tied to the beech tree inside your gate.'

'Two strange horses!' exclaimed Mara.

'Let's see them. Bet I recognise them.' Moylan was on his feet instantly and was out of the door and running down the road between the law school, inside its huge round enclosing wall, and the Brehon's house a few hundred yards away. The others went after him. Mara followed rather more slowly, having stopped to wipe the names from the board.

The huge beech tree inside the wall of Mara's garden had just begun to break into delicate, pale green foliage. It was a lovely sight in the spring, though in the summer it cast a dense, heavy shade. Mara had planted bluebells to grow underneath it and the combination in May was always beautiful when the bulbs came into flower beneath the tree buds. To her annoyance the two horses had trampled the fragile fleshy leaves of the bluebells and had broken most of the stems which were loaded with their tight dark blue buds ready to unfurl once the sun returned.

'Whose are these horses?' she said in annoyed tones. She could see now what had happened to Turlough. Two visitors had arrived and Turlough had whistled up Bran from his watching post outside the gate and had taken dog and horsemen on one of his favourite walks across the stony clints and grykes of the stone-paved fields opposite her house.

'That horse belongs to Tomás, and I suppose the other one belongs to his son. Fine horse that – a bit of Arab breeding in it?' Moylan gazed enviously at Adair's horse and then gave a whistle. 'I know that horse. The O'Lochlainn allowed me to try its paces last week. He said that he might have a buyer for it – a man with a son of about my age – one of Garrett MacNamara's relations from Thomond, he said.'

Mara looked thoughtfully at the spirited young horse energetically stamping on one of her precious bluebells. Ardal, she knew, sold his horses for a good price. This would have been an expensive purchase for Tomás and probably, a few days earlier, would not have been something that he would have contemplated.

The death of Garrett had made a difference to that family.

'I think that Tomás and his son have paid a visit to the king,' she said aloud. 'They've gone for a walk together, I'd say.' It would, she knew, be Turlough's way of dealing with a situation, of getting to know a person. He was a big man, her husband, always a little too large for any room that he was in, a man who liked to be out-of-doors with his hounds, striding across the land like any farmer. She thought about it for a moment and then turned to Fachtnan.

'Could you take the scholars back to the schoolhouse, Fachtnan,' she said. 'Go over that passage from Cicero with Hugh, will you?

Moylan, Aidan and Fiona, I want you to study that case I left ready for you. Discuss it and determine what the judge's verdict will be and what the fine should amount to; Shane, I want you to go through the law books and find out as much as you can about "sick maintenance", especially what the law says about the physician's house for those who are seriously ill. Nuala, will you come with me?'

Nuala watched the scholars go with an amused smile on her face. 'I suppose when we come back I'm going to be asked to admire Shane's work,' she remarked. 'Now, don't try to look innocent, Mara. Remember that I've known you all of my life. I know how you like to get your own way. You want to see me installed at Rathborney and caring for my heritage. Anyway, how are we going to find the king and his visitors? Search the one-hundred-square miles of the Burren?'

'Easy,' said Mara. She bent down, picked a flat blade of grass, held it between her hands and blew a penetrating musical note. 'Don't tell Brigid,' she said, her eyes scanning the flat grykes of gleaming limestone. 'She's been forbidding me to do that since I was five years old. Ah, here he is. Here's Bran. Can you see him? Yes, I thought so – they've gone over towards . . .' She had been going to say 'Caherconnell' but then she stopped herself. Caherconnell had been Nuala's home, the place where her mother had died and her father had been murdered; the place which should have been hers, but which was now occupied by her stepmother's son. With a glance at the girl's face she said gaily, 'Bran will lead us to them.'

'He looks so extraordinarily beautiful bounding across the grykes, doesn't he?' Nuala, also, did not want to talk about Caherconnell and the snow-white wolfhound seeming to almost fly across the gleaming silver of the limestone made a good alternative subject for conversation until he arrived panting, his long sleek tail wagging vigorously and his brown eyes full of love for his mistress.

'Do you remember his mother;' said Mara, patting the big dog's shoulder and stroking his narrow head. 'She was my dog and his grand-mother was my father's dog. They were both the usual grey in colour, but when Conbec had a litter of puppies, her last litter, one of them, the biggest of them all, was snow-white and that was Bran. And, do you know, she was enraptured by him. It was no wonder that he grew bigger than the rest; she favoured him all the time. All the other puppies went to new homes but I felt that it would break the old girl's heart if I gave away Bran, so he stayed. His mother used to lie on the rug in front of the fire just watching him play – Shane and Hugh were young at the time and they would roll on the floor with him and she would watch him with big soft eyes. I've never seen a dog with so much love for her offspring.'

'Mother love; you're brooding on mother love, aren't you?' remarked Nuala shrewdly. 'You're thinking about what the boys said of Cait, aren't you?'

'Tell me about that blow on the head,' said Mara. 'You were so busy explaining medical features in such detail to Peadar that I didn't take everything in. Could that blow have been dealt by a woman?'

'By Slaney, or by Cait?' asked Nuala.

'Either.'

'Difficult to be certain,' said Nuala thoughtfully. 'Slaney has the weight and the height to deliver a blow like that, but I wouldn't be certain about Cait, though sometimes these small, thin women are quite wiry and she might be a lot stronger than she looks. A blow on the head, anyway, doesn't necessarily mean that the victim was standing up. She could have dropped something, asked Garrett to pick it up, then hit him quickly as he bent down. It was a single blow and I fancy he died instantly from it.'

'I miss you and your brains when you are not here,' said Mara with an appreciative smile and then decided to say no more. Nuala was intelligent and independently minded. She would make her own decisions despite what Mara or her uncle Ardal O'Lochlainn might urge. It was best to leave her to think over the possibilities of setting up a school and a hospital for the sick at her property at Rathborney and to weigh that up against the prospect of journeying to Italy again and becoming more learned in her profession. So she resolved to keep silence until Nuala herself spoke, but when she did so, after they had walked in silence for about five minutes, it was only to point out that she could hear Turlough's voice.

'He's telling them about the battle of O'Briensbridge,' said Mara. 'That means he's in a good mood.' Turlough, of course, had a great trust in those over whom he reigned and so far he had never made a mistake. She hoped that Tomás would prove worthy of that trust.

It would be very embarrassing if he were designated as chieftain of the clan on one day, and arrested for murder on the following day.

Eleven

Di Dliguid Raith & Somaíne
*(On the law relating to the fief and profit
of a lord)*

*All clients of a lord must pay an annual rent: in
the case of a lowly farmer this may take the form
of an animal; a two-year-old bullock from an*
ocaire *(small farmer); and a milch cow from a*
bóaire *(substantial farmer). In addition each
client pays a food rent which consists of fixed
quantities of bread, wheat, bacon, milk, butter,
onions and candles. He swears to provide
hospitality for his lord and to join a reaping
party if he is required and at the hour of his
lord's death to dig the grave mound and to
contribute to the death feast.*

'So, he talked you over.' Mara set her heels to
her Arab mare, Brig, and drew level with
Turlough as they rode together up to Carron to
take part in the inauguration of the new *taoiseach*
and the burial of the former one.

Tomás and his son had been invited back to
supper and Teige O'Brien and his eldest son had
joined them. Turlough had come to bed in such
good humour and so full of love for her that she
had not liked to spoil the atmosphere by hinting
that he should have waited to consult her before

agreeing so readily to the inauguration before the burial. And then on the following day he had gone hunting with Teige.

The king looked at her uneasily. 'Seems like a good fellow, Tomás,' he said tentatively.

'As long as I don't need to accuse him of the murder of the former *taoiseach*,' agreed Mara. She said no more. There was little use since all had been agreed between the two men.

In any case her mind was preoccupied with the news that Cumhal had given her just before she set out. Setanta, who fished from the port of Doolin in the neighbouring kingdom of Corcomroe, had sent news that Stephen Gardiner was now staying there. Setanta had seen him talking to Cait, the wife of Tomás, who had come to select fish for the inauguration feast. Strange, thought Mara – still, perhaps there was nothing in it. Cait might be the sort of woman who felt that she had to oversee all household matters. But, as for Stephen . . . In her mind she composed a message to the Brehon of Corcomroe, informing him of the trouble which Stephen Gardiner had tried to stir up in the kingdom of the Burren. She would have to be tactful; relationships between herself and Fergus MacClancy, the elderly Brehon of Corcomroe, had not been cordial since the time when she had dismissed his nephew, Boetius MacClancy, from her law school.

The day was as cold as the preceding ones but she was warmly dressed in a robe of thick purple wool over her white *léine* and her cloak was double-lined. A sudden shower burst through soot-black clouds and stoically she pulled up the hood and patted her horse consolingly. The double ceremonies of inauguration of the new *taoiseach* and the burial of the former one had to be got through and then they could both get back indoors, Brig to the warmth of her stable and Mara to pick up the threads of her investigation again. At least, she thought, I can plead that I have much work to be done and so avoid all the merry making.

'You don't suspect him, surely.' Turlough sounded shocked.

Mara sighed. Tomás had been labelled by her husband as 'a good fellow' and now he could do no wrong in Turlough's eyes. 'I am convinced that someone killed Garrett MacNamara and left his body to be trampled by the stampeding herd of cattle,' she pointed out and, when he muttered something about the O'Donnell and his marauding scoundrels, she continued, 'Turlough, this is not a crime that you can lay at the door of the O'Donnell, or of any of his henchmen. Someone here in the kingdom of the Burren killed Garrett, and the probability is that they killed him for gain, for his wealth, or for his position.'

'Here's Ardal,' said Turlough with relief. 'Don't worry, Mara. Bet you will find that it was one of the cattle raiders; it stands to reason,' he added before hailing the O'Lochlainn with a voice reminiscent of a bull. 'Nuala, here's your uncle,' he shouted over his shoulder. 'You can't have her back, Ardal,' he joked, 'she's much too useful to us at Thomond. Did I tell you what Donogh O'Hickey said about her? He rates her as highly as his own son and that's something coming from O'Hickey – the foremost physician in Europe,' he boasted.

'Nuala is her own mistress,' said Ardal. There was a hint of frost in his voice. He had never approved of his niece Nuala and her studies and would have preferred to keep her at his castle of Lissylisheen after the death of her father. His idea was that Nuala could be a hostess and mistress of the castle until he could arrange a good marriage for her.

'Ride with me, Ardal,' said Mara, allowing Nuala to take her place beside Turlough. He was as fond of the girl as if she were a daughter of his and she would keep the king amused during the short ride to the inauguration place of the MacNamaras and really, she told herself, there was no point in her repining over this decision of Turlough's. Tomás MacNamara would be inaugurated, whether she liked it or not. But then her work had to recommence. Chieftain or no chieftain, the truth about the death of Garrett MacNamara had to be uncovered and then it had to be laid bare before the people of the Burren.

' "Crime must be followed by retribution",' she murmured and then smiled as Ardal looked at her in a startled manner. 'One of the sayings of the mighty Fithail,' she said lightly. 'We're off to the inauguration of the new *taoiseach* for the MacNamara clan.' Her eyes invited him to explain what he was doing on the road to Carron. This ceremony would be attended only by members of the clan.

'I thought I would go to the graveyard at

Carron,' he said, looking a little embarrassed and then when she looked at him with curiosity, he said uneasily, 'my steward tells me that there aren't many preparations made for the burial of Garrett – just a small hole dug – no pipers, nothing.'

'A small hole,' repeated Mara. Her scholars behind her had fallen silent at Ardal's words. This was unprecedented. She looked over her shoulder at her scholars. 'Who can remember what it says in *Di Dliguid Raith & Somaíne* about the death of a lord?' she asked and brooded on burials that she had attended. When Garrett's father had died, the clan had shown their love and respect by excavating half of the hillside and covering the enormous mound with stones of white quartz.

'I have a few men lying idle at the moment,' said Ardal in a low voice to Mara after he had listened with grave courtesy to Moylan's repetition of the law, emphasising the size of the lord's grave mound. 'I thought I would lend a hand with the grave and the burial mound. We'll be out of the way by the time that you all come back from the inauguration. It doesn't seem right, somehow, perhaps the new *taoiseach* didn't know . . .' And then he said no more.

Mara wished that she could ask his opinion of Tomás but she was conscious that to do so would seem to undermine Turlough's opinion. She trusted Ardal more than she trusted most, but as Brehon of the Burren she knew that every single one of her words bore weight and that her opinions could be tossed from mouth to mouth and gain momentum and different shades of meaning on their journey. So she murmured, 'That is good of you,' and then changed the subject. Ardal, she knew, never had men lying idle. All work was meticulously planned and checked and the schedule announced at the breakfast that he held every morning for his workers. If he spared workers for this act of charity it was because his soul was appalled at the lack of respect for the former *taoiseach* of the MacNamara clan.

'My boys are very envious of that horse young Adair MacNamara was riding,' she said lightly. 'Moylan thinks it is the one that he tried out for you a little while ago.'

'Yes, I sold it the very next day,' said Ardal readily. 'Tomás sent word down from Carron – you know the clan had gathered there when the news that the old *tánaiste*, God have mercy on him, was nearing his end. I invited him to bring the lad down and to take his pick. I always like to match a horse to a rider.' Ardal's eyes wandered to the rough pony from Connemara that Fiona was riding. He opened his mouth and then shut it again.

Mara noted the look, but she had other things on her mind than Ardal and his interest in Fiona. So Tomás had bought that horse, splendid and expensive, she was sure, for his son well before there were any prospects for him to become *taoiseach*. Unless, of course, he thought that he would be elected *tánaiste*. That office, however, had no monetary value. The clan paid tribute to the *taoiseach* only.

'Was Jarlath home at that stage?' she enquired

and Ardal looked surprised at the change of subject.

'Yes, he was; in fact, he came with them. Nice fellow, Jarlath,' he said with more enthusiasm than he had shown when discussing Jarlath's cousin, Tomás. He looked over his shoulder and smiled tenderly at Fiona, though his words were addressed to Moylan.

'Any time that you scholars have some leisure you are welcome to come and try out my horses. I've just finished training some young ones.'

'Good breeding?' enquired Moylan.

'Certainly, a couple of young stallions and one beautiful mare, a Spanish jennet, a lady's horse – you wouldn't be interested in her, Moylan.'

'You could get Fiona to try her out,' said Moylan innocently, and Mara suppressed a smile. In Moylan's eyes, Ardal was an old man and could have no interest in Fiona. Fachtnan, however, might be more percipient. Mara hoped that he was not hurt. He was a modest young man and would not fancy his chances against the wealthy and prestigious chieftain of the O'Lochlainn clan.

But Tomás! Mara forgot about the tangled love affairs around her and concentrated on her task of solving the murder of Garrett MacNamara. Tomás bought an extremely expensive horse for his son – and he, apparently, had six other sons. How could he have afforded to do that unless he had known that he had glittering prospects opening out in front of him?

And Jarlath? Mara had not realised that he had arrived a week before. And so, of course,

230

had the others; including Stephen Gardiner. There had been plenty of time for Stephen to have played his little game, to have worked on Garrett, and probably on Slaney; to have held out the prize of an earldom, a visit to London probably where Slaney could refresh her wardrobe and meet the handsome young king and his beautiful Spanish wife. London would have suited Slaney. She had made no secret over the last four years of how much she had hated the countryside. Rhona may have kept in the background until Stephen had done his work, perhaps she had stayed elsewhere for a while. Mara had a strong notion that Garrett had only just met his son; it would have been impossible not to have noticed the likeness instantly.

Jarlath and Tomás; it's interesting, thought Mara, how both of them had got what they wanted. Tomás was now *taoiseach* and Jarlath was the sole owner of the fleet of merchant ships.

And why had Jarlath sold his ship to O'Donnell? Did he plan that he would buy a splendid new ship within a short period of time? Was Garrett's silver still carefully locked away in the strong room of the castle, or had the key been found and the stores rifled? And how much was Garrett's share in the merchant ship business worth to his younger brother, Jarlath?

'Ardal,' she said, interrupting his enthusiastic description of his little Spanish jennet, 'tell me something, Ardal.'

Always the soul of politeness, he moved back up beside her and she put her question to him.

'Immense!' he exclaimed. 'I envy Jarlath. The

world is opening up. There was a time when trade was just with England, France and Spain and even then to have a ship was to be rich, but now! There's the Spice Islands – ships are criss-crossing the oceans laden with goods from there. And the last time that I was in Galway there was talk of a sea route to China. Think how easy it would be to bring back silks by sea than with the long years of travel across land. That young man will make a fortune, Brehon, or I will be most surprised.'

'I see,' said Mara. Now that she had her information, she wanted to spend the rest of the journey to Carron with only her thoughts for company. Over her shoulder she said, 'Shane, do you remember how, when you were younger, you always wanted to go to sea? Well, you must hear what the O'Lochlainn has to say about the exploration of the oceans.'

The ancient inauguration site of the MacNamara clan was in a strange hidden site. Mara was not fanciful, but the place always seemed to have an eerie atmosphere of primeval times long passed. It was in one of those hanging valleys which slotted into the limestone hills around and appeared even more secret and verdant because of the smooth shining stone surrounding them. One by one the party from the law school dismounted and tied their horses to the ancient large low-branched ash tree at the entrance.

Theirs were the only horses there, but a subdued murmur of many voices from above them told Mara that the clan had arrived. No doubt those from the Burren had either walked or left their horses at the castle above.

'You go first, Shane; the rest of you follow him,' she said in a low voice. It was fitting that the king should be the last to arrive. She tucked her arm into his and held him back while Fachtnan ushered the scholars along the narrow path of deeply scored limestone which descended into the small valley. A strange and eerie place, she thought, as she paced beside her husband; some pine trees grew on either side of the path, their enormous roots, swelling like claws from the stony ground, their grey-blue branches meeting overhead and casting a deep gloom over the passageway. A tiny stream twisted its way down beside the path leaving small islands and promontories for the ferns which grew in clumps beside it. A pretty place on a bright spring day, thought Mara noticing some pale yellow primroses nestling among the glossy green of the hart's tongue fern's strap-like leaves, but today in the dark and the rain there was something eerie about it. She had pushed back her hood to do honour to the occasion but was aware of steady drips going down the back of her neck from the spiky foliage overhead.

'I'll get through this as quickly as possible – skip a few of my ancestors,' whispered Turlough, but Mara frowned at him.

'Do it right and in a couple of hours we'll be sitting by the fire and you'll have a bottle of the best burgundy you've ever tasted – a present from the mayor of Galway himself,' she murmured, keeping her face solemn and dignified as they emerged from the path.

The small valley was crammed with people, all in their best clothes and all getting very wet. In front of them was Tomás MacNamara, dressed in a white *léine* and a mantle made from pure white lamb's wool. His face bore a look of almost saintly dedication with his brown eyes bent onto the ground. His wife, Cait, stood well back from him, but oddly her eyes were not on her lord, but on the prettily-flushed, petulant face of her eldest son who stood beside her. The boy, Mara noticed with a slight flicker of malice, was looking worriedly at the harm that the rain was doing to his finery and more interested in that than in the ceremonies.

Tomás was led in procession to the cairn and he stood there, calm, and impassive, seemingly unaware of the rain which had now begun to fall heavily again, splashing in small runlets down from the stony hillside, spraying on to the golden celandines and the delicate petals of the wood sorrel. Turlough, never one to mind the rain, stepped forward and stood out in the open, impervious to the downpour, while others moved as near to the overhanging rocks as they could or shrank back into the pine-covered pathway. Fintan MacNamara, the blacksmith from the Burren, approached Turlough and handed to him the ceremonial rod – a newly-peeled, straight, narrow branch from the nearby ash, a tree that was sacred to the MacNamara clan. A very ancient right, that of handing the rod to the king would have come down to Fintan from ancestors – perhaps going back to the distant past of legends. It showed, thought Mara, that the MacNamara clan were Burren in origin and she felt even more regretful that so many of the clan members now lived outside the kingdom.

When Tomás reached the foot of the cairn, King Turlough Donn touched him on the head with the white rod.

'Do you swear to be my vassal?' he enquired in a pleasant, conversational tone that seemed to imply that a negative answer could be received as easily as an affirmative.

Tomás, however, rose to the occasion. He had a pleasant voice, with a good timbre in it and he pitched it carefully to fill the whole valley as he swore on his hand to be the king's vassal in accordance with the ancient Brehon laws.

'And I swear to maintain my lord's boundaries,' he said, paused, looked around.

'And to escort my lord to public assemblies,' he continued.

And then, with war-like emphasis: 'And I promise to bring my own warriors to each *slógad* and to support my lord in the uprising.'

And then he dropped his voice slightly and said with emphasis, 'And in the last hour of my lord, I will assist in digging his grave mound and will contribute to the death feast.'

Turlough heard this unmoved, though Mara usually could not repress a slight shudder. Today, however, she was absorbed in watching Tomás's face, while Turlough enumerated his ancestors from the great Brian Boru down through the

235

following four centuries. Was it the face of a man who had finally attained his dream; the face of a man, perhaps, who would be willing to kill in order to find himself in the position where he was at this moment? But his face told her nothing. It was calm and dignified.

Then Tomás bowed to King Turlough Donn and encircled the cairn three times, sunwise, before climbing solemnly to the top of the mound. He lifted up the white rod and held it high above his head. There was a great shout of 'the MacNamara' from the clan of MacNamara. This was the naming ceremony and without this he would not be the *taoiseach* of the clan.

Tomás allowed the echoes from the rocks around to die down before holding out the white rod for silence and then in a sonorous voice he swore to serve his people and to protect them in return for a just rent and a fair tribute. Thus was Tomás MacNamara inaugurated as *taoiseach* of his clan, only four years after the inauguration of the murdered man whose body still remained to be buried. He waited for a moment for the cheers to die down. This was the moment when Mara expected to see him look at his wife, Cait. But his eyes were turned in a different direction and were fixed on the impassive face of Jarlath who was standing at the back of the crowd, half-hidden by the immense bulk of the blacksmith. Mara's eyes followed his but Jarlath did not return the gaze, only stared straight across the small enclosed hollow, appearing to fix themselves on a small crop of pale-green sheath-like leaves from the deadly nightshade plant.

And then Tomás looked back again at his clan and this time he spoke with a note of iron in his voice.

'And on this day, a day that will always be sacred to me, I swear to the MacNamara clan that whoever was responsible for the secret and unlawful killing of the last *taoiseach*, my cousin, Garrett MacNamara, then that person will be pursued and will meet with the full penalty of the law.'

There was a buzz of conversation from the listening people as he stepped down and moved away from the cairn. Several faces were turned towards Mara and with difficulty she preserved an impassive face. *How dare he take my office upon himself*, she thought but said nothing. He had not even looked towards her and may not have meant an insult, she told herself. In any case, now was not the moment to quarrel with a newly elected *taoiseach*.

Mara waited for a moment until Tomás stepped forward to speak informally to Turlough and then she went across to Jarlath and smiled at him in an easy way.

'Any regrets?' she asked as she had done before and he answered her with a broad smile.

'Not in the least,' he assured her.

'You looked pensive for a moment,' she said, probing a little more.

'I was thinking about the sea,' he said. 'There's a nice wind getting up. Coming from the south-east, too. Just the wind that I want. I could almost feel how good it would be to be out there on the ocean. Too many people around here; I feel hemmed in.' Jarlath looked around him with an air of restless dissatisfaction. 'Everything is the same as when I was a boy. It wouldn't suit me. I like new places, new sights, and meeting new people.' He glanced down at her with a smile. 'You should try it yourself sometime, Brehon; you would enjoy it, I think. Come with me on a voyage.'

'You're only saying that because you want to conceal that you are secretly wishing to get away from me and my questions as soon as possible.' Mara laughed as she spoke, but she watched his face narrowly and thought that he looked slightly taken aback as though she had uncovered his thoughts. 'I don't think that I want to get any wetter than I am at the moment,' she went on, smoothly covering her words of any covert intention. 'Is the burial going to be straight away?'

'Straight away,' Jarlath assured her. 'Tomás has given orders that the coffin is to be taken to the churchyard on a turf cart. It will be waiting for us there.'

On a turf cart! Mara stared at him with astonishment. Even the lowliest cottager in the kingdom would have a better burial than that. When the father of Garrett and Jarlath had been buried, men had fought for the privilege of carrying the coffin. And so many had there been to share the burden that the little piles of white quartz stones, placed by the mourners at the traditional stopping places down the steep hillside, still appeared like a long line when seen from the valley below. But to be conveyed to the burial place on a turf cart! What an end to a man's life, she thought. Not a bad man, either, just awkward and ill-at-ease with his fellow creatures – married to a different woman he might have eventually become well-liked and esteemed by his clan. A surge of anger filled her. Immediately she stepped forward and took her place at the foot of the cairn. Instantly every eye went to her and then conversations finished and there was silence except for the trilling of a pair of tiny gold crest birds.

Mara waited until all were looking at her and then said in low, but clear tones, 'Now we need to honour the dead and to escort the body of Garrett MacNamara to his final resting place.'

Keeping her head high, she put her arm into Turlough's and turned down the path.

'Don't slip,' said Turlough as she strode out, almost dragging him in her eagerness to get to the road and to save Garrett's body from the final indignity. 'What's the matter?' he asked, always sensitive to her moods.

Tomás has arranged to have Garrett's body awaiting us at the churchyard – carried there by a turf cart – and Jarlath, Garrett's own brother, told it to me without a qualm, she almost replied, feeling her anger almost choking her. But she closed her lips firmly. Before Turlough had become king of the three kingdoms, there had been constant wars, clan were set against clan, all of them warring to become the most powerful. The MacNamaras were the second most powerful clan in the three kingdoms and there had been battles between them and their overlords, the O'Briens. Since the inauguration

239

of Turlough the enmity and rivalry had become dormant; it was not for her, the wife of the king, to fan the hidden flames. She would do her best for Garrett, try to ensure a dignified burial, solve his secret and unlawful killing, but she would do it herself and not involve Turlough more than was necessary.

The body was already at the small graveyard at Carron when they arrived. And yes, it lay on a four-wheeled turf cart, the coffin perfunctorily covered by an old tarpaulin. There was a fair attendance of farm workers, though none, which Mara could see, of the indoor servants. No doubt they were back at the castle preparing a celebration feast.

Among the farm workers was Brennan the cowman, who was standing beside the coffin, and Mara went forward to greet him.

'A sad day,' she said. She had been to so many of those burials that the conventional words flowed from her lips without any thought of hers. She was touched by his presence, though. After all, he had been dismissed from his position as chief cowherd by the man whom he now came to honour. The place beside the coffin in the churchyard should surely have been Jarlath's but he kept his distance, talking to Father MacMahon in an animated fashion.

Brennan said something but she could not understand it. He seemed to be gobbling his words more than when she had met him with Cumhal. What an affliction it must be to have been born with a mouth that was unable to shape the sounds of speech adequately. Mara, who used a quick and clever tongue to steer her way adroitly through the potential flare-ups of a volatile and war-like people, found she could hardly bear to envisage a time when words would not work for her.

'I didn't quite catch that,' she said smiling at him in a friendly fashion. 'This rain makes such a noise . . .' She cast a look up at the purple sky and the large drops that were beginning to bounce upon the stones. It would get worse before long, she thought, and was glad that she had worn boots rather than shoes and had put on an extra pair of woollen stockings.

He repeated his remark patiently. He must be used to that, she thought, feeling desperately sorry for him and impatient with herself for not being able to understand. There was something about 'cows', she thought and she seized on this word and talked for a while telling him of Cumhal's high opinion of him and then, to her great relief, Rhona came forward. Neither she nor her son Peadar had been at the inauguration so they must have come down from the castle to accompany the body.

'Has Brennan told you the news, Brehon?' she asked; her hand on the man's arm and her broad-cheeked face lit up by a gap-toothed smile. 'The new *taoiseach* has given him his position back as chief cowherd – couldn't do without him, that's right, isn't it, Brennan?'

Brennan grinned bashfully, saying something, and Mara bit back an exclamation of pleasure as she picked out the words '*told her*' from his mangled speech. Instead she turned to Rhona and repeated all of what her farm manager, Cumhal, had said in praise of Brennan.

'Se . . . cow.' Brennan indicated Rhona with a smile that stretched his misshapen mouth and caused Mara to feel intensely sorry for him. The pulled back lip gave him something of the look of a seven-year-old displaying new, large teeth. She wished she could understand him better but refrained from looking for help.

'What did she do?' she asked with a friendly smile, nodding at Rhona and his own smile widened.

'No . . . fri . . . bull,' he said eyeing Mara anxiously to see whether his words would be understood.

'You've been tackling a bull!' exclaimed Mara, turning a look of mock-horror on Rhona. 'What! You, Rhona! Or was it your son, Peadar!'

'Peadar!' said Rhona. 'He's no cattleman; nothing interests him but herbs and medical matters. I was brought up with cattle; I was the only child of a cattle dealer. Not that there were any problems with this bull, were there, Brennan? He'd just got a bit above himself having run free for a few miles with all the cows. We got him back into the cabin, poor fellow, didn't we? He'll stay there until August when he can run free with the herd again. Good bull, isn't he?'

Brennan said something and Rhona nodded sagely, 'Yes, I thought that you would have had a hand in choosing him. Reminds me a bit of our Galloway cattle. Good bone.'

'I must go and see Father MacMahon,' said Mara, feeling that it was necessary to pull this burial party into order and at least to consign Garrett's body to the earth with dignity. Ardal had been as good as his word and there was an enormous mound of earth beside the grave and a collection of the highly valued quartz pebbles to place on top of all when the grave had been covered again. 'Goodbye, Brennan; I'm so pleased that you are now chief cowherd of Carron, again,' she said, making her escape quickly before there could be any more talk about cows.

But while making easy conversation with Father MacMahon she found herself wondering why Tomás, with all that he had to do, should have found time to reinstate a disabled cowherd. It showed, she thought, an unexpected side in his nature. She frowned slightly, turning to look at the threatening sky to explain her preoccupation when the priest looked startled. It was not of the rain, though, she was thinking. There was something strange about this. Unless, of course, Rhona had interceded on Brennan's behalf. That, however, was unlikely, thought Mara. Was there a chance, perhaps, that Tomás feared that Brennan might have seen something? After all, his cottage was not far from the spot where Garrett's body was found. She decided to postpone her thinking to the time when she was warm and dry and turned to see what the stir of people from the gate might mean.

'The O'Lochlainn must have sent him,' muttered Niall MacNamara. There was a look of shame on his face, and on the faces of the other MacNamaras from the Burren. Where was

243

the MacNamara piper? wondered Mara, watching with approval as O'Lochlainn's own personal piper came through the gates and went up to Tomás. Probably back at the castle preparing jubilant melodies to celebrate the inauguration of the new *taoiseach.*

'Shall we gather around the graveside, Father?' she suggested to the old man. 'Perhaps you would consult with Tomás about who should share the honour bearing the coffin with himself and Jarlath.'

Without waiting for an answer, she just glanced over her shoulder to make sure that he spoke to Tomás and then she went up to Fintan. 'You, as bearer of the rod, should be one who will carry the coffin to the graveside,' she said firmly. 'Let me go with you to Jarlath.'

In a few minutes she had it all arranged; it was only in the sudden silence after the piper ceased its wail, when the coffin had been successfully lowered on ropes into the grave and before the priest had begun to intone the words of the great psalm *De profundis clamavi ad te, Domine*, that her mind suddenly cleared. And it was only then that she fully understood how Garrett MacNamara had lost his life on the evening of the cattle raid of Bealtaine.

Twelve

Bretha Déin Chécht
(Judgements of Dian Checht – a mythological physician)

A physician needs public recognition before practising in a kingdom. He must be learned in the ways of the body; must know the twelve doors of the soul – the twelve ways in which life may be extinguished; he must know the seven most serious bone-breakings; and be able to classify teeth and find an answer to their problems.

A physician's house should be free from dirt, should have four open doors, and should have a stream of water running across it through the middle of the floor or else nearby. It needs to be set in a quiet place with no noise from talkative people, from fools quarrelling or from dogs barking.

'I've made up my mind.'

Mara turned a distracted face towards Nuala. Turlough had left at noon to go to another inauguration in Ossory. She had given herself and her scholars time to get warm and dry and to have their usual midday meal and then she had resumed teaching during the afternoon, but with only a quarter of her mind on the task. The other three-quarters ranged over the situation at

245

Carron. What was best to do? It had always been her philosophy to take full responsibility for any actions of hers – and that now involved carefully thinking through consequences before making any accusations. In the end, she dismissed her scholars to have half an hour's exercise before their evening meal, thankful that she had Fachtnan to take charge of them. Now she looked unseeingly at Nuala who had followed her over to the Brehon's house and then was aware of the silence and the puzzled look on the girl's face as she waited for an answer.

'You've decided,' she said. Earlier in the day Nuala had been talking to Brigid about a new gown for a celebration at Thomond to celebrate the birth of one of Turlough's latest grandchildren. 'So did you decide on green or saffron?' she asked, trying to force her voice into a note of enthusiasm.

'Not that.' Nuala sounded exasperated. 'I'm not talking about gowns. I'm talking about my future. I've decided to come to the Burren and live at my house in Rathborney. You're right. It's a great house and would make a perfect teaching hospital.'

Mara's eyes widened. 'That's wonderful,' she said with absolute sincerity. 'What made you decide?'

'I suppose it was Peadar,' said Nuala thoughtfully. 'I've been thinking, watching you at work, how much your scholars learn by doing things, by being with you. Yes, they have to have book learning, too – but I remember when I was a child what a struggle it was to understand my

246

grandfather's notes and how much I wished that I had someone to show me how these drawings applied to a real human body. I learned a lot about how to teach when I went to the medical school in Salerno in Italy, but I would like to teach the way you do – seizing opportunities from real life and applying them to the stuff you find in books.'

'Perhaps one day the medical school at Rathborney in the Burren will be as famous as the school in Salerno,' said Mara enthusiastically. 'Well, everything is in good order for you. Fachtnan rides down there once a week and makes sure that the house is kept warm and the farm is well-attended to. He has been your faithful steward.' She ended on a lighter note and saw the flush come to Nuala's cheeks.

'I think . . .' she began and then she stopped. They had been standing at the doorway into the house and both heard the sound immediately. A horse been ridden at breakneck speed. A moment later the beautiful Arab horse that Mara had last seen being ridden by Tomás's son came thundering down the road. At the same minute, Moylan, attracted by the sight, came running down the road between the law school and the Brehon's house.

But the horse was not ridden by its owner. Instead of the elegant, beautifully-dressed figure of Adair MacNamara was Peadar. Peadar with a white face and fear-filled eyes.

'Brehon!' he shouted, sliding from the horse and allowing Moylan to catch the bridle. 'Brehon! Something terrible is happening. My mother is

247

gone to Galway so I had to come to you; you'll have to stop them, Brehon. They've got her!'

'Who? Your mother? Rhona?' Mara turned an alarmed face to him.

'No, I told you; she's gone to Galway. It's Slaney; the wife of . . . of my father.' His voice rose to squeaky heights and then broke abruptly on a half sob. 'I didn't know what to do.' He looked at Nuala. 'I couldn't do anything,' he said apologetically.

'How on earth did you get Adair to lend you that horse? You've ridden him to the ground,' said Moylan angrily. He plucked a handful of last year's dead grass from the ditch and began rubbing the foam and sweat from the animal's legs and flanks.

'I had to; they've got her, out in the circle; below Carron.' Peadar turned a sob into hiccup and brushed his hand across his eyes. 'What do you care about a horse?' he raged in his high, half-broken voice. 'They've got the woman out there. And I've seen the firewood.'

'Where?' asked Nuala, but Mara had immediately known where he was speaking of and she felt her lips turn cold. She knew that lonely circle at Creevagh and she knew the tales that people told in whispers about things that had happened there in old legends. Brigid's words about Tomás's unpleasant grandfather came back to her.

'Cumhal,' she called, but to her dismay it was young Dathi who appeared, saying that he didn't know where Cumhal had gone. Still she had to go now before anything happened. She would

248

have to rely on her status in the kingdom to give her authority. 'Dathi, we'll leave this animal with you, but saddle a horse for me. Moylan, you and Aidan saddle your horses now and be ready to come with me.'

When they had gone, she turned to Nuala. 'Are you willing to take on Peadar as your apprentice, Nuala?' she asked. 'You're sure?'

Nuala nodded; her face serious and concentrated.

'I want him out of the way and safe and I want no one to be able to get hold of his patrimony,' said Mara. 'Fachtnan, you get your writing materials and go with Nuala and Peadar to the schoolhouse. Draw up the apprenticeship agreement and have it signed – Peadar is old enough to sign it himself as he has no living father. Make sure that Nuala has all the powers over him according to the English law of apprenticeship. When you have done that, lock it into the box in the press. I'll leave you in charge. Settle Nuala and Peadar down in Rathborney and then follow us to Creevagh – Fiona, Hugh and Shane can stay with Nuala. Help her in every way, won't you, and, Nuala, on my return I will be bringing you Slaney, your first patient. I must get her away from that crowd. With the help of God,' she added. She was not given to these pious appendices to her words, but this time, thinking of how she would have to confront the might of the MacNamara clan on her own, except for a couple of young lads, she felt that she would try to get all the supernatural help possible. The thought of Ardal O'Lochlainn and the army of men that he usually had working around his farm crossed her mind but she dismissed the idea. This would have to be carefully done.

'Let's go,' she said when Moylan and Aidan returned and set such a pace on her mare that she soon outstripped them and had to wait beside Caherconnell, Nuala's old home, in order for them to catch up. She had no real fear of aggression towards her own person; her status as Brehon of the Burren had given her complete confidence in her ability to handle a crowd, but she did want her entrance to be as impressive as possible. She rode in silence, turning over in her mind what was best to be done. If only she had got rid of Stephen Gardiner! It had been a shock to hear from Cumhal that he had gone – not to Galway, but only a few miles west to the kingdom of Corcomroe.

'Look down there, Brehon,' said Aidan after a while. Mara checked her horse and looked down. They had been climbing steadily and had passed through the area of common land, known as the High Burren. Far below them, where the high clint-paved land fell away into a small valley, there was the townland of Creevagh with its large ancient enclosure. Mara stayed very still and signed to her scholars to wait in silence. Both were, like herself, dressed in serviceable dark grey wool cloaks, felted and treated until they were almost impervious to wind and rain. In the gloom of the late afternoon, with the heavy sky above giving little light, they could watch without being seen.

The enclosure at Creevagh was a large one

measuring about a hundred feet across its centre. Uniquely it had two dolmens – the one situated within its walls and the other one in another enclosure just outside. Each was almost the same in construction – a flat stone rested upon three massive upright stones, giving it the look of some strange, prehistoric altar. When Mara was young, Brigid had told her that the dolmen within the first circle had been used for burial of good souls who would go to heaven; and the second dolmen had been used for the evil souls who were doomed to go down into the fires of hell. A sunken passageway, about the depth of a man's height, had been made by hacking through the stone and was constructed to join the two enclosures. Some years back, a farmer, rescuing a sheep which had become trapped within the stones, had come across a pile of burned skulls and bones and this had seemed to lend credence to Brigid's story. Most people avoided the place, especially at evening and during the great festival of Samhain, when, it was rumoured, the dead came back to life.

Today, on this wet May evening, the main enclosure itself was packed solidly with men – no women or children, noticed Mara, but the sunken passageway was empty and a fire burned beside the second dolmen. Not just beside it; realised Mara after a moment, as the flames leaped up. There was a ring of firewood all the way around it.

'Pine,' whispered Moylan, and Mara nodded. He was right, she judged. An aromatic smell filled the air from the thick black clouds of smoke that rose upwards. The fire had only just been started, she reckoned, but it would be a huge one. Enormous heavy branches of pine had been layered in almost a complete circle around the dolmen, leaving a small gap in front of the foremost supporting stone.

And around that stone was draped a heavy iron chain. Mara drew in a long breath. What was happening? The flames were getting higher, the fire burning in that exuberant way of pine; now she could see that the area outside the enclosing wall of the second dolmen was piled high with more pine. Trees must have been felled to accumulate as much firewood as this.

'Just the crowd from the castle – none of the MacNamaras from the Burren, I'd say,' said Moylan in a whisper. 'What are they doing, Brehon? This is MacNamara land, but it is not a sacred site, not like the inauguration place. I've never heard of anything been held there.'

'Nor I,' said Mara in a low voice, straining her eyes to try to see the faces. 'Not in my time, nor in my father's,' she added, 'but Brigid said . . .' And then she stopped as the words of the legend came back to her: '*And they shall be purified by fire and it shall be lit at Creevagh, the place of the branches . . .*'

'That's Tomás MacNamara there talking to them all.' Once more Aidan's long-sighted eyes had identified the figure in front of the crowd.

'And Stephen Gardiner standing beside him; what's he doing?'

'Let's go down there,' said Mara tersely. She had intended to wait until the arrival of Fachtnan, but now a terrible feeling of dread was coming over her.

'Yes, you're right, that's Stephen Gardiner,' said Aidan. 'He's come back into the kingdom, Brehon. How dared he?' He sounded very bellicose, not at all like the usual, easy-going Aidan.

But Mara did not smile. She was filled with a great feeling of apprehension.

'If we go across this field, Brehon, we'll be much quicker than by the road,' said Moylan. 'I know this place. I've come up here hunting with the O'Brien lads. The ground is rock a few inches below the soil. We won't slip.'

'Yes, you're right, both of you, it is definitely Stephen Gardiner. I didn't recognise him immediately. He's usually so colourful.'

And it was true. Stephen, who was usually dressed in blue or crimson velvets, now wore a black gown and a flat black cap. Mara went ahead of her two scholars, signalling them to be silent and then stopped at some distance from the entrance to the enclosure beside a moss-overgrown well. She dismounted quietly from her horse and handed the bridle to Moylan. The crowd stood with their backs to the entrance facing the small, low dolmen ahead of them. Behind that dolmen were three men.

Stephen Gardiner stood beside Tomás facing the silent crowd and now his voice rang out, the words blown away from the law school party by the northerly wind. There was a third man there also, a youngish man with a short, sparse red beard, and a huge stomach, half concealed by

253

his cloak. His was a familiar face and Mara drew in a sharp breath of fury at the sight of him.

'Boetius MacClancy,' she breathed and her scholars looked at her with wide eyes. Boetius MacClancy was a cousin of Fergus MacClancy, the Brehon of the nearby kingdom of Corcomroe. Mara had been persuaded to leave her law school in his hands for a short time while she recovered from the birth of her son. An opinionated and stupid young man; he had been a disaster in that post.

'I thought he had gone to London,' said Moylan quietly.

'Yes,' murmured Mara. 'And I thought we had seen the last of him.' She compressed her lips. Boetius was a troublemaker and she didn't like to have him here on the Burren. And why had he not come to see her and announce his presence, as would have been the correct procedure? Her first impulse was to push her way through the crowd, but her second was to wait. Most of these men were very drunk, she recognised. A few even had leather flasks slung over their shoulders and she guessed that they contained the strong, honey-smelling, and very potent mead that was always served at celebrations.

'What's that?' Aidan's voice had a quick note of alarm. Mara looked at him. They had known Boetius well, but Aidan wasn't looking at him, but at something else.

'It's Slaney,' breathed Moylan, but Mara found it hard to credit.

What she had first thought to be a bundle was really a woman who had been placed in front of the first dolmen, bound and gagged, standing there in front of the three men, Tomás MacNamara, Stephen Gardiner and Boetius MacClancy. It was Slaney, Mara now realised, but only a quick eye would have recognised her.

Slaney had been a tall, massively built woman with an enormous bosom and a stately air. Mara had never seen her in anything other than the finest gowns of silks and velvets. Now, she slumped there, a dazed and sagging figure, wearing a plain linen petticoat, her hair, unbound and uncombed, straggling down her back.

'My friends, my brethren,' shouted Tomás, 'you all know now how your *taoiseach* met his death – not in battle, no; not from old age, no; not from a fatal sickness; no . . .' He paused at each successive 'no' and the crowd groaned in response. 'Your *taoiseach* was slain by a herd of cattle. But what sane man in his senses would go and lie on the path before a stampeding herd? And yet, the facts are there. His broken body was left behind them on the roadway.' He paused, lowered his voice, and then said with a throb of sincerity, 'But, my friends, and fellow clansmen, what made him do that? Had some evil influence placed a spell upon him? Was there . . .' Suddenly he stopped and Mara could hear a soft sigh run through the crowd. 'Was there . . .' He dropped his voice dramatically, before continuing, 'was there a spell placed upon him by someone?' Here he paused for the words to sink in.

Mara took three quick strides forward, but then stopped in the shadow of the entrance arch. She would wait to hear all before interrupting, she thought, leaning into the ivy-covered stones. She saw Moylan tie up the three horses at a distance and then he and Aidan crept forward and stood in the shelter of the surrounding wall.

'But who did this?' continued Tomas and now his voice was so low that some of those at the back strained to hear and looked in puzzlement at their neighbours.

'Who was it?' he shouted, now raising his voice to its utmost power. 'Was it a witch?' He used the English word 'witch' and Mara was now near enough to see puzzlement on the faces of the clan.

'*Witch* . . .?' The word was tossed from one to the other in a half-whisper from pursed lips – a whisper that swelled like the beginning of a storm wind.

'*Cailleach,*' amended Tomás and then there was a horrified silence.

Mara half-shivered – the *cailleach* was an elemental power, a creature who was half-woman, half-spirit, the spirit of winter, a power which brought cold winds, and tempests; a woman who came to rule as the days shortened, carrying a *slachdan* (wand of power) with which she shaped the land. Brigid's tales about her powers had given Mara some sleepless nights as a child. For a moment she stood frozen, but then she pulled herself together. The legend of the *cailleach* belonged to childhood; but the threat of being a witch that now lay upon Slaney was of much more serious consequences. Mara's father had brought back from his journey to Rome tales of a terrible witchcraft trial that he had witnessed in Italy where what seemed to be a harmless old woman had been accused of various crimes and had been burned to death at the stake. Could this be the intention, here in the Burren, where no one had the right to take a life, even from one judged guilty of the most terrible crimes?

'Moylan,' she whispered almost soundlessly in his ear. 'You and Aidan must ride back as fast as you can go. You go to the smithy, Moylan, send Fintan MacNamara here and any of his men, and Aidan, you go to Lissylisheen and send Ardal O'Lochlainn with as many men as he can muster. Go as fast as you can. Oh, and Moylan, take my horse; it's faster than yours.'

Trained to instant obedience from their early youth they were off, doubled down, but running like hares. She hardly saw them take their horses, but was reassured a few minutes later when she looked up at the road on the hillside and saw the two figures galloping along the road leading back towards the west. Now she would have to play a waiting game. Let them talk themselves out and then *she* would talk. The longer the MacNamara clan stood here in the damp and cold, the greater the chance that some of them at least would begin to sober up.

'My friends,' said Stephen, his well-trained voice filling the space well. He paused to allow the echo to throw back his words, and then continued, spacing the words well in order that all was clear. 'I come from England, from the king of England, the Great Harry, as we call him.

He has chosen your clan as the most amenable here in these kingdoms. There will be rich rewards for you all and for your leader if you will accept the laws of England and give true justice to those who have lost their lives through murder. I tell you, my friends, your laws are bad and evil. Under your laws a woman can murder her husband freely; little penalty attaches to it. Do you, can you, approve of such licence to kill one who should be her lord and master? If this woman here—' and he indicated the bound body of Slaney – 'if this woman here can be allowed to kill her own husband without paying the penalty then, my friends, the walls of civilisation will break down.' Stephen stopped for breath and Tomás hastily translated. Quite a few of the audience knew English, Mara guessed, because the pause before Tomás had taken up the rhetoric had been filled with soft murmurings as neighbour explained to neighbour.

'But don't ask me,' exclaimed Stephen, opening his two arms widely and then pointing suddenly to Boetius MacClancy, 'ask this man here, a lawyer, a man who is learned in both English law and in your laws. He knows the truth. He has studied both sets of laws; he speaks your language; he will enlighten you.'

Mara clenched her teeth together tightly, but did not move. Let them finish, she thought. Her keen eye noticed an uneasy shuffling among the crowd. One man took a leather drinking vessel from his pouch, held it open above his mouth and then, in disgust, shook the last few drops from it. The crowd was beginning to sober up.

The mead, she hoped, would by now have run out.

Boetius, much as she despised him, had been well-trained. He went through the points in favour of Slaney's guilt, enumerating them one by one on his fingers: of her greed for money; of her knowledge of her husband's will, leaving her the entire contents of the castle; of her rage when her husband introduced a new wife into the castle; of her fury that another woman's son, not any son that she might produce, would now be an heir to his father's lands and possibly to the leadership of the clan.

Mara waited in the shadow of the bunched clusters of ivy, determined not to interrupt him, willing him to go on as long as possible. Her mind followed the journey that Moylan would take, across the rocky terrain of the High Burren. How long before he reached Fintan? And how long would it take Aidan to reach Ardal O'Lochlainn? She hoped that Fintan would come first. The blacksmith was rod holder to the clan here in the Burren. His influence might prevail to shame those gathered here to burn to death a drugged woman. But a clash between the O'Lochlainn and the MacNamara clans might result in open warfare.

The men, gathered into the confines of the enclosure, were beginning to get restive. Boetius, happy to have an audience, had begun to slow down, dragging out every point. He would not hold them for much longer. By this stage all present had been convinced of Slaney's guilt; they were anxious to get on with the shameful, furtive business. But perhaps a few of them, she hoped, might be beginning to have doubts.

'And then this woman, this creature—' Boetius pointed at Slaney – 'she took the filthy drug that she had made from the root of cowbane and she disguised it with mead and handed to it to her husband to swallow. And then when she knew that he was seeing visions she persuaded him, in the ways that such women use, to go down and to stand in the way of the marauders and the stampeding herds. She—'

'What are your qualifications, Boetius?' enquired Mara stepping forward briskly and nodding graciously at those who drew back in stunned astonishment. 'Have you ever progressed beyond the grade of *aigne*? Ah, I thought not, what a shame,' she said as he gaped at her. 'An *aigne*,' she explained condescendingly to Stephen Gardiner speaking in English now, 'is the lowest grade of lawyer in our system of laws. I have a couple of boys in my law school who will shortly be sitting the examination for this qualification. I'm sure that they will pass and I do hope that they will continue their studies and will progress to a higher grade. An *aigne* is only allowed to practise in the lowest forms of courts and cannot ever be a judge.' And then slowly and carefully, in tones of warm assurance, she translated her remarks to the crowd, explaining to them carefully that she was the only one present who had the right to pass judgement.

'The matter of the death of your late *taoiseach*, Garrett MacNamara, will be dealt with by me at Poulnabrone, the judgement place, in a couple of days' time,' she assured them. 'I invite you all to be there where I will present my findings to you and will sentence the guilty person.'

For a moment she thought that all would be well. There was a stunned silence and men looked at each other uneasily and muttered. Boetius opened his mouth, displaying his rather unpleasantly yellow teeth, Stephen Gardiner shuffled uneasily and bore the look of a man who sees his enterprise beginning to disintegrate, but Tomás stared straight ahead and there was no hint of relenting in that stern face. His son, Adair, Mara noticed, did not appear to be amongst the men within the enclosure. But was all this for him, so that Slaney would be denied her inheritance and there would be adequate silver to make Tomás and his family rich and powerful? And what role did the adoring mother, Cait, play in this accusation of Slaney?

The rain softened into a mist and a strong gust of wind blew the aromatic pine smoke into their faces. The fire flared and now Mara could see that each man held an unlit pine branch in his hands. *Creevagh* the place of the branches, she thought and had a moment's insight into secret rites and shameful burnings that might have been held in this place. Tomás, she remembered, was the grandson of a man who had owned these townlands. A strange, unpleasant character, about whom there had been terrible rumours, Brigid had said. And there was a strange, unpleasant look about his descendent, she thought as the blank, almost-black eyes stared at her with a look of fury.

261

'So I ask you now, good people, to go in peace, back to where you came from and to leave the legal affairs of the kingdom to me,' went on Mara smoothly. Tomás, she noticed, had, with three other men, left the enclosure and gone along the sunken passage towards the second dolmen, where the fire flared and crackled. No one else stirred and so she talked on, telling this crowd of men from Thomond all about Poulnabrone and the ancient dolmen and about how her father had practised there and how she had qualified as *aigne*, then as an *ollamh* and finally as a Brehon.

But then she stopped in dismay as she saw all eyes leave her and go towards the sunken passageway.

Tomás and the others had returned, each with a short, blazing branch of pine. They went from one to the other of their clan members. And each man held out his branch of pine and waited until it, also, flamed up. The gloomy enclosure was filled with flames and smoke and a chant began.

'*Cailleach, cailleach, cailleach,*' hissed the men from Thomond. Tomás moved amongst them touching some men on the shoulder and then, two by two, twelve men advanced towards the slumped-over figure of the unconscious woman.

Thirteen

Cáin Adomnán
(The law of Adomnán)

According to the law of Adomnán, the killing or the injuring of a woman is twice as serious an offence as if the same crime was committed against a man. As Jesus venerated his mother, so too should all women in the kingdom be venerated and no man's hand lifted against them to do any serious injury.

Offences against children and clerics are to be also severely punished.

As the twelve men took their places, six on either side, a hand seized Mara and she felt herself clamped to the curve of a protruding stomach. The other hand went across her mouth and she found herself wordless and impotent in the grip of Boetius, a man whom she despised and disliked. She froze and waited.

'Men of the Jury,' called out Stephen in shrill and rather uncertain tones. 'You have heard the evidence. You know that this woman, Slaney MacNamara, is accused of the crime of treason in that she murdered her husband, Garrett MacNamara. How find you? Guilty or not guilty?'

'Guilty or not guilty?' translated Tomás into

Gaelic, an impatient note in his voice. He did not look towards Mara, but kept his eyes fixed on his makeshift jury. Mara contemplated biting Boetius and jabbing him sharply in the stomach, but could not bring herself to do it.

'Guilty,' shouted the twelve men in unison, and almost before the words were out of their mouths, the crowd took up the chant of '*Cailleach, cailleach, cailleach.*'

The inert form of Slaney, her eyes wide open and almost totally black, was dragged towards the passageway by two of the jurors; Boetius tightened his hold on Mara.

'You will want to see justice done, Brehon, will you not?' he said in her ear, and there was such a note of gloating in his voice that Mara decided not to struggle but to walk with him as well as she could. He was getting pleasure from this, she could tell, and was revenging himself for the humiliation at her hands some years ago, when she had dismissed him from her school and from her kingdom.

The narrow passageway leading out of the enclosure had been hacked out of the rock to a depth of about five feet. Mara was quite a tall woman, but only part of her head was above its steep-sided walls which were dripping with moisture. About thirty paces long, she thought, endeavouring to step out as briskly as she could. Her flesh crawled at Boetius's clasp which was almost an embrace, and if she had a knife, she thought grimly, she would have undoubtedly used it. But her knife was in the satchel attached to her horse and, though useful for trimming pens and cutting tape, it probably would not do more than annoy Boetius.

It was a scene from hell, she thought. The end of the sunken passageway rose up and rounded out into a small enclosed circle that was almost completely filled by the dolmen. Huge branches of pine had been piled almost to the height of the surrounding wall. The place was full of smoke and shadows and the strong smell of burning wood. The fire rose high in the circle around the back and the sides of the dolmen at the end of the sunken passageway, encircling two of the upright stones that supported the table slab. Some branches had fallen in front of the third upright – a flat-sided piece of limestone encrusted with outcrops of gleaming quartz – and a man armed with a huge iron bar was carefully raking them to one side. Mara eyed the long black iron chain that was looped over it, and knew instantly what was intended. But there was nothing that she could do except pray that the boys would bring help before the final tragedy. About half an hour since they had gone, she calculated. She was glad that she had told Moylan to take her horse. Brig had been a present from the king, a well-bred horse with Arab blood and a horse that could almost fly when spurred on, but the distance to the smithy was so great that she suspected that he might only now be arriving.

And even now men were propping Slaney up against the stone and winding the great loops of the chain around her, pulling it in tightly under her bosom and tying the two ends into a knot.

Not hard to undo, thought Mara. A chain meant to hold someone would normally have had the ends softened with red-hot tongs and then hammered together by a blacksmith. But there was no blacksmith there and Slaney was so drugged that she knew nothing of what was happening and slept on.

When the flames began to lick around her flesh, though, she would probably be shocked out of her stupor and perhaps make an effort to escape. What would happen then?

And then came a tiny miracle, an answer to the prayers that were flooding through Mara's mind. A sudden gust of wind eddied through the enclosed space and smoke filled all eyes. A glowing fragment of smouldering pine was blown up against Boetius and Mara smelled the stench of burning hair as his red beard flared up. With an oath he released her and she sprang away from him picking up the iron bar and standing with her back to the limestone upright slab, beside the body of Slaney.

'I swear that I will beat out the brains of any man who comes near to me,' she roared using the full power of her well-trained voice. 'Get back all of you; get back, I say. How dare you take justice into your own hands?'

Swiftly she swung the bar, raking the burning branches so that more glowing embers flew out on the wind towards the crowd. They pressed back, those still in the passageway, being trodden on by their fellows who were escaping from the shower of burning embers.

'Think shame to you,' she screamed, not caring

266

for her dignity or for anything other than the overwhelming desire to save this unfortunate woman from an appalling death. 'The poets and the legend makers will sing of this deed of yours in the years to come, won't they? They will tell how the mighty MacNamara clan, the sons of the warriors from the sea, took an old, sick woman and tortured her. Will you tell that story to your grandchildren?' Again she swung the iron bar and again the wind blew the embers.

Her throat was beginning to fill with smoke though and the fire was licking at her boots and at her drenched woollen mantle. She could not hold them off for long. She remembered a story of the boy who was surrounded by wolves up on the mountain peak of Cappanawalla. He had kept the animals at bay all night long by flinging burning spars of wood at them.

Immediately she seized a brand from the fire and hurled it at Boetius and heard him yelp; she felt an immense inner satisfaction which compensated for the pain of her scorched hand.

'And this one for you, Stephen Gardiner,' she shouted pulling out another one. 'Go back to London and tell Cardinal Wolsley about your experiences among the *wilde Irish.*'

Then she saved her voice, just hurling the flaming branches as fast as she could at anyone that came near. It was amazing, she thought contemptuously, that they did not band together and capture her, but there was a primitive fear of fire among all people of the Celtic race and the wind had risen to storm force and it seemed to hurl sound and smoke down the sunken passageway, choking and blinding those crowded in the narrow walled space.

'Let's burn the two of them,' shouted someone, and then men hissed hoarsely, '*cailleach, cailleach, cailleach*,' but the chant had lost its potency and the words were swept away by the surging wind that now rattled through the stones of the enclosure.

However, the wind, Mara realised a moment later, brought its dangers. The gusts that swept through the dugout enclosure fanned the flames of the easily ignited pine branches. The fire roared like a wolf, the flames leaping up to the height of the stone table and beyond and illuminating the white faces and black eyes of those who pressed to the front to glimpse the human sacrifice.

And then the wind caught the flames and they curved around to the front of the dolmen where Slaney lay slumped in stupor, bound by an iron chain to the limestone slab. And Slaney, unlike Mara, was not wearing a mantle of heavy, felted sheepswool, soaked with rain. She was clothed only in a thin *léine*, a garment made of easily-inflammable linen threads. The flame licked around the corner and then found the material and blazed. Pain penetrated through the drug-induced stupor and Slaney screamed suddenly. The result was odd. Suddenly all chanting ceased. Half a hundred pairs of dilated black eyes stared at Mara and Mara reacted immediately. Lifting the skirt of her mantle, and feeling with thankfulness how soaked with rainwater it was, she dropped to her knees beside Slaney's inert form and bunched the material over the flames. They went out immediately and although the woman sobbed with pain, at least she was no longer on fire. A strong smell of scorched linen, mixed with the stench of scorched flesh, filled the small round enclosure where the dolmen ended the sunken passage. There was a gasp from the crowd, but whether it was horror or excitement was hard to tell. Mara used her iron bar to clear the burning branches away from Slaney, but was conscious that the fire was gathering strength and that soon they could both be engulfed in its flames.

At that moment, when she had almost despaired, the purple sky fulfilled its promise. An icy rainstorm poured down, small frozen balls of hail bounced on the flames. The air was winter cold and the rooks overhead cawed as though they could not wait to get home and away from man's cruelty. The wind had dropped and the heavy downpour seemed to quench the enthusiasm of the surrounding clan members. They blinked and looked away, many raising a hand to pass it over their eyes. Not all of those who had been at the castle were present, thought Mara suddenly and her optimistic nature took comfort in that observation. Perhaps there were still some sane members of the clan back in the castle. Perhaps someone might come to their rescue.

Slaney shrieked again. This time it must be from the agony of her burns. Mara herself felt that the burning pain in her hands had been relieved by the shower of frozen hail, but Slaney was a different case. The linen petticoat had gone up in flames and there was an ugly bright-red stripe down the woman's left thigh. By the light of the fire, Mara could see huge blisters bubble up from the flesh.

And then, unfortunately, the hail storm ceased almost as quickly as it had begun. The dull grey of the smouldering pine branches reddened and new flames began to lick upwards. Boetius wrenched the iron bar from Mara's hand and deliberately raked the crackling branches towards her. Mara swallowed hard, sending as much saliva as possible down her smoke-filled throat. The crowd in the passageway were surging forward. 'Burn, burn, burn,' they shouted and there was an insane, high-pitched note in the voices which made her knees tremble. She blinked hard and gathered all of her strength, trying to ignore her inflamed throat and her streaming eyes.

'Tomás MacNamara,' she called, keeping her voice at a level that it would reach his ears, but not attempting to make it reach to the back of the crowd, 'Tomás MacNamara,' she repeated, 'as *taoiseach* of the MacNamara clan, you have sworn loyalty to your overlord, King Turlough Donn O'Brien. What shall you tell him when next you meet?'

He stared at her blackly for a moment. There was almost an insane look in his dark eyes, but then he blinked hard and held up a hand. The chanting died down and the place was silent except for the roar of the flames and the harsh cawing of the rooks overhead. Mara quickly pursued her advantage.

'I swear to you, Tomás MacNamara, that if this affair goes ahead, that will be the end of you. You will be as nothing in the land. I shall condemn you. You will be an outlaw, a wanderer on the face of the earth. You will lose your honour price.' She paused to allow this to sink in; only a fugitive and an outlaw did not have an honour price; *lóg n-enech* (the price of the face) was the backbone to Celtic society. A man who lost that was a man without rights, a man who could be driven from the kingdom or killed with impunity.

At her words, suddenly something seemed to come over Tomás's face, almost like the expression of a man rousing himself from a dream. He blinked hard once again and passed a hand across his face. A shadow of hope began to steal into Mara's brain. Quickly she resumed talking, forcing the words out from her rasped throat, reminding him of the clan's reputation for hospitality, of the great deeds of his ancestors, of Sioda the Mighty . . . but she was not allowed to go any further. She had been conscious of an exchange of glances between Stephen Gardiner and Boetius. Stephen's mission was to stir up trouble between the clans – Turlough had been right when he had spoken of that. A man of burning ambition was this Stephen Gardiner; a young man who would do anything to raise himself in the favour of Cardinal Wolsey and of the king of England. And Boetius was his tool. He had lost Garrett, who had been so willing to bend the knee to Henry VIII, but now he had Tomás under his thumb. And suddenly she realised that now the stakes were higher. Not Slaney's death, not just a way of bringing English laws and English punishments into the Gaelic west of Ireland was his aim, but the death of Mara, Brehon of the Burren and wife of King Turlough Donn. This would immediately cause an all-out war between the O'Brien and the MacNamara clans – and in that war England, through the agency of O'Donnell, would send arms and men to assist the MacNamaras and hope that the death of their life-long enemy, Turlough Donn O'Brien, would be the outcome.

At that moment both Stephen and Boetius had re-started the chant of '*burn, burn, burn*' and it was taken up by the men packed into the narrow passageway. The only hope that Mara had was that another cloudburst might quench the flames of the fire. It was beginning to emit less heat, she noticed. More branches were needed to keep it going, but there seemed to be no effort made to fetch some from outside the enclosure. She looked up to the heavens, but the clouds were parting. Another of those sudden changes in weather that were so common to the west of Ireland appeared to be about to happen and she could do nothing about it. She opened her mouth to threaten Tomás again, but this time only a rusty croak was emitted. She boiled with frustration that her most potent weapon was now lost to her. She thought briefly about Brennan the cowman and wondered whether the frustration of all that rage and sense of injustice trapped behind a mouth that would not obey had played any part in the murder of Garrett. And then, of course, this was a man that understood cows, she thought, and shot one more glance at the sky.

But the rain had completely stopped now and a faint shaft of sunlight appeared in the western sky. Mara, dry-mouthed and still choking, looked instinctively towards it.

The land to the west of the enclosure, the stony slabs of the limestone plateau that formed the high Burren, had been empty a minute ago, but now up against the sky, etched in black, were the forms of some riders. Six men on horses, riding flat out, the horses stretched to a fast gallop. Could either Moylan or Aidan have managed to make contact? Were these riders coming to her assistance, or were they, as she tried to tell herself, nothing whatsoever to do with her?

Afraid to hope, Mara looked away. The clan members still chanted in dull tones and had not noticed the direction of her gaze, but Stephen Gardiner had begun to turn his head to follow the direction of her eyes. Rapidly she snatched a burning brand from the fire and moved it across his face. He drew back instantly, waving a hand to dissipate the smoke and then wiping his eyes with his handkerchief. Boetius was tenderly feeling the bright red bald patch on the side of his chin and she hoped maliciously that he would never again be able to sport that trimly pointed English beard. Once again she swiped the air with the brand, praying more sincerely than she had ever prayed in her life, that she could keep their attention from these racing horsemen.

Slaney moaned in pain and then cried out shrilly. She was beginning to come to her senses, thought Mara compassionately, and there would be no comfort for her in that. Better a blow across the skull, such as had killed her husband, rather than a slow death in the torment of a fire. She prayed again for rain; at least that eased the pain of burns, but no rain came and the late evening sunshine brightened.

And then there was a shout – more like a roar from a bull than the utterance of a man. Mara thrilled to the sound. She knew that man; it was Fintan the blacksmith, his mighty voice had been honed from a childhood and boyhood spent in a smithy full of the beating of iron. It penetrated the brains of the chanting men and an uncertain note came into the sounds.

The floor of the sunken passageway was so low that men found it hard to see properly over the walls and those at the back pressed forward so that those in front were pushed up and into the small round space encircling the second dolmen and its surrounding fire. A shout of pain and a stream of curses came when a few legs came into contact with the smouldering fire.

Two minutes later with blood-curdling yells, Fintan and the largest of his forge workers, came in through the enclosure, behind the compressed throng of MacNamaras. They cleaved their way through and stood brandishing enormous hammers. His brother, his son, his neighbours and some of his forge workers, all armed with fearsome throwing knives, stood above, peering down at the corralled men.

'Give the word, Brehon, and we'll slaughter the lot of them,' shouted Fintan.

Miraculously Mara felt her gullet expand with relief. She coughed once and waited for a moment, shaking her head to Fintan's suggestion. The smoke was dying down now and she opened her mouth, drawing in a gulp of damp air and allowing its coolness to soothe the inflammation in her throat. There was a sound of more horsemen now and to her immense relief, Aidan's head appeared at the top of the wall. He did not have the O'Lochlainn with him but the dependable face of Fachtnan leaned down from beside him and Nuala was by his side and behind her, Cumhal, Mara's farm manager, and his workers.

In an instant Fachtnan had leaped down, dislodging a few clansmen and he held up his arms for Nuala. She handed her medical bag to Aidan and slipped down into them instantly. Even in the midst of her pain and her anxiety, Mara noticed how Fachtnan held Nuala for a minute longer than was necessary and that it was Nuala who freed herself.

'Are you all right?' she asked Mara, taking her medical bag and bending over Slaney.

'Something for my throat, Nuala; I must talk!' whispered Mara hoarsely.

The wonderful thing about Nuala was her quick wits. In an instant she had produced a flask from her bag, handed it to Mara, saying 'marsh mallow root; just keep sipping it,' and then had applied herself to soaking pieces of linen and layering them onto Slaney's leg.

Mara swallowed a gulp of the mallow root

275

solution and then another. She took in a deep breath and when she spoke her voice was strong enough to be heard.

'All MacNamara men from Thomond, except Tomás MacNamara, are to be escorted from here to the boundary between the kingdom and Thomond. They will not be re-admitted to this kingdom except by the direct order of the king. These two men, Stephen Gardiner and Boetius MacClancy are to be chained – Fintan, will you see to that?' She waited until the two men had been seized and then continued, 'And, Fintan, I want them driven along the road to Abbey Hill and then released once they reach the road to Kinvarra at the boundary of this kingdom.' Mara took another sip of the cooling mallow root drink and addressed them severely. 'If either of you, Stephen Gardiner, or Boetius MacClancy, appear once more in the Burren, I will cry you to the heavens as an outsider and an alien and you will have no protection under the law.'

They did her will, quickly and efficiently. The men from Thomond were relieved of their throwing knives by Balor, Fintan's giant-sized worker. The sight of him, holding a hammer above their heads, made the knives come tumbling out and Balor placed each neatly on the top of the rapidly cooling dolmen. Fintan, in the meantime, softened the ends of the iron chain in the remaining embers and then shackled the two men, Stephen Gardiner and Boetius MacClancy. They were driven off by two of Mara's workmen who nodded at the directions given to them by Cumhal.

276

There was one more task to be done before this ugly business was finished. Tomás MacNamara was leaning against the wall and she went over to him. He looked up at her with very black eyes and then, suddenly and unexpectedly, vomited on the ground in front of her feet. Mara frowned. But there was no way that a man could do this for no reason so she went across to Nuala.

'Look at this man's eyes,' she asked and walked back beside her. By now Tomás had sunken down and was crouched on the ground, his head supported on his hands. He looked up at them with a dazed expression.

Nuala bent over him and pulled down the lid of the large, black-pupilled eyes and nodded.

'Cowbane,' she said. 'He's been dosed with cowbane. He'll recover. Let him walk around in the air for a while.' Rapidly she went back to Slaney, holding the woman's wrist in her hand and counting anxiously.

'Cowbane,' repeated Mara to herself. It was as she had thought. She remembered the rows of the very black eyes watching her. Tomás, she recollected from her first meeting with him, was, like his son, Adair, a brown-eyed man; brown-eyed, but not black-eyed. Who had fed him and the men from Thomond with cowbane? It would have been easy to put it into the mead – only very small quantities were enough to ensure that the drinker had strange dreams and strange fears. *Allucinari*, that was the word she had come across in her readings of the classics, she remembered. That's what the man was suffering from.

And not just Tomás. Again she cast her mind back to her mental picture of the men who crowded into the sunken passageway; the men with the black staring eyes. Almost the entire party had been doctored with cowbane.

But, by who?

She thought she knew the answer.

And why?

She knew the answer to that, also.

There was only one person who could have done this and that person was Cait, the wife of Tomás. And why? Well, the reason was obvious when Mara thought of the adoration in the woman's eyes when she had looked at her beautiful young son. Tomás's downfall would have been Adair's opportunity. Mother love, she thought as she nodded to Cumhal's plans to fetch a cart from a nearby neighbour in order to convey Slaney back to Rathborney.

She sighed. There was one more task to be done before she could rest and nurse her sore throat and burning hand. She watched the men from Thomond being driven off towards the eastern boundary between the Burren and their own kingdom and she waited until Stephen Gardiner and Boetius MacClancy had been dragged up to the road leading to the north. Only then did she mount her horse and sign to her two scholars to accompany her.

She would not seek her bed until every flask, pot, ewer, pitcher and bowl from that pernicious stillroom at Carron Castle had been emptied in front of her eyes onto the cobbles of the castle's courtyard. The rest, she thought, could wait until the morrow. She left Tomás to his wife's care; he seemed to have sunken into a wordless, sightless, immobile state and it would, she thought, as she appointed two of her workers to stand guard over the castle for the night, be useless to question him at that moment.

Tomorrow the truth would emerge.

Fourteen

Críth Gablach
(Ranks in Society)

A bóaire *(a substantial farmer) is a man of three snouts:*
1. *The snout of a rooting boar that cleaves dishonour in every season;*
2. *The snout of a flitch of bacon on the hook;*
3. *The snout of a plough under the ground;*
So that he is capable of receiving a king or a bishop or a scholar or a brehon from the road, prepared for the arrival of guest-company.

Here is the record of the possessions of a bóaire

He has twenty cows, two bulls, six oxen, twenty pigs, twenty sheep, four domestic boars, two sows, a saddle-horse, an enamelled bridle, and sixteen bushels of seed in the ground. He and his wife have four suits of clothes.

Mara slept badly and only dropped into an uneasy doze just as a blackbird piped a tentative whistle outside her bedroom window. When she woke her scorched hand was stiff and sore and she ached in every limb. There was a noise downstairs from the kitchen and she lay there for a while half-hoping that Brigid would bring her some breakfast in bed just as she would have done when Mara was a child and suffering one of her rare illnesses.

But when the door opened it was Nuala and her medical bag who appeared and Mara welcomed her with relief. From time to time, during the night, she had swallowed sips of the marsh mallow root drink and now the flask had been emptied. Her hand was painful, but that didn't matter; her voice was of more importance. There was something she had to do today. Garrett MacNamara's killer had to be confronted; a confession had to be made and a day appointed for the sentence of retribution. Wordlessly, she looked at Nuala and silently opened her mouth to allow the girl to inspect her throat.

'Getting on really well; much less inflamed; bound to be a bit sore first thing in the morning. I've brought you some more of the syrup. I've had Peadar out in that marshy piece of earth near the river first thing this morning and he brought me back a root of the mallow. I had him grind it and make a new supply. Drink this.' Nuala's voice was so full of energy and well-being that Mara began to feel better.

She tilted the goblet, drank and felt a soothing coat of mucous liquid, flavoured with honey, slide over the sore tissues in her throat and closed her eyes with relief. She eyed the well-stoppered flask with approval. It could be carried in her satchel, she thought as she enquired about Slaney.

'I've dosed her fairly heavily with poppy juice so she slept the night through, but it is a bad burn – she's a fat woman and it has burned almost to the bone. I've left Peadar in charge of her; that man in Scotland, the herbalist at the friary, taught him a lot. He is going to be a good apprentice,' said Nuala buoyantly.

'Perhaps he should have been the one to come here to renew the bandages on my hand,' said Mara, watching Nuala at work with a slight smile puckering the corners of her lips. There was an air of suppressed excitement and pleasure under the girl's professional manner. Was it relief at having finally made a decision to come back to the Burren? Or was there something else? She had known Nuala for her entire life and had seen her in all moods; but she had never seen the brown eyes sparkle quite as they were doing at this moment. Mara held her breath.

'I wanted to see you,' said Nuala. She gave a half-laugh. 'It was quite a night,' she said lightly. 'Fachtnan and I brought your two boys back up to the law school once everything was in place. We were a bit worried about you. And then Aidan came crashing in, saying that the O'Lochlainn and his steward were missing – they had gone to Coad races with quite a few of his men and it was thought that they would stay overnight with Teige O'Brien. Aidan came to ask Cumhal what to do. When I heard about Slaney, and about the fire, I thought I should go too. Aidan kept saying that the Brehon would rescue the woman and Fachtnan, of course, agreed with him, but Cumhal; I've never seen him so worried. I thought he'd kill his horse the way he rode that cob across the limestone pavements with the rain making everything slippery.'

Mara smiled. It was good to know that the members of her law school had such faith in her, but she thought wryly that Cumhal may have known better. He, like Brigid, would have remembered the ancient tales of Creevagh, the place of the branches.

'And when you got back to Rathborney . . . Fachtnan went back with you, of course . . .' Mara said gently, eyeing the flush that came to Nuala's cheeks. The colour suited her olive skin and brown eyes and Mara smiled appreciatively. Fiona, of course, was extremely pretty, but Nuala, in some moods, was beautiful. She could imagine the rest of Nuala's story. She and Fachtnan would have worked together – as they had done in the past. Nuala would have been totally involved in saving a life, easing pain and Fachtnan would have been observing her, his boyish love for her reawakening and . . .

'You're beginning to guess, aren't you?' Nuala said now, her red lips parting over strong white teeth.

'Tell me,' said Mara and Nuala threw her arms around her.

'Fachtnan asked me to marry him,' she said in Mara's ear and then straightened herself in a slightly embarrassed way as there was a perfunctory knock on the door and Brigid came in with a wooden platter and mug of milk.

'Oh, Brigid, toasted goat's cheese, how lovely,' said Mara. She didn't think she could possibly eat it, but she wanted to give Nuala a moment to recover.

Brigid, however, was not deceived. She put

down the mug and the platter on a small table by the bed, but never took her eyes from Nuala.

'Don't tell me . . . he . . .' She began and then took the girl by the hands, pulling her close and then suddenly hugging her. Nuala returned the embrace whole-heartedly.

'I'm betrothed, Brigid,' she said happily. 'Fachtnan has asked me to marry him.'

'And about time too,' said Brigid severely, stroking the glossy black hair with a gentle hand. 'Prettiest girl in the kingdom. If I haven't said that to Cumhal again and again . . . And how's the Brehon, this morning.' She looked intently at Mara and said firmly, 'I'm keeping you in bed all day today. You've got black circles under your eyes and you're as white a bowl of whey. Fachtnan can tear himself away from Nuala and take over the teaching today. Moylan and Aidan are still in bed and I'll let them have their sleep. Hugh and Shane are having their breakfast with Fiona who's in a sulk about missing all the excitement. Aidan was in a state last night when he couldn't find the O'Lochlainn, Brehon.'

'It all worked out for the best,' said Mara firmly. 'I must see Aidan and tell him that. When it came to it, Cumhal and his men managed much better and kept everything under my control.'

'You do look pale; you stay in bed as Brigid says,' said Nuala looking at her with her physician's expression. 'I'll tell Fachtnan to give your message to Aidan. I heard him—' again she flushed prettily – 'I heard him telling the two boys last night how well they had acted. Fachtnan—' her voice lingered fondly over the name – 'always remembers to say the right thing. I must think of that with Peadar and my pupils to come; praise them for what they do right. Now I'd better get back. That hand will be all right for a few hours, Mara. Just don't use it. Brigid, you keep her in bed.'

Mara did not argue as they both went out. Let Fachtnan manage the five scholars for the day. She would endeavour to eat as much of her breakfast as she could swallow – the blackbirds and finches outside her window would relish the rest of it, she thought as she struggled into a warm gown. At least the rain had stopped, she saw, as she went to the window with the pieces of bread. She opened the casement and placed the goat's cheese and bread on the sill. Brigid and Nuala were walking down the road together. Brigid was talking animatedly and the words 'midsummer wedding in the Brehon's garden when all the roses and lilies are out,' floated up to Mara. She smiled to herself and then sighed.

Before this happy event could take place, the case of the secret and unlawful killing of Garrett MacNamara had to be drawn to a conclusion, his killer accused and a fine imposed.

'Cumhal,' she called from the window. 'Saddle my horse, would you, and bring it around to my front gate. And Cumhal, could you accompany me and bring Eoin and a couple of the other men with you. We must go up to Carron. I have business at the castle.'

Mara remained alone with the woman; that was her choice. She had sent the reluctant Cumhal and his workers to accompany Tomás on his journey to see his king. There he would have to confess his involvement in the strange deeds at Creevagh and to await his judgement. It would be for Turlough to decide whether this man could now be deemed to be fit for such a high office as *taoiseach* of the MacNamara clan.

After they had left there was a long silence. Eventually Mara spoke, just making the simple accusation and then sitting back, curious to know what would be the response.

It came immediately. A resourceful woman! A hearty laugh and then the words followed fluently.

'I'm surprised at you, Brehon. How could you go so far wrong? Surely you can see now that it was a plot – nothing to do with me. In fact, if you want to know the truth, you made a great mistake when you allowed Stephen Gardiner to slip through your fingers.'

'Tell me about it,' invited Mara. She took another sip from Nuala's flask and sat back. Let the woman talk; the truth would prevail, sentence would be passed and justice would be done.

'He knew that the cattle raid would take place; you guessed that, I suppose.'

Mara nodded and took another sip. 'The murder is my concern at the moment,' she said. 'O'Donnell has been punished and I don't think he will be coming this way soon again.' She eyed the woman with interest. 'But why should Stephen Gardiner kill Garrett MacNamara? And how did he do it? Tell me that,' she asked.

There was a moment's silence. 'He had a weapon, a tool. He used the cowman, Brennan.'

'That is unworthy of you,' said Mara gently. 'And not very clever. How could Stephen Gardiner communicate with Brennan? The man speaks no English and only imperfect Gaelic. It was true, however, that the murderer had an accomplice—'

'Not Jarlath.' The words spurted out.

'Not Jarlath,' agreed Mara. There had been a time when she had puzzled over Jarlath's role. There was the affair of the sweets laced with cowbane – it had never really been established whether he had a hand in that. Mara had tried to see how there could have been a buried connection, a partnership of interests between him and Stephen Gardiner – after all, Jarlath had been the main beneficiary from Garrett's death, but Fiona's argument had prevailed. A man who threw away half of his inheritance was not a man who would murder for greed.

'No, of course, not – you had fixed on Slaney, hadn't you? But now that she may die, you are moving the guilt to my shoulders. You want to have your victim in court, don't you? You needn't tell me that you don't enjoy standing up there at Poulnabrone and dictating to all those men.' The voice was harsh now – a woman fighting for her future and her happiness – and for her son.

'I considered Slaney, naturally. Garrett's will has left her a rich woman and of course someone like Slaney would find it hard to suffer the insult of another woman being taken into the household and a son, not of her making, being set up as the heir.' The denial of the existence of the chain had focussed the thoughts of the law school on Slaney, but in the end Mara saw it had probably just been a matter of stubbornness on Slaney's part and frightened lies from the servants. The tale of the violent quarrel between Garrett and Slaney had come from one source only.

It had been a difficult case, acknowledged Mara. There had been a time when she had certainly considered whether there were international links to this murder, but, of course, in the end, it had come down to something far more simple: the overwhelming love of a mother for her son. Cait, of course, had been Stephen Gardiner's willing tool in the matter of drugging the mead. The vision of her beautiful son with the title of Lord Mount Carron, and an estate to go with it, was a bribe that could not be resisted by her.

And mother love, also, in a very different woman, had resulted in a more serious crime: the secret and unlawful killing of Garrett MacNamara.

'When I spoke of an accomplice,' she said softly, 'I did not mean a human one. You kept your own counsel and trusted no one. I'm sure that you have been in the habit of doing this. No, your accomplice was a dumb animal, a bull.'

Rhona froze. Her grey eyes widened and she sat very still.

'You were used to cattle; you told me that. You were the only child of a cattle dealer.' Mara looked up at the powerful woman. Large hands, heavy muscular arms, wide shoulders, she had probably done a man's work from a young age.

'I thought that there was a connection between the cattle racing out of the barn to join the herd, but originally I had not thought of the bull,' she said. Her mind went to Setanta's story about how her little villain, Cormac, had placed the cat on the sheep's neck, set the whole field running and excited the sheep awaiting sheering to burst out from the cabin at the top of the field.

'I'm used to bulls,' said Rhona indifferently. 'You have to show them who is in charge and they usually accept that. They are stupid animals.'

'Takes a bit of courage, though, to do what you did,' said Mara admiringly. 'I presume that Garrett was dead when you dragged him into the bull's cabin. You found the chain in there, of course. There would always be a few spare chains in places like that. You guessed that there was going to be a cattle raid; perhaps got the information from one of the men on the boat. They would not have guarded their tongues with a woman from Scotland.'

'Do you know how I did it; how I attached Garrett to the bull?' Rhona looked at her with a half smile.

'I've had many hours trying to work that out,' admitted Mara, 'but eventually I thought that you must have used something like a piece of wood, or a piece of twine, something that would snap eventually as the bull crashed down onto the road. That cabin is not too far above the road, but the hillside is very steep there.' She thought back and remembered the broken gorse bush. That was probably where the maddened creature shed its load.

289

'It was easy, really. The farmers use a small bar of iron to thread through the chain to a hasp on the wall; I looped the chain around Garrett's ankle and then attached it to the ring through the bull's nose, but I just used a piece of wood, instead of iron. Then I released the first chain and when I went out I closed the door, but only slid the latch in less than an inch. They're stupid creatures, bulls, and he probably thought he was still chained and locked inside the cabin – until he heard the noise of the herd and then, I knew, that he would make for the door, dragging the body with him.'

'So Garrett was trampled underfoot while you were miles away on Mullaghmore Mountain. You pretended that you wanted to go back to Carron when I invited you to come home with me, but I suppose you were just bluffing. I thought afterwards that it was not within your character to bother about making friends with Slaney. In any case, I had already got the impression that you would not stay and become a second wife to Garrett once your son had been acknowledged and his rights established. And when I saw that you were already pregnant, well I knew that you never had any intention of doing that. Now,' Mara's voice sharpened, 'tell me how, and why you killed Garrett.'

'You tell me,' said Rhona. She gave a glance around and deliberately got up, carried her chair and placed it close to the door. Mara eyed the powerful shoulders and the stony face, but she continued. The truth had to be known and then she would dictate what came next. Her throat was sore and her hand burned and throbbed but she allowed no weakness to appear. She knew what Rhona meant by having power over a bull if you believe in your own superiority. Her own life had shown Mara how to use this power.

'When the maid servant spoke of seeing Garrett go up the stairs towards the main bedrooms in the middle of the day,' she said in calm, unemotional tones, 'we assumed that he was going to Slaney's bedroom. You yourself reported hearing a fight between them, but of course that was not true. Garrett came to your bedroom. That is correct, isn't it?'

Mara waited for a moment, but no answer came, so she continued, 'I have to guess now, but I suspect that Garrett forced himself on you and when you refused his attempts at love-making he threatened to repudiate Peadar.'

'He said that he would accuse Jarlath of being the father and then that would account for the likeness between himself and my son. After all, a boy can resemble an uncle almost as easily as a father,' said Rhona dully. A heavy flush spread over her weather-beaten cheeks and Mara nodded understandingly. Peadar's grin and remark about his mother came back to her. Rhona, she had thought, when she saw that sideways view of her on the edge of the hillside, was pregnant – probably with the child of a man back in Scotland. And, of course, the brehon in Scotland would have explained to her that her son's inheritance would be safe once Garrett had acknowledged him in public.

'You were not prepared to accept Garrett's offer of a marriage in the second degree because

291

you were already in another relationship,' she said tolerantly.

'But I wanted the boy to have his rights. He is Garrett's son,' said Rhona quickly. 'My man, back in Scotland, he is just a poor fisherman. He could not give the boy the future that Peadar wanted.' Her colour rose again. 'I hit him over the head with a chair. I suppose that I could pretend that I didn't want to kill him, but I did. I knew I would not be able to talk him around. He was a stupid and stubborn man and I was glad when I saw that there was no life left in him. I waited until everyone had gone into the hall for the midday meal. I was going to bury him, but then I thought of the cattle raid that would come in a few hours' time. Garrett knew all about it and he told me that he was going to organise his own cattle to be shut up in the barn – he asked me to help him. He had to promise Stephen that he would not tell anyone, but he did not count me as anyone.'

'I see,' said Mara. 'It was as I had thought. Now we come to the legal business—'

'Now we come to the parting of our ways,' interrupted Rhona. She rose to her feet and Mara saw that she had the key to the door in her hand. 'I am going to lock you in; I won't harm you. I respect you and I like you, but this bedroom is a long way from the kitchen and it will only be when you are missed from the law school that you will be found here. By that time, if I take the fastest horse in the stables, I will be in Galway. I have already arranged for one of the fishermen to give me a passage back to Scotland – paid for it with the silver that Garrett gave me to buy a gown worthy of one of his wives. I shouldn't have come back today, but I wanted . . .' Here her voice faltered a little, but she controlled it almost instantly. 'I wanted to say goodbye to Peadar – perhaps you'll do that for me,' she finished.

'No need for that,' said Mara. 'Stay and tell him yourself. This is not England. No one will burn you to death, or hang, draw and quarter you. Admit your guilt, pay your fine and then the scales of retribution are balanced and you are free to do what you wish.'

Rhona laughed harshly. 'I have no silver, no cows. I know what the fine would be. I asked Fiona and she told me. A secret and unlawful killing of a *taoiseach* would bring a fine of forty-six ounces of silver or forty-six cows, that's what she told me. I can't pay it myself, but my son could pay it by selling his substantial farm and losing his status as a *bóaire*. And then what would become of all his dreams? I will not do that to him and you cannot make me. I may not have your brains and your education, Brehon, but I can look facts in the face and I can take care of my son.'

She rose to her feet, but Mara remained seated. Rhona was right. Physically she would be no match for this woman and she had no intention of trying.

'No one can make your son sell his farm without the permission of his master,' she said mildly as Rhona opened the door and inserted the large key in its lock.

'Master?' Rhona whirled around, but Mara waited until she had closed the door again.

'Peadar was apprenticed yesterday according to our laws,' she said mildly. 'This means that his master, Nuala the physician, is now answerable for his actions in law, she will be required to authorise such business deals or marriage contracts as he, her pupil, might wish to make. Peadar cannot sell his farm unless Nuala gives permission and that she will not do as it would not be in his interests. Nuala,' she ended with a smile, 'was brought up amongst lawyers and she has a great respect for the law.'

Rhona sat down heavily.

'But how do I pay the fine?' she asked.

'That,' said Mara 'is a matter for me to think about. It's a complex and difficult point. You are here in this land as a stranger, but yet you did not come unasked or uninvited, but came in the company of a man who is the brother to the late *taoiseach* of the MacNamara clan. I'm inclined to think that Jarlath will have to pay your fine, and don't worry, the fine is paid to the nearest male relations of the murdered man – that is to Jarlath and to your son Peadar. Jarlath can well afford to do this.'

The law, thought Mara as she watched relief flood into the woman's grey eyes, always had the answer. A little good will on all sides would see a happy future for Rhona and her son, Peadar. What was it, she mused, that the great Fithail, had to say about an affair like this?

'The law of the land makes smooth all the pathways of man.'